To Steve enjoy

STOLEN

Arthur Allison

Published by

MELROSE
BOOKS

An Imprint of Melrose Press Limited
St Thomas Place, Ely
Cambridgeshire
CB7 4GG, UK
www.melrosebooks.co.uk

FIRST EDITION

Cover by Melrose Books

ISBN   **978-1-912026-56-2**
        978-1-912026-57-9 epub
        978-1-912026-58-6 mobi

Printed and bound in Great Britain by:
Berforts South West Limited
17 Burgess Road
Hastings
East Sussex
TN35 4NR

Contents

1

Africa

There are a number of majestic rivers flowing through the rift valleys of Africa. They are Africa's lifeblood, but none are greater than the mighty Zambezi. Half of all the wildlife in central Africa is dependent on the Zambezi for survival.

In the late afternoon, the colour of the water swirling around the hidden boulders buried deep in the middle of the river was a deep green; so dark it was almost grey. Foreboding whirlpools and small waves pushing against the flow gave a hint of the power and the danger that ran beneath the surface. Closer to the river bank, the colour was different: here, where the mighty river flowed over the rapids and smaller rocks, there were multitudes of golden sparkling ripples, twinkling like small diamonds in the late afternoon setting sun. Shadows from the heavily leafed giant acacia trees and tall ilala palms stretched out across the river from the opposite bank. Darkness was now approaching.

Night in Africa falls quickly, like a giant, dark curtain descending upon the earth; this was something Michael Ashton had momentarily forgotten. He was casting out a thin silver lure with a deadly triple hook beyond the swirls of the rapids into the main river for what seemed like the hundredth time. Here I am standing at this magnificent river's edge he thought, five miles upstream from the Falls themselves; this is my river, my land, pure paradise. My soul remains here wherever I am in the world.

Michael had spent half his life in Africa and the other half in England, which was now his home.

Even at a distance of five miles, the water created a low thundering sound as it plunged over the Falls themselves, sending up a spray which the wind carried hundreds of feet into the air. The dull roar seemed an echoing warning of its awesome power to those on the river: beware, show respect. "Mosi-oa-Tunya" the locals call Victoria Falls – the smoke that thunders. They believed whoever angered the mighty river would answer to "Nyami Nyami", the half-serpent, half-human river god that the local people both feared and worshipped.

Michael looked up as the darkness descended; he knew this was his last chance to hook that elusive tiger-fish before packing up and heading out of the national park, back to the small town of Victoria Falls. He could think of no other national park in Africa – or anywhere in the world – that allowed visitors to leave their vehicles amongst the wildlife and set up on the river bank to fish. The evening breeze was slight, and he heard the familiar distinct guttural cough of a male leopard above the early evening sounds. About a mile or so away, he guessed.

His mind drifted back to when he was a young boy, and he and his family had done an overland safari across the desert plains of Botswana and Namibia. *I was so lucky to be brought up with nature and seeing so much of wild Africa, but today it's an ever-shrinking wilderness*, he thought. He recalled learning about the true meaning of sunset from an old bushman tracker. The family were sitting on one of the famous red dunes in the Namib Desert. Michael was spellbound by the deep crimson sky, and the red glow over the dunes reflected in the faces of those around him. Michael could not keep quiet and exclaimed at the pure beauty of the event. The wily old bushman turned to the eager young boy as they squatted together on the high red dune watching the burning orb of the sun quickly sinking below the horizon. He signalled to Michael to be quiet. He stared at young Michael and then, as he began to speak, made the bushman guttural clicking sound.

'To learn about nature, boy, you don't watch the setting sun or speak out aloud, you close your eyes and listen to it. Listen for the night sounds awakening and the daylight sounds going to sleep. The air around you, feel it; feel the cool air descend on the desert. Listen to the new night birds and nocturnal animal sounds. It will teach you far more about your surroundings. It is better to feel the world around you than just to see it.' *To this day I still close my eyes when nightfall comes*, Michael thought.

Suddenly, the line cracked taut as if running into a brick wall, and his chain of thought was broken. Tiny shimmering droplets of spray flew off the line as it twanged. Michael's forearms stiffened and strained, the force of the strike sending a shockwave of pain through his muscles. Instinctively, he pulled back on the line, whipping the rod hard and high to set the vicious triple hook of the lure. He could feel the fish fighting back, angered and surprised by this thing in its mouth. The lure set, game on. The tigerfish broke the water just above the rapids, bursting out of the water in a kaleido-scope of silver and orange, desperately trying to throw off the lure and its triple hook by tail-walking, mouth open wide. Man versus predator.

Although it only averages 6.5 kilograms in weight, a fully grown tigerfish is one of the deadliest fighting fish in the world, attacking its prey, other fish, at such speed that it can de-scale its victim instantly. Only the majestic marlin tail-walks with the same fury and in the same manner when hooked. Pound for pound, the tigerfish is a harder fighter.

Michael knew only too well from past epic battles with tigerfish what to watch for. One second of slack line, or too much strain, and the magnificent fish would win. Slowly, and using all his fishing skills, he tried to turn the battle in his favour by tightening the drag on the reel. The strain was enormous; hunter and prey were in a physical stand-off. In his mind he played out the fight and the perils it carried with it, using all his knowledge: don't let him run across the rapids or the line will be shredded on the buried rocks; don't hold him too tight or he will snap the line above the steel trace that holds the lure; don't let him rush back at you. The battle for supremacy raged on for fifteen minutes. Michael's body was finely honed; he was super-fit and muscled in a solid way, rather than muscle-bound. At six feet three inches, he was a powerful individual, one who could not easily be crossed. Even so, his body was taking strain. *Damn*, he thought, *either I get him into the shallows near the sandbank quickly, or I will be in big trouble with the park rangers.* He briefly thought of cutting the line, but his subconscious drive to win shut it out just as quickly as it had come to mind – Michael was not one to walk away from a challenge. From across the water, he heard the call of the rare and beautiful Pel's fishing owl. The night sounds were approaching fast as darkness threatened to descend upon the land.

He knew that leaving the national park after dark was a big no-no and then you had to take into account the dangers of travelling after nightfall in big game territory. Slowly, inch by inch, he wound in the line, using brute force more than finesse. Out of the corner of his eye he saw a small ripple in the river that hadn't been there a moment before. About twenty feet out in the swirls, a dark gnarled snout and a pair of evil-looking deep yellow eyes were drifting slowly towards Michael. It was an eight-foot-long Nile crocodile, and it was drifting easily with the current towards the calmer water near the bank, moving slowly towards its potential victim.

Its eyes watched the movement on the bank, looking for a wrong move or sign of weakness. Its predatory eyes, just narrow slits in the gnarled skull, stared unblinkingly ahead, coldly focused on its intended prey. The eyes appeared to be saying, 'Just make one mistake my friend – one false move, just one.'

Michael felt a shudder pass through his body at the sight of an old adversary from years before, and he subconsciously took a half pace back on the sandy beach. The crocodile, seeing the corrective movement eased past, not five feet from the bank. One lazy flick of its tail and it was gone, as suddenly as it appeared, in the knowledge that it had been rumbled by its intended prey.

Slowly, the fight with the tigerfish was starting to turn in Michael's favour: each tail-walk was less fierce than the one before, each run on the line slightly less aggressive. Finally, after what seemed an age, Michael got the mighty fish up onto the beach. His arms were aching and sweat was pouring from his back and from under his arms, creating dark patches on his khaki shirt. He stepped forward quickly, placing his boot on the tigerfish's tail and slipping his fingers into the gills of the fish to force open its mouth. The slightest mistake in releasing the lure would result in a multitude of three-inch razor-sharp teeth ripping open his hand and probably devouring a finger in the process. Using a pair of pliers, Michael slid the barbed hook rapidly backwards, releasing the lure in a twisting movement. The mighty fish lay glistening in the sand at his feet. He slumped back onto the sand, which was still warm from the setting sun.

He looked at the fish's silver scales and bright orange stripes, its fearful teeth now clamped shut, its body still convulsing with fatigue from the fight. *A great fight and a noble adversary*, Michael thought. He was always enraptured by the sheer thrill of taking on a tigerfish and winning. He raised his bottle of lager, recovered from the sand next to his boots, and said out loud, 'I salute you; you are a mighty warrior. Now let's get you back into the water to grow some more and give somebody else in years to come a tremendous fight.'

In a single fluid motion he raised himself from his

haunches, walked to the river's edge, holding the fish firmly in both hands. He knelt down and gently pushed the tigerfish away from the shallows into deeper water. The fish remained motionless for a few seconds, then its tail gave a rapid flick. The water rippled, then there was a silver flash, and the tigerfish was gone, back into the depths of the mighty Zambezi.

Michael wearily collected his fishing tackle and turned away from the river, then climbed up the still-warm sandy beach. Reminded of impending nightfall by the crimson setting sun, now low above the palms, he broke into a sprint up the beach towards his Toyota Land Cruiser. He stopped only to throw in his portable barbeque, folding chair, keepnet filled with tilapia and pink-bellied bream caught earlier and the remainder of his six-pack of beer into the back of the cruiser. The cruiser's big diesel engine kicked into life, and the lights already had an effect on the dusk. Better get out of here in a hurry, mused Michael, I'm not looking forward to the bollocking and maybe a fine from old Shadreck, the head ranger. Perhaps a bribe of a couple of bream might help, and oh yes, he would love the remainder of the beer.

As the cruiser crested the sandbank, onto a dirt track leading away from the river, there was a sound of something crashing through the trees, and branches splintering and snapping on the left side of the vehicle. A young bull elephant, bellowing with rage, was charging at the cruiser that had just interrupted his early evening reverie. Michael could see the lowered head, the dust exploding off the elephant's back and the ground bursting with dust plumes as each foot thundered down; it was getting closer and closer to the cruiser. The weepy eyes confirmed that the young male was at his most dangerous: he was in musk, meaning he was very randy and angry!

It was now ten feet away and closing. The cruiser would buckle up into the night sky and flip over as though it were a leaf in the wind if the young bull hit the side of the cruiser. In desperation, he instinctively reacted by swinging the cruiser's steering wheel hard to the right, away from the immediate danger, off the dirt track through a thicket of jesse bush and thorns, and up a small rocky shale mound, missing the elephant and its charge by inches. The cruiser only just made the climb out before almost stalling, but it was enough to shake off the young male.

'Humans one, elephants nil,' Michael yelled into the early evening sky. What a near miss it had been was now slowly sinking in, and his body reacted to the close encounter with a massive rush of adrenaline. He swung the cruiser back onto the track, the headlights now starting to come into their own as darkness fell suddenly, like a giant blackout curtain dropped from the heavens onto Africa.

Automatically, Michael pushed the cruiser hard down the deep bone-shattering ruts along the rocky bush track. The rains had not yet arrived in Zimbabwe. The cruiser thumped and bounced its way towards the main gate leading from the park.

The engine roar, together with the rattling and teeth-chattering bumps created from the ruts in the hardened earth drowned out the rising sounds of the night. Suddenly, Michael picked out another movement in the bush close to the track. Stiffening his hands on the wheel, Michael tried to work out what had caused the movement. *Oh shit, not another elephant*, he thought; the last encounter was still very fresh in his mind. Almost instantly, his trained bush eyes picked up a lone old buffalo bull crashing through the bush away from the road and the cruiser, away from any danger, snorting with annoyance, mud flying off its back.

The worst kind of buff if you are on foot, he thought: old in years, short on temper, a loner living out the last years of his life away from the herd. These buffalo are called dagga boys, so named because of the way that during the hot daylight hours they seek refuge in thick black mud along the rivers and waterholes. They cover themselves in mud (dagga in the local Shona language) to stay cool and kill off insects missed by the oxpecker birds that seemed to live permanently on their backs.

Nearing the exit gate to the park, he caught a glimpse of a magnificent male leopard blending beautifully and gracefully into his surroundings, melting away into the undergrowth, only the flick of his tail giving him away. The movement would have been missed by all but the most trained eyes. It was only a brief glimpse of the most elusive of the big cats, but it was still mind-blowing and magnificent.

Leopards own the night around these parts, no wonder my cruiser has no effect on him, thought Michael. He wondered whether it might be the same leopard he had heard near the river. Perhaps the same leopard that was killing so many domestic dogs and cats in the village of Victoria Falls, itself within the national park boundaries.

At the gate, Michael skidded the cruiser to a halt in a cloud of dust, in part because Shadreck, the head ranger, had suddenly stepped out from the thatched gatehouse, an old AK-47 rifle slung over his shoulder. *Well at least he isn't about to wave it in my direction*, Michael thought. The usual dressing-down from Shadreck followed, a dressing-down for the late exit from the park. He said a lot about the arrogance of '*mukiwa*' (young white boys) as well. Shadreck knew Michael well though, so the lecture was good-natured. In fact, Shadreck had a sneaking admiration for Michael's bushcraft. The bollocking was followed by the two old friends giving each other the traditional tribal handshake. Michael handed over his gifts to Shadreck: a fresh bream supper for his family, and the remaining beers which would be reserved for him alone. They shook hands again in farewell and Michael set off homewards on the fifteen-minute drive for Victoria Falls village, a place which had, over the years, grown from a neat village into a sprawling, unkempt town.

2

Memories

Michael eased his body into a more comfortable position in the driver's seat of the Land Cruiser, then set off down the tarred road back to town. He was now driving at a more sedate pace than he had when exiting the national park. The newly tarred road wound its way along the river banks, past what was now the Zambezi Boat and Fishing Club. In a bygone era, this had been Imperial Airways' flying boat base. In the late 1940s and early 1950s, majestic Empire flying boats would land on the Zambezi and disgorge their passengers for their penultimate overnight stay at the magnificent Victoria Falls Hotel.

The far-flung reaches of the British Empire had been made that much closer by Marconi's short-wave radio and the Empire flying boats delivering the royal mail. Once ashore, the guests would be whisked away to their overnight hotel. Formal attire was required every evening at dinner, which was an adventure in itself. *Wouldn't do with today's 23-kilo luggage allowance on flights*, Michael thought, with a smile on his face, recalling some women he knew who would have turned the experience into a monumental fashion planning exercise!

Michael's annual 'farewell to Zimbabwe' bash was taking place at the boat club later on in the evening. *Any excuse for a piss-up*, he thought with a smile on his face, remembering many wild drinking parties and fishing barbeques that had taken place at the boat club. The road ahead was quiet except for a couple of warthogs scurrying around the roadside on their front knees, digging for grubs and insects. A few tour buses were heading to the jetties along the river to collect returning sundowner cruise guests. Night brought with it a cool evening breeze; he let it flow over his face and muscled arms. He passed the crossroads, which enabled drivers to turn off for the Elephant Hills Hotel on the left and the Victoria Falls Safari Lodge on the right, then slowed at the bend beyond. He knew from past experience that there were many accidents between people and animals at this point. It was a favourite crossing point for animals from the national park, both great and small, heading for the waterholes and green grass on the far side of the road.

Ahead appeared the dull, yellow-orange glow of lights. The electricity was poor, as a result of the antiquated under-capitalised power grid; it flowed into the leafy avenues of the so-called low-density housing areas of Victoria Falls village, where Michael's boyhood home still stood on Acacia Avenue.

Michael's parents, Geoff and Sue Ashton, had gifted the property to Michael's childhood friend Kevin Van Der Riet and his wife, Gail. In those 1980s, the Zimbabwean economy was crumbling and you couldn't sell houses.

Gail was an intelligent, attractive, tough bush girl. Her bark was far worse than her bite, and her tireless efforts to help underprivileged locals had earned her the nickname 'the angel of mercy' in the Falls. Both were third-generation Zimbabweans, of pioneering stock. Kevin had traversed Africa buying up crocodile skins from specialist crocodile farmers, and he was considered the best in his very specialised trade. All crocodile commercial farming is carefully controlled and above board. All farming is strictly controlled under the auspices of the United Nations World Wildlife Trust. Every skin is tagged and recorded. By decree, ten per cent of all farmed crocodiles must be released back into the rivers and lakes of Africa. *Pity that can't be done for elephants, too*, thought Michael: a carefully controlled and monitored culling programme would result in a legal trade in ivory, which would raise much-needed funds to finance the fight against poachers, as well as providing income for the local population and game reserves, thus boosting tourism and the local economy. *Shouldn't be that difficult*, Michael thought.

Michael's family had moved back to Cranleigh in Surrey, England in the late 1990s, but his father often reflected on the time the family had spent in Africa.

'Africa is an adventure, filled with wonderful memories,' he would say. 'I envy those still to discover Africa, for them, the very best of this planet and the finest experience of their lives is still to come.'

The family had emigrated from England under a special colonial office scheme in the early 1950s to live in what was then Southern Rhodesia, which itself was part of the Federation of Rhodesia and Nyasaland. It was a thriving British colony considered to be the bread basket of southern Africa. As a British colony, it had a governor-general, and an elected prime minister and parliamentarians. Things started to change politically and independence was granted to the members of the federation. Northern Rhodesia became Zambia, and Nyasaland became Malawi. This culminated on 11 November 1965 after talks with the British government failed to slow the pace of the handover to majority rule, when then-Prime Minister, Ian Smith, unilaterally declared independence from Britain. Thus began the so called UDI years. The country became engulfed in a terrible and cruel war, the so-called Chimurenga, or freedom war. Russian and Chinese-trained terrorists against the best bush warfare troops in the world. The fight would never be lost on the battlefield, but the price was high. Atrocities occurred on both sides, although the so-called freedom fighters seemed to save their worst atrocities for their own kind. This was a fight for survival, the days of sanctions-busting legends. The pioneering spirit brought the whites together in what was to prove a costly and futile endeavour to hold onto a small part of Africa for a few more years. The end was to come through the ballot box, after South Africa was persuaded to close the borders on its old ally.

Thus began the new dawn, a result of late British Prime Minister Harold Macmillan's 'Wind of Change' speech. A transition from a self-declared independent Rhodesia, to freedom! Zimbabwe was born under a very different leader, President Robert Mugabe. He was an intelligent man with three university degrees, schooled in Rhodesia by Jesuit priests. He started out making all the right noises: making speeches about unity and convincing the incumbent UK government that the white minority would be protected by the constitution for eighteen years. He promised the future would be about all working together in a new land. History tells a very different story.

As the Zimbabwean dollar declined and the family filling station and vehicle servicing business became difficult to operate under any sense of normality, Michael's father, Geoff, sold up as best he could, accepted a job near London as a financial advisor trainee and Michael, his three sisters and parents then returned to the green fields of England, to a semi-rural home on the outskirts of Cranleigh called Milkwood. The home was not many miles from Sandhurst where Michael had entered his young adult life as an Officer Cadet. The children had all grown up and left home by that point. Michael's sisters were all university graduates: two were doctors and the third a barrister in chambers in London.

Michael pulled up outside the house in a cloud of red dust. The fine red dust got in everywhere and covered everything at this time of the year. Most of the houses were stained with red dust before the October rains.

On the upstairs verandah stood Michael's lifelong friend, Kevin, looking through some night binoculars at movement in the darkened game corridor just outside the fence of the homestead. He put the binoculars down and turned to look down on Michael, a glass of bubbly in his hand.

'Come on up, Fonz; you're late, mate.'

Fonz was Kevin's nickname for Michael; he was so called because Michael had a habit of often brushing his short hair back off his face, like the Fonz from the TV series *Happy Days*.

'Glass of bubbly waiting for you, Fonz. Let's get moving.'

'Sorry, Kev. Quick shower, and I'll be there.'

Michael decided the tigerfish tale could wait. Kevin had caught some monsters in Barotseland on the Zambian side of the Zambezi – although Gail claimed she had caught larger. Kevin always said she managed to bend the camera lens.

In the hot refreshing shower, with the jets of water stinging his weary body, Michael's thoughts drifted to his life since leaving Zimbabwe.

He had excelled at his secondary school, St Saviour's College near Cranleigh, and had gone on to Merton College, Oxford on the back of 3 A-Levels and having captained the rugby first team. Standing six feet three inches tall and weighing 198 pounds (89 kilograms), Michael had been a blindside flanker, wearing the number six jersey and being the target ball carrier in the forwards collectively known as the scrum.

Unlike many school leavers, Michael did not use his gap year to take an extended paid holiday. Instead, Michael chose to attend a brigade squad army selection course. He learned very early on in the course that the eight weeks was an excuse to kick the crap out of civilians and discourage them from ever wanting to join the army.

Having survived the army's attempt to break his spirit and ability to think as an individual, he attended the Regular Commissions Board seeking sponsorship; not financial sponsorship, but the promise of a junior officer placement in a chosen regiment should he successfully complete his officer training at Royal Military Academy

Sandhurst.

Michael was offered sponsorship by the Household Cavalry, which he readily accepted. He wanted to be a part of the armoured regiment formation reconnaissance unit within the guards. The Life Guards and the Blues and Royals are the two most senior regiments in the British Army. Their 'public face', seen by millions of tourists every year, covers ceremonial duties including the Changing of the Guard at Buckingham Palace, the Trooping of the Colour at the Queen's Birthday Parade and mounted escorts for visiting heads of state. These duties, although very much part of the make-up of the Household Cavalry, were not foremost in Michael's mind when making his choice.

Armed with the promise of regimental sponsorship, Michael took up his undergraduate place at Merton College, Oxford. There he obtained a first-class degree in Military History and English Literature. As Michael was not one for academia, he was mystified by this achievement. On the sports field his love of rugby earned Michael a full 'blue'. He remembered with great affection his final match for Oxford: it was against Cambridge University – 'the annual Varsity Match' as it was dubbed. The game took place at Twickenham Stadium, the home of English rugby. There were 70,000 spectators and his enjoyment at winning by two points was only exceeded by his enjoyment of the pub crawl around Oxford's many taverns surrounded by a bevy of young ladies keen to show how much they admired his efforts on and off the field.

Michael had chosen a military career prior to going to Oxford, and so the following January, he entered

Sandhurst for the 48-week officer training course. The course taught leadership, how to take decisive actions under pressure, mentoring and caring for the individuals under one's command, and understanding military history and the strategic study of war.

Michael enjoyed the comradeship of his fellow officer cadets, and the time spent in the field, where he quickly earned respect for his leadership qualities. He also took pleasure in the stringent fitness regime and the social bonding of the young men when they were together in the mess or at dinners, as well as just being together as a thinking, communicating military unit.

The highlight was the sovereign's parade, which marked the passing out or commissioning of young officers. Watched by family, friends, girlfriends and VIPs, the Sword of Honour, the Overseas Sword and the Queen's Medal were presented to the top cadets, and followed by the adjutant riding his horse up the Old College steps through the grand entrance, followed by the graduating officer cadets. This in turn was followed by a formal lunch with family friends and regimental officers. The day was concluded by a spectacular celebratory commissioning ball, and, on the stroke of midnight, Michael displayed his second lieutenant's rank insignia for the first time.

Michael moved to the Household Cavalry armoured regiment barracks at Combermere in Windsor, as a new second lieutenant in the Cavalry Regiment. The regiment has an active operational role as a formation reconnaissance regiment, as well as its more famous ceremonial duties, and, at that time, everyone there was waiting for rotation to operational duties in Afghanistan.

The training Michael did at Combermere was focused on fast vehicle reconnaissance, especially Scimitar light tanks and Jackal 2 all-terrain armoured vehicle. They learned how to be 'the eyes and ears' of the battalion headquarters, radio operators received feedback designed to help commanders in the field to determine where to place troops, how to monitor enemy movements, and how to provide support for light artillery and mounted vehicles. Reconnaissance combined speed of decision-making and maximised effectiveness of available assets.

The company were flown directly from Brize Norton in Oxfordshire into Camp Bastion. Within two days of their arrival they were patrolling. This encompassed the so-called 'winning hearts and minds' as their war began in earnest. Michael quickly learned that even Sandhurst and basic infantry training with the Household Cavalry cannot prepare you for the fear and horror that is the reality of war. As the army moved further forward into Helmand Province, the need for on-the-ground patrols far exceeded the need for vehicle reconnoitring. The war was moving to a new phase, and winning hearts and minds on the ground invariably resulted in clashes with the Taliban, with mounting casualties and death on both sides. Michael never was convinced that any of the tribal leaders were fully onside with the allied troops, maybe through Taliban intimidation, perhaps just not wanting yet another army on Afghan soil.

The regiment were re-orientated and past basic infantry training was revisited in the confines of Camp Bastion. The heat was unbearable and made the training worse; each breath felt like swallowing fire. Dust accompanied the men relentlessly. After less than a week of re-training as a light infantry unit, Michael's platoon was airlifted by Chinook helicopter to an isolated fortified forward base deep in Helmand Province. In truth these bases, or checkpoints, were no more than four high, reinforced mud walls with observation towers, or *sangars* as they were known. The men in the base and not on patrol were able to provide support with light artillery and mortars, but only for short distances beyond the camp. Heavy machine guns, known as general purpose machine guns were placed in the *sangars*; the firepower they provided was awesome, but again they were only able to protect the camp or patrols near to the base.

The endless futile patrolling – 'winning the minds', as the commanders called it – continued day in and day out. Armoured reconnaissance vehicle patrols gave way to foot patrols, each one an invitation to the Taliban. They would often ambush patrols or blow them up with IEDs (improvised explosive devices). These devices had accounted for more dead and maimed soldiers than any other weapon in the Taliban's arsenal. The most frustrating thing of all for the soldiers on the ground was that you could not fight back; the enemy were not there, only the cursed device. IEDs cut through a man's arms and legs like a knife through butter. They tear chunks out of a man's flesh and torso. Some said it was better to tread on the device: that way you would never know the outcome – and who knew, maybe the 'seventy-two virgins' thing worked for both sides.

The patrols would follow dusty roads through small villages of mud buildings surrounded by high mud walls. Opium poppy fields, the main source of funding for the Taliban, were clearly visible behind the villages. The roads were bordered by small, foul-smelling ditches called *wadis* and sluggish murky streams, which made the terrain marshy and difficult. The patrols would pass villagers, who would watch idly from the roadside, never knowing who was friend and who was foe. Whenever the villagers mysteriously disappeared, the patrols would go onto heightened alert. When that happened, the Taliban was never far away.

On his second tour, Michael was wounded. The patrol were ambushed close to their small forward base in Helmand Province while returning from yet another patrol. A round from a Russian-made AK-47 had left a deep gouge in Michael's right arm, just below the shoulder, tearing the flesh and leaving a four-inch scar, then exiting into a mud wall behind some of the patrol. The wall had given some small protection to half of the platoon, but the other half had been buried in the mud of the small irrigation ditch on the side of the road and had taken heavy fire. The heavy machine guns in the *sangars* had poured down murderous covering fire, but still the Taliban had seemed to be everywhere.

The enemy fire had been so intense that Michael had called an air strike to provide cover so that the patrol could be extracted to their base, a mere 500 metres away. The firefight raged for twenty minutes, during which a corporal was wounded in the chest and went down like he had been hit by a bus; he didn't make a sound as he fell, a sign that the round had hit him hard, knocking him immediately unconscious. He would require immediate medical attention. Before the call for a medic had even been made, the platoon medic had, without a thought for his own safety, crawled over to the wounded man, who was lying on his back in the ditch, and administered vital early first aid. After what seemed an interminable age, an Apache attack helicopter had come in low and fast overhead. Rumour had it afterwards that it was flown by a royal. Its 30mm cannons had flashed, unleashing instant death, and pounding rounds ploughed into the mud walls and houses where the Taliban fighters were firing from. The mud walls were no match for the heavy shells and appeared to disintegrate in dust and rubble. The firepower from the Apache was awesome. Michael eased from behind the wall in a crouch, intending to order a section to provide fire support so that the rest of the troop could withdraw, but as he raised his body slightly, he was hit by a Taliban AK-47 round. It was like receiving a massive punch somewhere in his upper body. He was spun completely around. The round made a sound like an angry bee, and it echoed in his ears. His body was lifted off the ground and he landed heavily on his back. He felt a numbness in his shoulder and arm; at that point, the pain still had not registered in his brain. He dropped his weapon and spent the rest of the firefight in a purple haze as he was dragged by his webbing back to the relative safety of the compound.

The medic who bandaged him up and told Michael he was lucky. Had the bullet been a little squarer into his arm, it would have hit the bone and shattered his humerus, which would have resulted in the arm being blown off or being amputated in a field operating theatre. When he had been treated, the stretcher-bearers carried Michael and the corporal to the medevac site to wait for a Chinook.

The wound was still very much in Michael's mind, and now he subconsciously rubbed the scar in the shower. The action of rubbing the old wound snapped him out of his flashback memories. Realising he had stayed too long in the shower, he dried off and dressed quickly in standard bush gear, khaki longs and a khaki short-sleeved shirt with desert-coloured hide-bush boots. He ran upstairs onto the verandah and lifted a champagne flute off the silver salver.

'Cheers, Fonz. That was a long shower. Were you playing with yourself again, chum? Warned you before: you will go blind, or worse, it will fall off,' joked Kevin.

They raised their glasses high and clinked them together in salute.

'Fonz, the eyes, mate. The eyes,' Kevin scolded.

He was always going on at Michael about looking directly into the other person's eyes when raising a glass in salutation. Eye contact was a sign of respect, he would tell him.

'Sorry, Kev. Yes, you are right: the eyes,' responded Michael.

The two young men stood on the verandah, listening to the animal sounds coming from the darkness beyond the fence. Two young '*mukiwas*' drinking rosé champagne in the twilight as though it was a completely natural thing to do in the bush. After a few minutes of silence and a refill, Kevin turned from looking over the game fence on the front boundary of the property into the national park beyond.

'Grab the bottle, Fonz. Gail's already left for the boat club. Let's go have a party,' said Kevin over his shoulder as they headed downstairs to the cruiser.

3

Farewell to Africa

A gigantic hangover is bad enough on its own, but the next day, Michael had one in 38-degree dry heat while waiting to catch a flight from Victoria Falls to Johannesburg before getting an onward connection to London. It was hell. The overhead fan in the passenger lounge, which was the closest thing there was to air conditioning, barely fluttered; the motor made a sound which made him think that any moment there would be a bang and smoke everywhere. The lounge was crowded with tourists and businessmen, as well as people who had been visiting friends in Victoria Falls. The familiar buzz of many conversations taking place simultaneously in close proximity echoed around the crowded terminal. There were two local politicians trying to look both intimidating and important. They were surrounded by their over-dressed, overweight wives and a small, immaculately dressed army of children. A captain in the uniform of the Zimbabwean army momentarily caught Michael's eye, and he wondered briefly what would be taking him south to Johannesburg. A few diehards wandered around the miserable shops, looking through the poor excuses for duty-free goods. Michael stared at the flaking magnolia-coloured walls. There was a dark green painted stripe along the floor, masquerading as a skirting board. He watched a large spider edging ever nearer to a couple of unsuspecting flies on the ceiling above the sign that said 'Departures' – there was only one exit out onto the tarmac anyway.

After lounging as best he could for thirty minutes, he stretched and lifted his six-foot, three-inch frame off the black metal chair, one of many near the departure gate. Normally, his body was fit and taut, but today, he was somewhat worse for wear. He decided to make his way to the bar at the back of the lounge, where there appeared to be less light and where there was another fan which looked like it was working slightly better than the one he was sitting under. His light-khaki longs and khaki short-sleeved shirt and bush boots without socks were contributing, to some extent, to the smothering, stale nature of the air in the terminal.

'Cold beer, please,' he said to the barman, unfolding himself and propping up the bar by leaning on his elbows on the cool granite counter top. The barman, well turned out in a pseudo-colonial morning suit and white shirt accompanied by a huge grin, gave him a knowing nod and swiftly flipped the top off an ice-cold bottle of Castle Lager before placing it in front of Michael.

'Would you like a glass, sir?' asked the barman.

Michael responded by lifting the bottle to his lips and, taking a long gulp, downing half the bottle in an instant.

'Ah, the hair of the lion that bit you,' said the barman, adding that his name was Phineas.

'You mean the hair of the dog, Phineas,' corrected Michael.

'Ah yes, maybe, sir,' said Phineas, giving a huge grin, 'but you look like a lion bit you in the arse, sir.' They both laughed loudly at the joke.

Michael drifted across to a concrete bench built into the back wall of the bar. On it were large, colourful, animal-motif designed cushions acting as backrests. He sat down and leant back against the wall, which was surprisingly cool. He closed his eyes and let his mind drift back to the previous evening at the boat club, home of the two-dollar bottle of beer – bargain!

The previous evening had begun, as so many did when one was with Kevin, with two bottles of Rosé Brut Champagne (although the French would have had a fit at the use of the term, as the champagne was South African), and then a short journey out on the game drive road to the boat club. Drink-drive breathalyser equipment was rumoured to be arriving soon in Victoria Falls, just as soon as the local police raised enough money from their hand-held radar speed guns (reported to be the only way they got paid nowadays) to buy the equipment. They will make a bloody fortune, Michael smiled to himself thinking about it.

It was hard to believe that the large kikuyu grass lawn along the river's edge, which was now a place where most of the young white and black families on the river would gather for their weekend fishing parties and barbeques, had once been the landing stage for Imperial Airways' Empire flying boats. The only remaining reminder of that era was the metal bridge and rusty pontoon, neither of which were still in use, although there was a plaque stating that it had been used by Imperial Airways. After arrival, the lucky passengers would head for the Victoria Falls Hotel, which is still in use today – a beautiful colonial-era building overlooking the Falls themselves. The hotel, with its white walls and red-tiled roof, is a throwback to an era of luxury and decadence, the so-called 'white mischief' years. Old habits and standards die hard: the hotel still did high tea on the highly polished red concrete verandah.

As in previous years, Kevin's farewell speech to his mate was forgotten as the evening progressed.

'Fonz, you will be back next year; we will do it then,' Kevin slurred, giving the cheeky grin for which he was well known.

The beer flowed freely, and the floor around the bar area became a small lake; confirmation of a roaring trade. So-called 'shots', concoctions of liqueurs and neat hard spirits, were passed around and downed as toasts at any excuse. The laughter had got louder, the jokes had got worse, and the mingling and suggestive flirting, which was so much a part of these gatherings, began.

An expat, 'Zimbo', who was now a pilot for Emirates Air, sang his own brand of Zimbabwean folk rock. He was hugely popular with the young folk from the Falls area, and his singing was often drowned out by the raucous sing-alongs. At one point, he had sung 'Run Rhino Run', a song he had written about the dangers rhinos all over Africa were facing. Some of the young men had developed a dance routine to the music, young men playing the part of poachers and rhinos alike, prancing and dancing around the bar area, knocking friends and onlookers flying about the bar. The culmination of the dance was the inevitable death of a couple of the rhinos. The local anti-rhino poaching ranger, a strapping young lad called Sean, played the part of the head of the poaching gang, leaping all over his mates as they lay on the bar floor. Ironic, Michael had thought.

At some point, Michael's head started spinning from the combination of champagne and at least half a dozen beers with the odd 'shot' thrown in, combined with the huge writhing, dancing, singing, sweating melee of bodies. Eventually, he found himself out on the lawn near the water's edge, listening to the calm sound of the river flowing downstream. The night sky was cool, considering the rains were yet to arrive. A full African moon lit up the river banks and glistened on the water, giving life to the shadows. Thinking that he had seen a lone, old, bull elephant under the ilala palm near the jetty gently swaying from side to side, Michael peered into the shadows. In the trees, the cicadas, known locally as Christmas beetles, were sending out their mating high-pitched screech, which they made by rapidly rubbing their legs against their bodies. Local folklore claimed that some over-zealous beetles rubbed so hard they exploded. *Poor buggers*, thought Michael.

'Michael?' came a soft voice from the shadows under the baobab trees in the direction of the parking area. 'Is that you?'

Michael turned to see Sally Morton, the wife of a local private hunting concession owner. Michael had met Rob Morton once. He was pleasant in a mundane sort of way, but was not somebody Michael felt completely at ease with. But he had spent a good hour talking to Rob at the barbeque, and the man knew his stuff when it came to hunting. Although it was controlled and done under licence, it was a vocation Michael had little time for. In his opinion, it was all about big money and very wealthy, ignorant clients.

He had met Sally several times, at Gail's Africa Café and around the village. He had also chatted to her once at a private game camp upstream in the national park. He had always thought she looked really good. She took good care of herself and obviously kept herself fit with exercise and workouts.

'Hi, Sally.'

Michael turned towards Sally as she walked slowly over towards him on the lawn. The moonlight was fully on her back. She was wearing a white, ankle-length kaftan-styled, loose-flowing dress. The moon added a further dimension, creating an X-ray image; it looked like there was little else underneath the dress. Her body looked perfect in the moonlight: she had long, lithe legs, a small waist and breasts which fitted perfectly into the top of the dress. The shape of her breasts were hidden by the shadows, but they strained gently against the little buttons below her neckline. Two of the buttons were open, but the secrets within remained just that – secrets… Michael recalled a photograph he had seen in some celebrity magazine of a young Princess Diana taken in her courting days shortly after her engagement to Prince Charles.

'How are you, Sally? I didn't see you in the bar, but that's not surprising with all those reprobates milling around. There was a real crush tonight.'

'I came down tonight with a couple of girlfriends. There's always good music, and we wanted to have a laugh. Somebody said it was your farewell party. Are you off back to England?'

'Yes, it's been a great three weeks – gone too quickly. Still, I always come back to get my adrenaline fill of Africa. Hopefully I'll be back next year again – or sooner, perhaps. Kevin is like a brother to me, and it's like coming home.'

'I don't know how you cope with living in England. All that awful weather; no wonder they call it Mud Island. I saw Gail the other day; she said you were no longer in the British Army, but had been working for some undercover outfit for the last couple of years. Sounds a bit James Bond. Do you travel the world in your job? Are you licensed to kill?'

'Nothing as glamorous as that, Sally. Besides, as the head of MI6 said to a parliamentary committee recently, James Bond doesn't really exist. I work for a company providing security and protection of UK citizens' assets. It's a job I know and do well, one I enjoy doing. All a bit boring, really.'

'Were you ever in Afghanistan when you were in the army, Michael?' asked Sally.

'I was, a couple of tours; it seems like a long time ago now. It's gone into a box of memories that doesn't often get opened. Why don't you let me buy you a drink, Sal?'

'Thanks, Michael, but I was thinking of going home. It's nearly midnight, and the noise and the crush is all a bit much for me. My friend Sarah is supposed to be giving me a lift, but she has her sights set on that new Lodge manager, Clive. She says she is going to give him a welcome to the Falls he won't forget and further his education. Knowing her, she will follow him into the gents if she has to! Isn't that romantic – not!'

'Needs must I guess,' shrugged Michael. 'Tell you what: why don't I run you home? I'll get the keys of Kev's truck; you are just in the village near the game fence, aren't you? I'll drop you off and be back to collect Kev in no time.'

'Are you sure that's okay? I could always call Rob and ask him to come and get me; he is not into loud parties.'

Most likely sitting in his lounge cleaning his rifles and listening to Jim Reeves, thought Michael. A little cruel, mate, he immediately scolded himself – Rob wasn't that bad.

'I'll just grab the keys from Kevin and be back,' said Michael.

As he walked away, he chuckled to himself: of course James Bond exists; we just don't publicise the fact.

They drove back into the village in silence, but it wasn't unpleasant or awkward. Michael had to concentrate on the road and the shadows beyond, and he strained his eyes staring into the darkness, which was not surprising considering the amount of alcohol he had consumed. The silence allowed him to focus on the night sounds and smells drifting through the open windows of the cruiser. His senses picked up a soft, sensual fragrance coming from the passenger seat where Sally was sitting, with shoes kicked off and legs tucked up underneath her. Her back was against the doorframe, and she was facing Michael, her eyes drifting slowly over his well-built frame. *Hmmm, Chanel N°5*, he mused – my kind of girl.

As he drove through the electrified gates in front of

the white-walled bungalow, his headlights picked out a large, flat area of kikuyu lawn, where there was a scattering of small mopani trees and what appeared to be tropical flower beds. The electrified wire fence was there to keep out the elephants from across the road, which formed the natural boundary with the national park. The six-foot-high iron fence on the park side of the road had long since been ruined. President Mugabe's cabinet didn't regard national parks as high priorities for funding.

Michael followed behind Sally towards the front door and noticed the ever-present red mud stains on the lower white walls, a constant reminder of the rains still to come. The first rains would reduce the stains to light brown.

'Come on in,' Sally said, glancing over her shoulder.

Michael entered the lounge area, which, like so many colonial homes in Zimbabwe, was filled with furniture hand-me-downs from parents that seemed to belong to an age past – the fifties, mostly. *Retro, they call it in London*, Michael thought.

'Drink?' Sally asked.

Michael hesitated briefly, knowing that booze was hard to come by at times in the Falls.

'Do you have any Scotch?' he asked tentatively.

'You're in luck. Scotch coming up. It's 25-year-old Macallan. My folks brought it up from down south when they were last here. Water? Ice?'

'On the rocks thanks, just ice. Will Rob be joining us?'

'Be right back,' Sally answered and disappeared down the passage.

When Sally returned, she was holding a glass of red wine in one hand and the Macallan whisky in the other. She had changed from her white dress into an exquisite full-length silk and lace black nightdress, totally see-through. There were no panties and no breast protection, other than the lace top which pulled at her full nipples. Michael drew in his breath sharply.

'Oh my God, Sally,' was all he could stutter. 'But where is Rob, is he…?'

Sally cut across Michael's question. 'I lied. Rob is on a hunting safari, and I need the company. No, actually, I need you Michael. I have done for a long time.'

Michael recovered from his initial shock and walked towards Sally, who in turn was backing up against the wall, placing the drinks on the sideboard as she did so. Michael reached towards her and pushed her up against the wall. Sally lifted her left leg and wrapped it around Michael's hip, causing the nightdress to ride up, and exposing a beautiful leg and the promise of an inner thigh. Michael kissed Sally lightly on her mouth, slowly tightening his grip around her back as he did so. Her lips parted and Michael's tongue moved deep inside her mouth. Their kissing became hungrier, more explosive and Sally pushed her lower body hard against Michael's taut stomach muscles. Michael swept Sally up and moved effortlessly to the couch. As he laid her on the cushion her right leg shifted to the floor, and she opened up her legs in a slow, sensual movement. Michael watched as she lifted her mons Venus towards him; she was almost completely shaven. Michael sank to his knees next to the couch and gently started to kiss the heart of her femininity. His tongue feverishly sought her and she writhed, uttering small mewing sounds.

'No, Michael, come into me, before it's too late,' Sally cried out.

Michael rose and in one movement placed his hands on the backs of Sally's thighs, then entered her as he knelt above her. They were both locked together in nature's special dance, where the mind goes blank and passion and climax roll like thunder through the brain. The red strokes.

They lay in each other's arms, sweating, eyes closed as the faint but overpowering human perfume enveloped them both. Neither spoke for some while, and then Sally stirred, got up and squeezed past Michael. Her nightdress was lying on the floor alongside the couch.

She walked to the lounge door, smiled, looked fondly at Michael and then turned out the light, and as she closed the door behind her called softly, 'Don't waste the whisky, angel, my very own 007, please lock the door on your way out.'

With that, Sally was gone.

Michael lay back on the couch, still in the red zone, caught by surprise at Sally's sudden exit. *For the best, I guess*, he thought. What more is there to do or say without getting into awkward discussions? He rose from the couch, dressed quickly and picked up the nightdress, then brushed it against his lips before dropping it on the couch. He walked to the sideboard, lifted the Macallan and downed it in one gulp. *Bloody shame*, he thought: it's pure nectar, to be sipped and savoured.

He gently closed the door and slipped out into the still-warm night. His thoughts briefly turned to Kevin. *How had the silly bugger got home?* he wondered.

Michael was shaken out of his pleasant reverie by the static from the public address system.

'Your attention, please. We are boarding flight BA 1426 to Johannesburg now. Proceed at once for boarding, please.'

No further pleasantries, no business class and gold card holders, not even women and children first. Michael hauled his body off his seat and followed in the general direction of the heaving throng towards two ground handlers, who were collecting boarding passes, tearing them in half and handing them back to passengers as proof of permission to board.

Out on the tarmac Michael was at once hit by a blast of hot air. The sun was bathing everything around in a hazy shimmer. Up the stairs – no air bridge here. He was greeted by a very smartly dressed young black female cabin attendant.

'Row ten, Seat A, sir – on the right. Thank you,' she said.

Michael shuffled towards his seat, which was behind a couple of young female German backpackers. Although they were attractive, they clearly had not seen a shower in a while. Michael reached his seat and discovered Seat B was at this point still empty. *Would be great if that remained the case*, thought Michael, throwing his rucksack into the overhead locker and easing himself into the narrow seat. The last thing he remembered before nodding off was reading a sign on the aircraft bulkhead which stated that the route was flown by Comair in partnership with British Airways.

A gentle hand shook his forearm.

'Please put your seat in an upright position and

fasten your seatbelt, sir,' whispered the same young lady who had greeted him on boarding. 'We will be landing at O.R. Tambo International, Johannesburg in ten minutes,' she said.

Michael always wondered why they called it O.R. Tambo and not by the ANC founder's full name, Oliver Tambo.

The aircraft, a Boeing 737-200 series, bucked wildly and slammed from side to side as it approached the airport underneath huge, dark cumulonimbus clouds. The pilots knew only too well the unpleasant landing conditions that would be created by the hot, high veld late afternoon.

The high veld, as Gauteng Province is known, is famous for late afternoon summer thunderstorms, full of dark violent clouds, sweeping rain accompanied by electrical storms and lightning that thunders down onto the earth below. It's an almost daily occurrence, and a thing of frightening awe and beauty, but it's always over in the matter of an hour, leaving the smell of newly mown grass and a drop in temperature in its wake. Spectacular, but not great when you are landing.

The pilots knew exactly how to handle these conditions: fast and down, in that order. No clever flying; just getting the job done. The Boeing 737 slammed into the runway, then lifted into the air again briefly. Just as it appeared half the passengers were about to let out a scream, the intercom came to life.

'Whoa, big fella, whoa,' one of the pilots said, affecting an American drawl, calming the sense of near-panic.

One of the cabin crew immediately followed this up with 'Ladies and gentlemen, welcome to O.R. Tambo

International. Please remain seated…'

Michael's mind drifted off, so he didn't hear the rest of the announcement. He watched the aircraft cut across one of the main runways, making its rumbling and bumpy way to its slot in a bay alongside the domestic terminal. As soon as the seatbelt sign had been switched off and the jet engines cut out, Michael rose, grabbed his rucksack and moved quickly forward, moving past several rows of disembarking passengers to ensure he was off quickly.

As the airport switched into night mode, catering trucks and cargo loaders scurried around, their head-lights and orange flashing warning lights on their roofs orchestrated chaos. Michael arrived in the duty-free departure area of the airport, having cleared customs and immigration formalities. He chose a seat in a fast food outlet with a 180-degree vision of the aircraft stand apron and all the movements on it. He could clearly see the aircraft as they thundered past on the main runway, towards the rotation point, the point of no return. The spray from the now distant storm created a smokescreen effect as the giant planes lifted quickly into the night sky, their landing lights piercing the blackness like powerful torches.

Michael ordered a beefburger with bacon and mushrooms, together with a couple of Peroni beers. *Getting two saves ordering again*, he thought; waiters are trained to ignore you after the first delivery of food. When the burger arrived it was huge, and came with onion rings and a side salad. Michael was already on his second beer and was feeling almost human again. He felt the effects of the abuse of his body the previous evening fading rapidly. He felt relaxed and comfortable. Suddenly, he felt the hair on his neck stand up, and his army training kicked in. He glanced rapidly around the restaurant, scanning to find the source of his concern. His eyes caught those of the army captain he had seen in the departure lounge at Victoria Falls; he was staring across from the other side of the restaurant. Their eyes only locked briefly before the captain broke eye contact. *So he is travelling onwards, going somewhere else*, thought Michael. Where to? What is his business?

The captain must have been staring for a while, and he had aroused Michael's survival instincts. *You're being paranoid, old son*, thought Michael. *It's a free world, and people in uniform are not uncommon.* Indeed, in Michael's own line of work he often had to wear paramilitary uniform. Michael dismissed his thoughts, but not before snatching a quick photo of him using his mobile phone, in case he needed it for future reference. He paid for his meal, left a good tip, then wandered around the fully stocked and varied duty-free shops. *Like two different worlds*, thought Michael, recalling the poor excuse for duty-free available at the Falls.

Boarding began on the BA 56 flight nonstop from Johannesburg to London at 2000 hours. This time, it happened in an orderly fashion: children and old folks went first, and they were offered assistance; they were followed by the privileged few in first class, although Michael suspected they had been boarding from the outset through the desk area with a dark blue strip of carpet and a vase of wilting roses, signifying the check-in was for 'special' passengers; then the corporate air miles collectors, the businesspeople, and the gold and silver card holders. Michael noticed that this still didn't stop a few passengers from trying to jump the queue. He smiled at the exercise in futility. Finally, the great unwashed shuffled forward. Michael held back, happy to wait, as he would be sitting down for the next ten and a half hours until they reached Heathrow.

After getting on, he made his way to the back of the economy section, where, on a Boeing 747-400, you can find two seats against the outside bulkhead; there it's less hassle and less movement. He placed his old rucksack in the overhead locker and settled into his seat, discarding the earphones before tucking the pillow behind his back and stowing the blanket under the seat in front of him. He looked across the aisle and saw the two German girls across the far side. *I wonder if they've found time for a shower*, he thought. Right on time, the jumbo jet pushed back, and without further ado, trundled down the taxiway, then turned briefly at the entrance to the runway where the engines were run up to maximum power with the aircraft brakes still on. Then, as the brakes were released, the aircraft began moving. The engine's reassuring rumbling was replaced by a roaring crescendo as the aircraft thundered down the runway. The Rolls-Royce engines pushed the aircraft into a gentle rise off the runway into the night sky. The 747 gracefully commenced its climb to 35,000 feet in a northerly direction.

After a few minutes, the engines cut back from full throttle. There was a pinging sound as the seat belt signs were switched off, and the cabin crew immediately sprang into action. Michael declined the evening meal, instead ordering two small bottles of good South African Cabernet Sauvignon. He was rewarded with three bottles by a petite blonde-haired member of the cabin crew. She smiled at him, obviously thinking he was cute. *Really cute guy, wouldn't throw his slippers out from under my bed*, she thought. Michael returned her smile, then stretched out as far as possible and opened the first bottle. After putting aside half of the third bottle, he immediately started scratching around, trying to locate his eye shades. Yet another result of his army experiences: sleep when you can, fall asleep as quickly as you can, for as long as you can. Sometime during the night, he felt the cabin attendant gently placing his blanket around his upper body, letting her fingers linger on his forearms. He half-smiled in his sleep.

4

London

Immigration, which had been given an all-new public image and logo as the 'UK Border Agency', was quick and efficient and Michael used the new eye technology entry queue. He rode down on the elevator to the baggage hall and was pleased to note that his baggage was already on Conveyor 5, the Johannesburg BA flight number clearly indicated on the TV monitor screen above the moving belt.

A brief saunter through the green 'nothing to declare' route and Michael was clear through to the glass and steel Terminal 5 Arrivals area. Staying on the ground floor, Michael made his way to the taxi rank immediately across the road outside International Arrivals. A number of the iconic black cabs edged along to swallow up arriving passengers, all strictly controlled by a couple of no-nonsense controllers. As Michael squeezed his frame through the door of the cab, he turned around, and for an instant, thought he caught a glimpse of the young Zimbabwean army officer getting into a cab two back from Michael's own. *Must be some sort of military attaché in the London Embassy*, he told himself.

Michael shut the door and called out to the cab driver.

'Wimbledon Village, please, mate. Bottom end of

the high street, please.'

'Righto, guv'nor,' called back the cabbie as he pulled away smoothly from the rank. Unlike their American counterparts, all black cab drivers in London have acquired 'The Knowledge', which involves months, sometimes years, of training, requiring them to gain a detailed knowledge of 25,000 London streets within a six-mile radius of Charing Cross, as well as all the major arterial routes serving the Greater London area. Another requirement for 'The Knowledge' is a good knowledge of buildings and places of interest in the city.

The early morning rush hour had not yet got into its stride, and the autumn sun was only just above the horizon, giving the London sky a watery, yellow-grey hue. The cabbie opted for a quick dash down the A4 to Brentford, then went down the Kew Road and over the Thames, passing the Royal Botanic Gardens fondly known as Kew Gardens, 121 acres of magnificent garden flora and fauna from all four corners of the Earth. Less than two miles later, the cab entered Richmond Park, one of Michael's favourite places to spend his leisure time, with something over 2,300 acres of forests, gardens and wildfowl ponds, through which herds of fallow and red deer roamed freely. The park was criss-crossed by cycle paths, footpaths and bridleways, offering shared access for all. Michael had done a number of charity runs around the park's six-mile perimeter.

He fondly recalled some close encounters of a more amorous nature, like being in some ferns with a lady friend just as a ride from a local riding school came by, and having to scrabble around in the grass for her black bra. Or another time with the same nature-loving lady, her skirt around her waist, a pair of white lace knickers in one hand, and the other holding onto a young sapling for dear life as Michael stood behind her with his jeans around his ankles, his legs taut and thrusting forward. He was just about to reach a magnificent climax when she had hissed, 'Hurry, Michael. We are about to have company.' Michael had climaxed with seconds to spare, before two ramblers wandered past, grinning from ear to ear, and the sapling finally stopped waving around as though it were in a hurricane. 'Lovely day for it!' the male member of the party had called out.

Suddenly the cabbie's voice cut into Michael's thoughts.

'Where exactly do you want to be, guv?' he asked.

He had dwelt on the park and all his memories for so long that he had not realised they were on Wimbledon High Street.

'Just on the traffic circle by Le Pain Café, please,' Michael replied.

From there it was a short walk down Grosvenor Hill to the brownstone art deco apartment block where he shared a three-bedroom first-floor flat with his best friend and fellow ex-Sandhurst officer cadet, Edward Hunt. He was, however, not in the apartment when Michael arrived. Probably at the gym or out jogging on Wimbledon Common, Michael assumed.

Edward was just back from a routine watch and listen assignment on behalf of a wealthy Far Eastern client of Excalibur Securities Limited, the private security company they both worked for. Owned by an ex-SAS colonel, Donald Torrens, Excalibur provided all forms of security, surveillance and protection to wealthy clients across the globe. Business was booming, and Torrens kept it close to completely legal by remaining tight with old contacts in the spy industry, often taking on jobs that government ghosts such as MI5 and MI6 didn't want to be seen being actively involved in. Torrens also had more than a passing acquaintance with Sir John Reid, GCHQ's boss man.

Michael threw his rucksack on his bed, stripped off his khaki bush-wear and headed for the shower. The apartment had been reconfigured by Michael when he purchased it to create two en suite bathrooms, leaving a very small third bedroom, which now doubled as an IT room and office room. Michael and Edward had shared the apartment since leaving the army and joining Excalibur Securities.

Michael took his time in the shower, luxuriating in the hot water. He had turned the rainforest shower head so that the jets provided a mild stinging sensation. Stepping out of the shower he dried off vigorously, put on a plain black T-shirt, blue denim jeans, socks and a black roll neck sweater, then wandered around the flat, before sitting down at the dining room table, intending to go through all his mail, which Edward had neatly stacked against the toast holder. Nothing of great importance: a few bills and a couple of interesting-looking invitations to dinner parties.

He wandered through to the office and switched on the computer, then went quickly to his personal email account. The first email that caught his eye was an instruction from Colonel Donald Torrens to be at Excalibur's Old Bond Street offices at 0900 hours on Monday morning for an assignment briefing. The email was thinly disguised as a market update and strategy meeting for heads of departments.

Michael heard a key in the apartment door and the awkward movement of somebody struggling to open it with only one free hand.

'Is that you, Edward?' Michael called over his shoulder.

'It certainly is,' came the reply as Edward staggered into the kitchen, juggling half a dozen grocery bags. 'How was Zim, you lucky bugger?'

'Had a great time, Ed. Good to see all my old mates and get back into the bush. The rains were just beginning, and there were a lot of young animals around – good time for the carnivores.'

'Starting to get cold here; won't be long before the clocks go back. Going to grab a shower and then meeting up with my sister Millie for lunch. You free this weekend?'

'As far as I know. I was thinking of going down to Milkwood in Cranleigh to see my parents. Why? What's up?'

'Millie is having a party down at my mum's place in Challock this Saturday. She is doing out the barn and has organised a band; some guys are doing a barbeque. Mind you, it will be a bit bloody cold, but hey, that's England for you. She is inviting some of her friends from her old City firm. Could be quite a hoot, knowing Millie.'

'Yes, that sounds like fun. Count me in. Let's meet up at the Dog & Fox this evening for a couple of beers. We can catch up then.'

Michael spent a couple of hours going through

emails, sorting out his accounts and just chilling around the apartment. He thought briefly of a trip to the gym, but decided to catch up on some sleep, which was just as important, he argued with himself.

Edward arrived at The Dog & Fox about seven that evening and found that Michael had got them a small table up on the elevated section of the bar, close to the big picture window that looked out over Wimbledon Village High Street. Edward stopped at the already crowded bar area and signalled 'Drink?' to Michael.

Michael raised his near empty glass in reply, tapping it and giving a thumbs-up signal. Edward could see it was the remnants of a pint of Guinness. He ordered two more pints and pushed his way to the table.

'Thought we were in a recession?' Edward said as he sat down at the table. 'Where do all these people and their money come from?'

Michael shrugged and smiled at his friend.

'Cheers, mate,' he said, raising his glass in salute. Edward returned the greeting, raising his glass and clinking it against Michael's. Michael held his eyes for a second. Edward was as good as it got if you needed a rock solid number two; Michael considered himself lucky.

'*Slainte*,' responded Edward, using the Irish word for 'good health'.

The two friends talked about what each had been up to over the past couple of weeks. Edward reported that his last assignment had been mind-numbingly boring except for the five-star hotel and the heat of Dubai. The Guinness flowed freely as they talked.

'Monday will bring us up to speed,' said Edward.

'Torrens wants to brief us on a contract. Sounds as though we could be out of the office for a while.'

He was being deliberately vague, due to how crowded the bar was. Before Michael could respond, a couple of wannabe Sloane Ranger-type girls – attractive, put-on posh accents, early- to mid-twenties, carrying a bottle of Sauvignon Blanc – asked if they could join them at their table as the other tables in the bar appeared to be full.

'We were just leaving. You can have this table to yourselves,' said Edward. The younger girl, who had long, straight blonde hair, a short black dress, sheer black stockings and high heels cast her eyes downwards, obviously thinking that this was a pity. *Whoa*, thought Michael: *bet she could be trouble*. He smiled and waved as they pushed their way back through the now heaving mass around the bar and into the night on the high street. The two men wandered down the high street to a little French bistro they both enjoyed. Pierre, the maître d', greeted them warmly.

'Bonne soirée, messieurs, your usual table?'

'Of course,' responded Michael, with a chuckle.

There were less than 30 tables in the place, but the one on the far left at the back, facing the entrance, was as close as it got to being private. They both ordered *poulet Breton* chicken and *frites*, and, without being asked, Pierre placed a bottle of Burgundy and two glasses on the table.

The rest of the evening was spent in a relaxed mood. The closeness and camaraderie the two young men shared was easy to see. They finished the night with a short, slightly inebriated walk home.

5

Excalibur London

Anyone looking into the Excalibur Securities offices from street level around this time would have seen a neat but cramped foyer behind a gleaming, black-painted door with a silk finish, and a number of small, clear, square glass windows cut into its upper half. On the door itself were heavy polished brass finishes, a knocker, a buzzer and a Yale lock. The door was always locked, and gaining entrance required the visitor to press the buzzer and talk into a discreet microphone. The entrance foyer was compact and well designed, and the carpet was pure wool in a deep royal blue. Inside the foyer was a small marble desk, and underneath, out of sight, were a range of electronic communication devices from buzzers, intercom, radio handset and an alarm system. An ornate, expensive Far Eastern lamp-shade sat on top of a brass lamp, and there was a map of the world with certain countries highlighted on the rear wall. On the far wall was a small brass plaque stating that it was the office of Excalibur Securities Limited. No other information was on display. A small modern lift was the only visible sign that there was a way to reach the first-floor offices. The desk usually had a slender, attractive, dark-haired woman in her mid-thirties with piercing deep-blue eyes sitting behind it. Her standard reception attire was a charcoal pencil skirt, a white silk blouse, a navy-coloured designer blazer and black stiletto high heels. A small name plate on the desk gave her name as Ms. M. Mulvihill. She looked the epitome of a top receptionist; she had a serene, soft caring face with beautiful blue eyes, which only enhanced her attractiveness. First-time visitors were, without fail, both captivated and fooled by her appearance.

Nobody would have known from looking at her that this demure young lady had formerly been a lieutenant in a rapid-response infantry platoon, and that she was equally at home with an L85A2 assault rifle and an FN Minimi light machine gun as she was in a Sloane Square wine bar. Her family was from the Republic of Ireland, but Maria had been born in England; as a result, although she had returned with her parents to Ireland at the age of five, she was allowed to serve in the British Armed Forces.

The office entrance in Bond Street was surrounded by the London headquarters of some of the most famous and expensive fashion houses in the world, complemented at the end of New Bond Street by the timeless architecture of Burlington Arcade, a precursor of the mid-nineteenth century shopping galleries of Europe – all the hallmarks of a very expensive address. Just the sort of address and look one would expect of an exclusive company serving the super-rich.

On Monday morning at precisely 0900 hours, Michael and Edward were sitting in the Excalibur boardroom in New Bond Street awaiting the imminent arrival of their boss. They were fresh from a most enjoyable weekend in Kent; Millie had held a riotous party at Edward's mother's small estate there. Before making their way upstairs, neither of them had been able to avoid a little banter and flirt with Maria in reception. She had handled them with ease and a smile. *Damn*, Michael had thought, *what a stunning woman.*

'Boys will be boys,' she scolded them, half-smiling, as they headed towards the lift.

Whilst waiting in the boardroom, Michael glanced at the two silver-framed adages that Colonel Torrens had adopted when he was first planning Excalibur.

The first framed quotation was from William Shakespeare, taken from *Julius Caesar*: 'Cry "Havoc" and let slip the dogs of war'.

Framed alongside this was Nelson Mandela's now world-renowned quote: 'One man's terrorist is another man's freedom fighter'.

Since Colonel Torrens had formed Excalibur some five years before, their reputation for getting the job done quietly and to the complete satisfaction of the client had grown in the world of espionage and security. Michael and Edward had been two of the early original officer recruits, and as he waited, Michael reflected on what Torrens had told him about why he had started up Excalibur and why it had, so far, been successful and respected.

Torrens had seen the shift early. The enemy was no longer known and definable – as had been the case during the so-called Cold War, when you knew who they were, where they were and to a degree their strengths and ambitions. In essence, this was the classic cat-and-mouse Cold War scenario. Now that was long gone, except for the age-old spying game, which still existed. Listening in to one's enemies and friends was a daily routine.

Torrens had seen the gap before most in what was needed to fight modern enemies: the IT terrorists, shadows in the night; coercion and subversion through social media; Western governments hard pushed daily by the massive increase in terror threats to their own security counter-measures always one step behind.

Britain was no different. Its police forces, special terrorist units, the border agencies and Secret Services, supported from time to time by crack military units, were fighting a daily battle to contain the threat. MI5, MI6, GCHQ and other lesser-known 'spook' agencies, both overt and covert. The best men and women in government service anywhere in the world all challenged daily. Sifting through millions of phone calls, a number which had been swelled recently by the increasing use of mobile phones. There was a vast array of internet traffic to monitor, which was a nightmare in itself. Many terror groups recruit from within, looking for home-grown terrorists, British nationals, and this just made the task harder.

The common goal of all the 'spook' agencies was to keep the homeland and its borders safe. As well as monitoring what was going on internally, an unwritten practice also involved keeping the enemy out. A major part of this strategy involves placing the armed forces, when called upon, into countries where the perceived threat is highest, thus keeping terror away from home. Problems arise when the intelligence services have no clear friends or foes in a particular country, Syria being the current prime example. There are a number of extremist groups who all want a new Syria, as well as many different splinter groups backed by countries with their own agendas. Identifying friends and foes is a nightmare. Nobody wants to be the government that supplied the portable ground-to-air missile that brings down a civilian airliner. Especially a friend of significant worth like Israel.

Colonel Torrens, by putting together a group of highly trained ex-military men that could be called on to assist in protecting British assets and citizens abroad, was giving the government more options. This was a force that could fight dirty; they were military operatives that could break the rules when necessary. They had proven invaluable in dealing with hostage situations where the 'friendlies' were not to be trusted. Torrens' company had proved to be a valuable ally and addition to the government security agencies in a number of situations, including protecting mining interests and other capital assets such as pipelines, and dealing with Somali pirates and other terror groups that were attacking Commonwealth countries' shipping. *He was a clever military man*, Michael thought.

Colonel Donald Torrens, dressed immaculately in a classic Bond Street navy blue pinstriped suit, a white shirt and a Guards tie, strode into the room carrying a small memory stick. He inserted this into the computer, which was connected to a state-of-the-art projector positioned at the end of the antique mahogany boardroom table, then turned to Michael and Edward.

'Welcome, chaps. I trust your leave was relaxing, Michael,' he said, in a manner that didn't require an answer.

He clicked a small buzzer which simultaneously turned down the boardroom lights and closed the blinds on the boardroom windows.

A screen dropped down from the ceiling, and an aerial photograph appeared on the screen of what looked like a small mine, some outbuildings and a couple of Land Rovers. There was mining equipment all over the place, and the area was muddy with tyre tracks from heavy vehicles and equipment. It was surrounded by a ten-foot-high heavy mesh fence with large automatic gates attached to concrete pillars, and surrounded by lush, dense forest full of impenetrable jungle-like undergrowth.

Torrens spoke from behind the projector.

'Right, listen up. Gentlemen this is Mankula Mine. It's in the DRC, also known as the Democratic Republic of the Congo, about twenty miles upstream from the port of Matadi on the Congo River. Matadi is itself the furthest upstream ocean-going port on the Congo; it has a mile-long granite waterfront and is the strategic import and export harbour for the DRC. It's First World around the harbour: good tarred roads, government buildings, a couple of high-rise commercial developments and one or two half-decent hotels. But outside the port area, conditions are Third World in all but a few residential areas. Untarred roads that turn to red mud in the wet, mud or breeze block single-storey buildings, corrugated tin roofs, some electricity. From here, rail traffic passes through the surrounding countryside to Kinshasa. As in the rest of the DRC, roads are not good – in fact, it's the least favoured transport network in the DRC.

'The mine belongs to White Cliffs Resources PLC and is principally owned by our new client, Sir Gordon

Ashton. His company is quoted on the FTSE 250 and is tipped as an up-and-coming small mining and oil prospecting operation. This particular mine has found diamonds in shallow alluvial soil, enabling easy extraction.' Torrens paused. 'Any questions so far?'

Both Michael and Edward shook their heads in response. Michael frowned briefly.

'Trouble?' asked Torrens.

'Sir, when I was in Zimbabwe, I spoke to some of the lads running large cargo trucking operations up through Zambia into the DRC, and they described it as 'the Wild West gone wilder'. Life is not high on the agenda and it's pretty hairy from what I hear.

'True, there are problems,' responded Torrens, 'but mainly in the south-east around Goma, where the M23 and other Hutu militia supported by Uganda and Rwanda have been operating. It's reported that ethnic cleansing is still being carried out in some areas. Since the last cease-fire things have been a little quieter. The UN currently has a peacekeeping force of over 18,000 troops in the DRC; this helps, but the DRC government also has armed forces from its other supporters and strategic partners – Zimbabwe, Namibia and Angola. These troops and their commanders are often distracted by a keen interest in acquiring a piece of the mining action in the DRC for themselves. So the problem remains: weird deals are being done by bad individuals on mineral rights that don't belong to them.

'Anyway, I digress. Let's just say the DRC has a huge amount of mineral wealth – estimated at $24 trillion, the equivalent of the combined GDP of the USA and Europe – and is having trouble in getting control of it. Too rich for its own good, you might say.

'It's more stable around Mankula Mine. Small-scale mining is not as prevalent in this area, so there are fewer hotheads. Our brief is to provide protection to the mine and its personnel, many of whom are British. There had been one or two minor skirmishes at the mine, but the guys on the ground put it down to petty thievery, but then, ten days ago, there was a small arms attack by unknown assailants, and that hammered home the need for protection. There were casualties during the attack, although none serious. The attack was thought to be an attempt to steal the mined uncut diamonds, which are stored in a large safe in the main compound offices.

'I want you two to put together a stick-strength size, say, of ten to twelve men, heavy firepower capability and get out there pronto. Set up a base inside the mine perimeter fence, set up comms back to us, secure the perimeter area around the mine and provide protection to the mine and its personnel. You, Major Ashton, will command the unit and Captain Hunt will act as second in command.'

Michael smiled. Torrens knew the two of them almost as well as if they were his own sons, but when he was choosing a leader he always addressed them by their old army ranks, as if to back up his choice.

Torrens continued, 'Take Sergeant McBride as your troop leader, as he has vast experience. For your stick NCOs select lads who are experts in using heavily armed fire-force weaponry. We have a couple of ex-SAS lads who can operate out of the area independently if necessary. The actual choice of which men I will leave to you, Michael.

'Select your weaponry, lightweight comms, computer satellite link kit and each man's equipment from Sergeant Major Nicholas down at the stores in Woking and I will clear it to Manston in Kent for our own C-130 flight out to Kinshasa. You will assemble all the weaponry and transport at Mankula's Kinshasa compound, then take the main Kinshasa coast highway as far as the turn-off to the mine, which is before the large road bridge across the river, some twenty kilometres this side of Matadi.

You will need both heavy and light terrain, so we will fly out a couple of the newer Jackal 2 armoured support vehicles and two long wheelbase Sabre Land Rovers; they will give you mobility. Probably get most of the kit on the C-130; if it's overcrowded, prioritise what is essential and then we can fly out the rest on the next run. I do not foresee much foot patrolling being necessary.

'Roger that, sir,' said Michael.

Torrens continued, 'Passports, health jabs, currency and visas from Maria as usual. Maria will be your headquarters satellite comms link under call sign Alpha One. She in turn will update me at all times.'

Edward, a solid second-in-command as ever, made rapid notes, nodding in agreement as he went. As with all operational outlines, Torrens had meticulously covered most of the troop movement to the DRC well in advance, although with their training and background, Michael and Edward could have worked it all out themselves. Still, it was good to confirm all the details regarding the troops on the ground with the boss.

Colonel Torrens ended by saying, 'Maintain a low

profile, especially where the weapons and other kit are concerned. You have been approved, but there is no need to broadcast information about our firepower; that might give people ideas about acquiring it.

'The client is keen to have you out there yesterday. The mine manager, a chap called David Smith, will give you a rundown on the day-to-day and the mine layout. He will travel down to Kinshasa to oversee your customs and immigration clearance. Any further questions at this stage?'

'What about the locals, sir?' asked Edward. 'Are we expected by the authorities and the local police and military in the Matadi area? I would hate to run into a firefight before we have even taken up our positions.'

'White Cliff Resources have cleared you from Kinshasa and on to Matadi, and also from Matadi to the mine. They have all the local government paperwork, but as you know, in Africa, often that is not worth the paper it's written on. They have their own government contact in the area: military chap by the name of Fabrice Bemba, a colonel, I think. So, for what it's worth, they are expecting an authorised and approved armed mine protection team.

'Gentlemen, that's our role and responsibility: protection of the mine, the personnel and the mine's assets. There are a lot of different armed groups out there, but that's not our fight and is none of our business. So watch the trigger-happy ones, especially the boy soldier groups high on drugs and witch doctor medicine! They call them invincibles!'

6

Airlift to the DRC

The two sticks of ten men spent four days down at the Woking barracks and stores. Time was set aside each day for the firing range. Twice a day, Edward led the men on a five-mile road run, and every morning commenced with the assault course and some limbering-up exercises. All the men handled the physical exertions with ease; no lingering ailments or injuries were sustained. Each man was assigned multi-terrain camouflage kit, osprey body armour and brown desert-style boots. As the stick were not expecting a full-on infantry role, headgear was left to personal choice. Most chose floppy camouflage hats, which provided protection from sun and rain.

The weapons included L85A2 assault rifles, standard infantry issue, 30-round magazines, 5.56mm round; 2 FN Minimi light machine guns, 2 L115A3 sniper rifles and a Heckler & Koch 40mm grenade machine gun which could be mounted on the Jackals. Michael also selected a '50-cal', which was a heavy 50-calibre machine gun or HMG. The Jackals themselves each carried L1A1 heavy machine guns mounted on a gun ring at the rear, which gave them the ability to swivel 360 degrees.

The heavy machine guns and grenade machine guns were tested on the vehicles on a specially adapted range while the assault rifles were tested and fired on the normal rifle firing range moving down the range running from 300 yards to 50 yards. The unique smell of gun oil, hot metal and explosives lay heavy in the air, bringing back memories to all of the stick – they had all fired weaponry in anger on their operations around the world.

Several boxes of the smoke grenades, high explosive and white phosphorus grenades were loaded on as well. Each man also had a Personal Role Radio, and there was a single Bowman secure VHF radio. Edward secured the computer equipment to establish a video link via satellite back to London. There were a variety of systems to aid vision, some of which were carried on their weapons: from the standard SUSAT 4 x magnification sight, used with the L85A2 rifles, to thermal imaging and night vision sights. Each man was given a choice to draw their personal favourite weapons. A couple of the lads drew handguns, while the two SAS lads drew pump action shotguns and an older-style FN MAG medium machine gun which could be mounted on one of the Sabre long wheelbase Land Rovers.

On their last evening at the barracks, the stick went into the Red Lion pub on the outskirts of Woking for a meal and a couple of beers. This should be a 'bonding session', not a complete piss-up, Michael had cautioned his men. The mood was upbeat and there was an air of anticipation; they felt they would do this job like professionals.

There was the usual discussion about weaponry, during which one of the SAS lads, Mark Jones, told the group that the L115A3 sniper rifle held the world record for the kill from the furthest distance by a sniper: in

Helmand, a Taliban commander had been taken out by a shot fired twelve feet high to the right from a distance of 2,815 metres; the bullet had travelled for six seconds before hitting its target.

'Yeah, but not by one of you lot,' shot back Corporal Rob Gibb. 'It was one of us from the guards.'

'We are normally a lot closer; we prefer taking out our ragheads with a knife from zero metres – something you probably would not be able to do because the enemy would hear you peeing your pants with fear,' shot back Jones.

Everybody erupted in laughter. Michael glanced around the group to detect if there was any animosity, but there was none – the group was solid.

As the publican rang the bell and called out, 'Last round, gentlemen, please,' Sergeant Sandy McBride stood up, looked around at the group and in a deep Scottish burr said, 'Come on, lads, drink up. It will be a long flight tomorrow, and there is no business class on a C-130.'

McBride was probably the most decorated in the stick, and to a man, they respected him. There were legendary tales of his bravery and the way he protected his men while in the Scots Guards regiment. The group rose as one and headed for the pub door.

The C-130 Hercules transporter, which was camouflage green and had no markings, rose off the long runway at Manston with ease, in the early morning, late October sunlight. As it climbed over the Channel, the passengers saw that Calais appeared bathed in a pale yellow glow. The four Allison turboprop engines chopped into the moist cold air, the plane's cargo of weaponry and men trussed up in its cavernous belly. Since all the kit and vehicles were on board (the load-master had done a brilliant job in getting all the equipment and the full stick on board), the men were seated in two rows of bench seats, facing each other across the fuselage. The fuselage was not insulated in any form, and the cold air and the roar from the engines made sleeping difficult. But the army can sleep anywhere, so it was not long before the conversation died down and heads dropped.

The fuel range of the C-130 required two refuelling stops at 'friendly' military air bases in Italy and Kenya. While there, Michael allowed the men to leave the aircraft, leaving two-man guard teams on rotation at the top of the rear-hinged loading ramp. The men were thus able to exercise and get a couple of good meals and refreshments from the canteen areas.

Just over 24 hours later, the C-130 began its descent into N'djili International Airport, Kinshasa. Clear skies made the landing straightforward, but there was the occasional bump, because the temperature on the ground was already rising, even though it was still early morning. The engines screamed as it landed, but reverse thrust quickly slowed the C-130, and it turned off the main runway halfway down. The aircraft was directed to the international cargo area. The C-130 drew up alongside a large steel and corrugated iron storage facility, which was painted a dull grey colour and had large sliding hangar doors. Two of the four pilots, who had rotated on the flight, shut down the engines and silence prevailed on board. The cockpit appeared overcrowded, with the pilot's, navigator's and engineer's seats all occupied. The relief pilots and loadmaster had bunked down in the rear near the steps up to the flight deck.

Michael addressed the team: 'Hang on chaps, sit tight, I am going to find our mine contact and see what is required to clear the aircraft and its cargo.

'Lower the ramp, loadmaster. Remember there are many inquisitive eyes around; be awake, guys.

'Mark, get down behind the ramp and cover with one of the sniper rifles. We need to have a clear shot on anybody making a sudden move.'

'Got it, sir.'

Michael moved up to the cockpit area, and the pilot in the left-hand captain's seat pointed out of the port cockpit window at two Toyota Hiace trucks with several people standing around them.

'Looks like your guys are here and waiting, Michael; the chap in the beige suit is signalling for you to join him.'

'Thanks, skip – good flight, thank you,' said Michael and he climbed down the cockpit stairs and out of the aircraft's low-slung side door. The man in the beige suit disengaged from the others and walked swiftly over to the aircraft.

'Welcome to the DRC. My name is David Smith, Mankula manager,' the suit said.

'Hi, Michael Ashton, Excalibur,' returned Michael. 'How quickly can we unload and get clear of the airfield? I am always uncomfortable in a sitting duck situation.'

'We are just waiting for Colonel Bemba's arrival. We have all the necessary paperwork and if you are set for rapid debus, we can clear the airfield to our Kinshasa offices. There is a large courtyard at the rear of the building with a high security fence; you can get organised there. There shouldn't be any problems on the city roads; the locals are used to seeing armed vehicles – it's part of the way of life here.'

As if on cue, a black Range Rover with blacked-out windows swung around the far end of the hangar and slammed to a stop a few feet from where Michael and Smith were standing. *Probably a gift from the United Nations that never reached the person it was intended for*, mused Michael.

From the front passenger seat a tall, slightly over-weight gentleman in a dark green uniform with several rows of medals attached lumbered out. He brushed down what appeared to be his full ceremonial military parade uniform and placed a cap with gold braiding and a huge badge on his head. His shoulder badges indicated that his rank was full colonel.

'Good morning, my name is Colonel Bemba of the Democratic Republic of the Congo's Army; I am attached to the Headquarters Division. I am here to escort you through all our formalities and see you get on your way.'

Michael's pale blue eyes fixed Bemba with a long, hard stare. Out of the corner of his eye he saw three other uniformed soldiers in what looked like camou-flaged battledress debus from the Range Rover and take up positions to the left and right of Bemba, but a good six feet further back. All three had AK-47 assault rifles, which were cocked and had the safety catches off.

'Tell your men to put on their safety catches and point those weapons towards the ground,' barked Michael by way of reply.

Bemba began, 'They are only…'

'Now,' cut in Michael. 'Look closely at the rear of the aircraft near the ramp, and you will see a man with a sniper rifle. One nod from me and he will take them all out and then you, all in a couple of seconds. Do it now.'

Bemba barked something in French to his men, who complied immediately.

'Thank you, Colonel Bemba. I can never relax when somebody is pointing a rifle at me – too many memories, too many mistakes.'

'Of course, I understand, Major Ashton. If you will follow me, we will go through customs and immigration.'

Bemba couldn't keep the annoyance at being pulled up in front of his men from showing on his face.

'Roger that,' said Michael.

He fell in with Bemba and his entourage, and they were joined by David Smith. The party made its way to the side of the grey hangar and into a long metal hut that appeared to have been made by welding a couple of sea containers together. Michael noticed Mark and another soldier running across the tarmac apron in front of the hut, then taking cover behind a number of aircraft storage bins. He also noticed a brief discussion taking place between Bemba and David Smith and a large brown envelope changing hands.

Michael shook his head and muttered to himself, 'Bad move, but hey, that's how Africa works, the fat cats get the cash while the little guys stay poor.'

Inside the hut the heat was unbearable. There were a couple of overhead electric ceiling fans rotating at full speed, but they were only pushing hot, stale air around the confines of the cream-painted interior. The smell of stale sweat permeated the air. A large, overweight man in what appeared to be the universal customs uniform with a little extra gold braiding waved a large rubber stamp high in the air and proceeded to smash it down on all the paperwork placed in front of him, not hesitating to look at what was contained in the documents. The banging was so loud that Michael feared it might trigger Mark and the other soldier with him into some sort of counterattack.

Within a matter of minutes, the papers were thrust back at Smith, then the big man grunted, '*Passeport.*'

Michael stepped forward and handed over ten passports, most of which were British. The big man flicked open each in turn, pausing when he got to Michael's passport.

'*Mercenaire?*' he asked.

'*Non, sécurité,*' replied Michael.

The customs man looked at Michael for a couple of seconds, then he smiled and shrugged and the passports were handed back unstamped. Michael wondered if that was because if the proverbial shit hit the fan, the DRC authorities could claim they had no knowledge of the group's entry into the country.

They all left the hut, relieved to get out into the fresh air. Bemba threw a sloppy salute to Michael, muttered a few words to Smith the mine manager and headed off with his bodyguards towards his shiny black Range Rover.

'Well, that was pretty straightforward,' said Smith as they walked back towards the aircraft. 'He was not amused at you ordering his men to lower their weapons.'

Michael shrugged and then turned to Smith. 'What is the going rate for importing a small army into the DRC?' asked Michael. 'While this sort of bribery and skulduggery is going on, poverty is not an option in Africa. Please note, David, that Excalibur is not involved in any way in the practice of paying bribes.'

In response, Smith shrugged and smiled. 'That's Africa for you.'

'Once you and your men are offloaded and in your vehicles, follow me through the airport perimeter gates and we will move to our company compound in Kinshasa. You will be able to rest up there. There are showers, and we can keep you in the back compound, away from prying eyes.'

Once the loadmaster had directed the vehicles of the C-130, Michael and Edward had a quick discussion on how the convoy should be formed. It was decided that the Land Rovers would bring up the front and rear with the two Jackals in the middle, these two vehicles carrying more men than they normally would in a patrol situation. Michael decided that they would make their exit fully armed and ready.

'No point in getting our arses shot off while our weapons are safely stored beneath the seats!' explained Michael.

Edward pointed out that Torrens had commanded them to keep a low profile, but agreed with Michael that a show of force would provide added protection. Every man was flacked up, with helmets and floppy hats, all weapons armed. They wore camouflage uniforms with grenades attached to their web belts; they were equipped with radios, the full nine yards. The machine guns were mounted on the Jackals along with the Heckler & Koch grenade machine gun. Edward noted that the SAS boys had mounted their MAG on the front dash of the Land Rover; both had their assault rifles and shotguns in a gun holder near the gear shift.

Michael climbed into the passenger seat of the lead, open Land Rover. The vehicles fired up and he waved the small, but heavily armed, convoy forward around the back of the main airport building and terminal, keeping to the perimeter fence and out of sight of any civilian traffic or passengers. There was no need to stop at the exit gates: when they reached them, the soldier manning the gatehouse stood stiffly to attention and saluted. *Probably our friend, Mr Smith, handing out envelopes again*, thought Michael, although the sight of heavily-armed army vehicles with a bunch of well-disciplined, serious-looking soldiers on board may also have had an effect. Outside the airport gates the convoy joined the normal traffic flowing towards the capital. The convoy was surrounded by civilian cars, taxis and lorries, together with smoke-belching, heavily over-loaded buses, their engines straining and their chassis buckled; all were pushing towards Kinshasa.

Once in the relative privacy of the Mankula compound, McBride quickly arranged the vehicles in a square laager with the equipment in the centre. He established static sentry posts and a larger patrol area around the compound. Some of the men were stood down, and some wandered off for showers. Gas cookers sprang to life with blue flame, some good old cuppas were brewed, and there was the sound of rations being opened and sorted out, along with muffled voices and the occasional laugh, signs of a camp settling down for the night. Michael established satellite comms with Maria in London; their call sign was Alpha One. He gave a brief, to-the-point, situation report, telling her that phase one was complete and the compound was secure. Michael mentioned the bribe situation and asked her to pass it on to Torrens. Maria agreed and Alpha One signed out.

7

Mankula Mine

As dawn was breaking, the huge red glow of the rising sun lifting from behind distant hills, the convoy drove out of Mankula's Kinshasa compound. Michael's Sabre Land Rover was in the lead, followed by the two Jackals. Edward was at the rear in the other Sabre Land Rover. They headed out onto the Kinshasa Matadi highway – Route Nationale 1, as it is known. Route 1 is one of the few fully tarred roads in the DRC. They knew that the distance they had to travel was 265 kilometres, which should have taken them just over three-and-a-half hours.

However, as the convoy soon found out, after the road left Kinshasa, it started to meander. They passed roadside stalls, hundreds of colourful little shops made out of corrugated iron, and pedestrians who seemed to be everywhere. The smell of roadside cooking, the sight of fresh food stalls alongside mountains of rubbish and the harsh blare of transistor radios at full volume only worsened what were already extreme driving condi-tions. Everywhere along the road and parked up was a melee of giant 36-wheeler haulage trucks, buses and cars. Driving right-hand drive vehicles on the left-hand side of the road only added to the confusion and the need for concentration. Progress became precarious and slow.

Michael, who was in the lead vehicle, suddenly snapped to attention as he saw a large haulage truck coming towards them; its brakes were screeching and there was blue rubber smoke rising from the road. Michael's eyes sought out the danger and he saw a stray mongrel dog disappearing under the front wheels in an explosion of bone and blood.

As they left behind the city and its sprawling shanty towns, the road started to wind its way up the surrounding hills and the landscape became more of a mixture of farmland and tropical foliage with ilala palms dotted around. The traffic had been bumper to bumper in the city, but at this point it thinned out and the tension among the men eased almost visibly.

Three hours later, the convoy started down the winding road towards the Congo River. In the distance they could see what looked like the large steel arches of a road and rail bridge combined, which crossed the river itself. As they came around the next long, downward-winding bend, they saw a large, metal sign on the left-hand side of the road indicating that Mankula Mine was 25 kilometres away. On the sign was a large arrow pointing down a red, muddy track surrounded by dense, bushy scrub and thick undergrowth.

'Turn in here, Sean, then pull up 500 metres down the track. We can regroup and close up a little there.'

'Roger, boss,' answered Sean Ahearn, an ex-Irish Guards infantryman who had three tours of Iraq and Afghanistan under his belt.

As the Land Rover slowed to a halt on the edge of

the muddy path, Michael reached for his personal radio.

'Charlie Two, Three and Four: this is Charlie One Sunray. Pull over behind my vehicle, Charlie Three, then take the higher ground off to the left of my position and stay sharp. I am not expecting trouble, but watch out anyway. Then all vehicle commanders on me to discuss our move on to the mine.'

'Charlie Two, roger that.'

This was followed by the same acknowledgement from the other vehicles.

Michael watched as Charlie Three changed to a low gear and the Jackal moved slowly up the hill to his left, the light machine gun pointed at the treeline. No sooner had all four vehicles stopped than all the commanders converged on Michael's Land Rover.

'As you guys saw, we have about 25 k's to go. The vegetation is heavy, but not so much that we won't be able to see into the bush around us. There is some cultivated land as well with papyrus, ilala palms and reeds closer to the river. Also, the odd baobab tree. We should pass a couple of villages closer to the actual river. Security at the mine has had a couple of punch-ups with armed gangs recently, so assume they are still in the area. Watch carefully for civilians near to the roadside. Stay open on comms. I want you, Sergeant McBride, to move up your Jackal to point.'

The commanders returned to their vehicles and the convoy moved off onto the thick, muddy, red tracks.

The convoy progressed slowly for about ten kilometres, during which a few civilian farmers were sighted and the occasional cattle, pigs, chickens and the forever present mongrel dogs. Suddenly, out of nowhere, two fighter jets screamed overhead at tree top level.

'Zimbo Hawk jets, boss,' yelled Sean over their afterburner thunder.

'Didn't see the markings. Well spotted, Sean,' yelled back Michael.

The jets suddenly climbed high into the sky. They were about five kilometres ahead and off towards the river, Michael guessed. They circled round, then went back in the direction they had come from.

'Fuck me,' came over one of the radios.

Michael cut it with a barked order.

'Split up off the road and fan out. We have nothing to match those bastards if they come back, so don't be a sitting target. Find cover in the trees.'

The convoy split up immediately, all going into the bush and getting under cover of trees and foliage.

Edward's Land Rover was the furthest to the north, nearer the river.

'Charlie One, this is Charlie Two. We can hear small arms fire over towards the north of us, and there is smoke rising from that direction. About two clicks away. Can we take a look-see?'

'Roger that, Charlie Two, but remember it's not our fight. Only if you perceive a threat to the mine can we think of getting involved. We will spread out and follow behind you at about 500 metres.'

Edward's Land Rover increased its speed towards the smoke while the other three vehicles formed up in in line abreast and moved slowly through the scrub and trees towards the smoke. Although the Hawk jets could still be heard, they did not reappear overhead.

Suddenly, Charlie Two's radio came alive, the sound

of gunfire and explosions clearly audible. What was more audible was the horrific screaming that pierced the ears of all those listening.

'This is Charlie Two. We are on the edge of a village. There are women and children running everywhere. There are guys in some sort of uniform firing directly into them, they are running parallel to us. Oh God, there are guys with machetes hacking at them. The huts are on fire. This is murder.'

Then there was a brief silence.

'Charlie Two, we are going to drive at these bastards and put a couple of bursts above their heads to cut them off. We can see some women and young females being dragged off towards their trucks. Some way off there appear to be army vehicles. They look like British Jackals, Charlie One. That just can't be. Commencing fire now.'

'Charlie Two, this is Charlie One. Do not engage directly unless you are fired upon; try to shelter the civilians. Remember it's not our war. Don't get involved, Charlie Two.'

The firing continued; now the remaining convoy could hear the sounds up ahead and see the smoke for themselves.

Edward looked on in horror in Charlie Two. As he was taking in the full horror of the massacre he saw two men armed with machetes closing in on a woman in rags and bare feet. She was running towards the Land Rover, carrying a small baby. The machete swung in the sunlight and the woman's shoulder and arm were hacked from her body. She fell screaming to the ground, blood gushing out of her torn upper torso, and the child fell from her grasp. The man gave a guttural cry, his face contorted in an evil grimace. As he raised the machete above the baby again, a single shot from an L85 behind Edward blew the top half of the man's skull into oblivion.

Edward knew instinctively that Tim Abrahams, one of the two ex-SAS boys in his Land Rover, had taken the shot. He knew as well that ice-cool control was needed to take even a single shot with a fully automatic weapon. Edward reacted immediately.

'Tim, aim high on full automatic above those gooks' heads. Robin, use the MAG to put down rapid fire in front of the gooks to stop those animals from chasing down those women. Tough shit if you hit a few of them.'

Then he turned to yell an instruction at Matt Tresman, the third soldier on the Land Rover, formerly a corporal in the Royal Marines.

'And Matt, use your grenade launcher to put a couple of grenades behind those trucks alongside the two burning huts now.'

The Land Rover immediately became a huge platform for firearms. Shell casings began flying all over the vehicle, the heavy hammering of the MAG and the distinctive thump of the Heckler & Koch Grenade MG competing in fire power ferocity with three L85s on rapid fire. The shellfire made the Land Rover start rocking wildly. The stench of cordite filled the air, temporarily blocking out the pervading smell of warm blood.

'Charlie Two, this is Charlie One. What the fuck's happening, Ed?' said Michael's voice over the radio.

Edward did not answer, concentrating instead on the

effects of the rapid fire going down around him. The running line of rag-tag bandits were charging onwards straight into the heavy MAG rounds, which were ploughing up the earth, blowing off their legs and limbs in the process. Mud and blood were spurting up from the red soil. They hesitated as the comprehension of what was happening to their comrades sunk in to their savagery-filled brains. There was another blast, and two more fell, their flesh and bone disintegrating, and the dishevelled line broke and turned. They ran towards the trucks, which were already moving off, in a desperate attempt to avoid the grenades.

'Cease-fire,' yelled Edward, and the air was filled with stunning silence.

'Who are those fuckers off in that clump of trees near the rocks? Twelve o'clock, three hundred yards,' shouted Matt.

Edward looked over at the sighting reference, and saw two sand-coloured Jackals moving away from the mayhem. Inside were troops in full army uniform.

'Permission to grenade them up the arse, skip,' called Matt.

'Negative,' was Edward's response as he trained his binoculars on the withdrawing Jackals.

'Skip, I saw them dragging some women over to those Jackals. The soldiers on board were not in the firefight,' Robin said.

Edward lowered his binoculars, frowning as he asked himself who the hell they were. They were British Jackals, he knew. Who could be using them in the DRC? His mind was dragged back to what was happening by the cries for help and cries of agony. Villagers somehow unscathed appeared from their hiding places and started to help the wounded and dying as best they could. One of the women from the village scooped up the crying baby lying in the grass in front of the Land Rover; the child's mother had already bled to death in the short grass. A group of women in tribal dress started a piercing ululating call, a unique chant made by rolling the tongue over the teeth to give off a high-pitched sound of anguish.

The other three vehicles pulled up in a cloud of dust and red mud.

'Ed, what happened?' called out Michael. 'What the fuck happened to "don't get involved"?'

'Michael, we drove straight into a massacre. We didn't start the firing; we acted purely in defence of the innocent,' yelled back Edward.

As if to strengthen his argument, Edward walked over to the mother holding the small baby. Taking the child in his arms, he said to Michael.

'This baby was about to be beheaded by that bastard we shot, who's now lying in the grass – well, what's left of him at least. What would you have done, Michael?'

'Okay, okay, sorry. I can see what you walked into. My fault for letting you go in the first place. Let's stay calm and help out here where we can.'

The ten men got into a sweeper formation and walked through the carnage helping the wounded into more comfortable positions, and handing out bandages and water bottles to the villagers. Two men, including Sergeant McBride, remained on a Jackal, manning the Minimi LMG, which covered the surrounding short-distance horizon. Mark Jones, a fully trained SAS medic, was helping the more seriously wounded with bandaging and morphine, and moving the wounded into the shade or propping them upright against the mud walls of huts. At least ten bandits had been killed in the short firefight; one was still breathing, and Michael could hear the rasping sound a man makes when he has bullet holes in his lungs. As the sweep line moved past him, he seemed to just stop breathing. Michael glanced over towards Tim Abrahams who had slowed and was bent over the man.

Tim shrugged as he straightened up.

'Poor bugger just gave up on life, boss,' the trooper said.

Michael thought he caught a glimpse of steel.

Michael glared at Tim, who just shrugged and rejoined the sweep line. The rest of the bandits had fled to their pick-up trucks and made good their getaway. Edward informed Michael about the army vehicles that looked like Jackals which had been among the trees in the distance.

'They did not take part in the fight, Michael. They seemed to be observers. Who the hell has our Jackals out here in the DRC? They were not like these other gooks; the troopers were in full, up-to-date, military kit and looked like soldiers.'

An elder in an old torn pinstriped suit and a dirty white shirt with a frayed collar was making his way over to Michael, flanked by two other senior male villagers. He walked up to Michael and stopped in front of him. His eyes were filled with tears, but his face was proud; he was still in control.

'*Ils ont pris nos jeunes femmes,*' the elder said.

'What did he say, Michael, my French is not great, did you follow that?' asked Edward.

'He said they took our young women,' replied Michael.

Turning to the dignified elder, who was trying so hard to stay controlled, Michael asked in broken French: 'Who has taken your young women?'

'Soldats,' he replied

'Who, these soldiers?' asked Michael, kicking at the blood-spattered body of a dead bandit, lying alongside his AK-47.

'*Non, les soldats*,' he replied in French. Michael nodded and turned to Edward.

'He is saying these dead gooks are not the soldiers; they must be the guys you saw in the Jackals, Ed.'

Michael put his arm gently around the elder's shoulders and said in French that he would do everything he could to track the soldiers and also to recover the young women. The old man held out a wizened hand and shook Michael's hand. He stared long and hard into Michael's eyes before squeezing his hand. His eyes held so much sorrow that Michael was forced to break contact.

'*Merci.*'

The old man turned and shuffled away, dragging his feet in the dust. Michael noticed that his shoulders had slumped, and he was visibly shaking.

Having done all they could for the villagers, Michael told the guys to mount their vehicles. He told Edward he would provide a full sitrep back to Alpha One when they reached the mine and try to get answers on who it could be that was operating British-made infantry armour-protected vehicles in the DRC.

The rest of the journey to the mine was uneventful as the men who had been caught in the firefight silently reflected on the murderous thuggery they had just witnessed.

The convoy pulled into the mine just as the red sun was beginning its rapid descent towards the horizon. Night sounds were already making themselves heard, Michael heard an owl off to the west of the compound.

The mine itself was smaller than Michael had expected. There was no mine pithead, as the mining was done by scraping the earth with shallow digger blades towed by JCB diggers. There were a number of shallow quarry pits where the earth had been torn away by the diggers. Outside of the fence were old, disused quarries; the mine had moved with the digging. Under corrugated iron lean-to roofing and supported by steel there was a motor pool which also doubled as a repair shop. Towards the hill at the back of the compound there was a small square with five or six small houses alongside patches of grass; poor attempts at gardens. An ugly, grey, two-storey administration building lay at the centre of the mine compound. This building was the largest of all. Alongside the admin building were two barrack-room-style bungalows, long rectangular buildings with small windows, set equidistant from each other, and with doors at both ends of the buildings. There was a large parking area and a turning circle just inside the gates as well as a number of medium-sized leafy trees providing shade and an area that looked like an outdoor bar and barbecue area.

Sergeant McBride was at once at work setting up sentry points and an OP (observation post) on top of the main mine admin building. The building itself was a flat-roofed, two-storey building built with clay brick under a large, flat concrete roof. There was a door and four sets of metal-framed windows on both the ground and first floor. The ground-floor windows had anti-rocket and anti-grenade steel cages around the frames. The building had, once upon a time, a coat of whitewash, but now, due to the weather, this was fading.

Two-man foot patrols were set up around the perimeter fence. They marched around it clockwise about two yards in from the fence, before returning the other way. The section itself was allocated one of the long bungalows, brick under corrugated iron, similar to a school dormitory in shape. A small bedroom at one end was laid out for Michael and Edward.

The section IT specialist and signals man was Corporal Matthew Birrell, a solid soldier with a very dry sense of humour. He was Royal Corps of Signals, but had been attached to the Grenadier Guards in Afghanistan. As soon as he had set up satellite comms in a small room adjacent to the admin building, but slightly higher up, on a small, raised rocky area, Michael made contact with Excalibur. Michael had ordered a large camouflage net to be thrown loosely over one end of the building, breaking the natural silhouette of the building and hiding some of the wiring and aerials.

'Alpha One, this is Charlie Two Sunray, copy?'

'Wait, One,' an unknown voice came back.

The response indicated that somebody was calling Maria to the Excalibur signals and operations room. A couple of minutes passed and then the radio came to life.

'Alpha One copied,' he heard Maria's voice say.

Michael replied, 'Alpha One, go visual for sitrep.'

'Roger. Wait, One.'

The laptop computer screen in front of Michael lit up to show Maria standing on her own in the operations room focused on the large screen in front of her. *That lady has something really special about her*, Michael thought briefly.

'Hi, Michael, we have a secure line. Send your sitrep.'

'Roger. Hi, Maria. We had no problems leaving Kinshasa and all went well until we started down the Mankula Mine track. We were buzzed by a couple of Zimbabwean Air Force Hawk jets, no contact. Then we saw smoke and I sent Edward on call sign Charlie Two to investigate. They came across what looked like a tribal massacre, or a case of ethnic cleansing. In order to protect civilians, Charlie Two was forced to engage what looked like armed rebels or bandits. There were no casualties on our side, but took out ten bandits. There were many civilian deaths and casualties, some nasty bullet and machete wounds, loss of limbs and body mutilation.'

'Copied, Michael.'

If Maria was shocked or taken aback it did not reflect in her face or her calm level voice. A true professional soldier.

Michael continued, 'Let Colonel Torrens know that we were pulled into a situation and did not start the fight. During the firefight we noted something else odd: as well as the local bandits, there were two armoured,

British-made Jackal vehicles parked off to the side of the village with eight to ten well-armed and uniformed soldiers on board. They took no part in the fighting, but the village headman tells me that several young women were dragged off to the Jackals. I need to know who is operating British armed vehicles in this part of the DRC. We should try to find out what it's all about. I promised the headman we will try to recover his young girls.'

'Copied. Seems very odd; will get back to you. I will brief Sunray Alpha One and get back to you 0700 hours tomorrow. Anything else?'

'Any news from Torrens on the bribe?'

'Colonel Torrens is not surprised: it's the way in the DRC. He will take it up with the client, but says it's not our problem. I will guarantee, however, that he sure as hell will have a little more input on your new sitrep. He made it clear that there would be no involvement in the country's wars; your task remains to protect the mine and its personnel.'

'Charlie One, roger that. I repeat we had no choice.'

Michael shut off the video link and signal. *I wonder whether Maria is as tough and hard-arsed as she makes out, or whether she is just staying on task*, he thought. He threw down the headset on the trestle table and moved out of the signals room into the warm night air. The smells and sounds of the night always had a calming effect on Michael. Day one down, and what a bloody awful day it had been. At least the team had not sustained any injuries in the firefight.

The night passed without mishap: the perimeter patrols saw and heard nothing and the OP on top of the admin building reported that all was quiet.

Michael got a half-hearted bollocking from Colonel Torrens on the satellite link up at 0700 hours. Maria was alongside him in the operations room. Torrens was too good a soldier to see everything in black and white; he realised that war was about instant decisions and to ignore innocent people being butchered was just not what a professional soldier is trained to do. This very situation was what had made Bosnia such a messed-up situation: the UN-mandated troops had been helpless to defend the population unless fired upon first. He made it clear that the section should avoid contact where possible and said he had received no intel on the Jackal armoured vehicles or their occupants, but was making enquiries through contacts at the MOD. The satellite link was brought to an end. Michael once again felt a slight unease at the unexpected presence of British fighting armoured vehicles. Supplying the DRC government with any form of military equipment was a serious no-no.

With the sunrise the mine came to life slowly. Trucks and machinery had started up and the shallow digging operation was beginning to flow. Small Oshkosh diggers were ripping at the red earth and dumping their loads of soil into hopper bins on the back of squat diesel transporters that rumbled off into a queue at the washing plant. Here, the soil was washed away and the remaining rocks and diamonds were sifted through a series of holes of varying sizes, before being washed again. Finally, the diamonds were dropped onto conveyor belts lined with thick grease, which captured the stones.

The dawn patrol around the perimeter fence was stepped down as the daylight gave enough clear vision into the surrounding trees and undergrowth which had been cut back for 100 metres from the line of the fence. The OP on top of the admin building was strengthened by additional sandbags and the occupants swept the surrounding countryside with powerful binoculars. A few of the men chose to sit up on the roof with those manning the post. Shirts were already off, and tanning appeared to be the main order of the day.

Life became more mundane and routine, and several days passed in an uneventful manner with no sign of the bandits who had attacked the mine compound. From the bush telegraph, they received messages saying that there had been no further trouble in the outlying villages either.

'Let's look up Smith and see what the recreation is like in Matadi. We can send the boys in for some R and R in rotation,' said Michael to Edward on the tenth boring, uneventful day there.

'Agreed, the lads could do with a break from the monotony and the mine. It's not exactly alive with wine, women and song,' answered Edward.

Michael and Edward set out to find Smith. Acknowledging the wave and thumbs-up from McBride, who was up on the roof, they made their way into the admin building looking for David Smith, the mine manager. When they entered, Smith looked up from a long table covered in technical drawings. He was engaged in some sort of discussion with a couple of tough-looking mining types. Michael detected what he thought were South African accents.

'Good morning, guys. Hope you all slept well, I know we did just knowing you were here and watching over us.'

'No problem. All quiet last night; no movement out there,' replied Michael.

'Meet Kobus and Jonnie Swanapoel. They are my mine foreman and shift boss respectively. Also brothers and very experienced in mining generally – their last jobs were on the gold mines in Gauteng near Johannesburg.'

That confirms my hunch about their accents, thought Michael.

Smith continued: 'Kobus is going into Matadi later on today. It's about an hour from the mine; becomes easier when you hit the N1 tar road at the end of the mine road. We have all our supplies, both mining and general, shipped up the Congo River and we collect them from the port. Also most of our foodstuffs and fresh vegetables. There is a hotel called the Ledya in the town with a decent swimming pool and a recreation area – although the food is average. There is an outdoor bar area and a billiard table room. They have a mini-zoo, but they keep the apes in dirty cages, and frankly, they are aggressive and dangerous. Some of your guys might want to get a break from this place and have a change of scenery. Kobus can show them the ropes. The hotel is on the N1, near the Boma taxi stand and before the road and rail bridge crossing.'

'Thanks for that, we were just coming to ask about that ourselves. We can send the boys in small groups a couple of times a week, if that would be any good. Edward and some of the lads can make the run today and test the water. Let us know about any no-go areas. We will keep the OP manned and foot patrols as well as radio comms at all times,' replied Michael.

'Jong, there are many don't goes,' said Kobus.

'Including where the ladies of the night hang out, unless your boys are looking for a good dose of AIDS! It's a crazy place: you can be in the First World, turn down a street, walk a couple of blocks and you are back in darkest Africa, mate. There are also plenty of those black bastards who will cut your throat for a few euros. Killing is a national sport – life is cheap,' pronounced Kobus.

Michael gave him a cold, hard stare – no expression, just an understanding that he did not value Kobus or his input. Kobus held the stare briefly then averted his eyes and turned away. Most men did. He returned to his conversation with Smith.

'We will send a couple of men in a Land Rover today. We can travel in convoy with Kobus.'

8

Matadi

Edward, Mark Jones, Tim Abrahams and Robin Gibb left in one of the Sabre Land Rovers from the mine compound shortly after 1000 hours, following the mine's three-tonne open-back Mercedes truck towards the main road and Matadi. After a brief discussion between Michael and Edward, they concluded that as the stick itself had not been attacked and the level of armed activity was low in the Matadi area they would only carry side arms and dress down in civvy clothing. There was not much they could do about the Sabre Land Rover, which was painted in a desert sand colour. Tim Abrahams, still thinking like an SAS soldier, hid his pump action shotgun in his gym kit holdall.

Michael set off with Sean Ahearn and Sergeant McBride in the other Land Rover. Corporal Matt Birrell was left as stick commander of the remaining men, and was also given comms responsibility, which was no sweat to the Royal Signals man. The men in the Land Rover were fully armed and an LMG was mounted on the roll bar behind the front seats, because they were headed back to the village that had been the scene of the massacre and firefight.

Upon arrival, Michael could see that members of

Médecins Sans Frontières, had set up a makeshift hospital in a couple of large tents. They had arrived after Michael had radioed the DRC headquarters in Kinshasa, telling them of the atrocities and carnage. Michael had a great deal of respect for their efforts in many war-torn areas of the world, and he knew that 80% of their funding came from public donations.

Michael leapt off the Land Rover and strode across to the first of the tents where he was met by an attractive lady who appeared to be a doctor. She was wearing dark slacks and a white coat, and had a stethoscope around her neck. Her hands were hanging limply at her side, and she looked tired and drawn.

'*Bonjour, Madame* Médecin. My French is not great, Doctor. Do you speak English?' asked Michael.

'*Je fais*, of course,' she replied, holding out her hand.

'My name is Doctor Marie Louise Ancelet. Are you the soldier who contacted us? If so, thank you for assisting these people and for carrying out immediate first aid.'

'It's the least we could do. We did not want to fight, but we could not sit by and watch a massacre unfold.'

'*Évidemment.* Sorry, I mean obviously. But as a soldier you will have seen this before, no?'

'Yes, but this is a first in that we were not the aggressor or under fire. We were here and able to help a little, although we were not here soon enough, or fully apprised of the attack. I am sorry we did not do more.'

'I understand. Are you okay yourself? How do you feel?'

'I am fine, thank you. It does not give me sleepless nights. It's what I am trained to do, and I do it well.'

'That is good, but it's also sad, *monsieur*, that humans can be trained to kill and not care.'

Michael opened his mouth to explain that when men or women joined the army they are fully aware that combat is an aspect of the job, but he stopped himself, realising that she might see it as self-justification. Instead, he asked how the wounded were coming on after the attack.

'We have transported the more seriously wounded back to Kinshasa and we have now only – uh, how do you say it – "walking wounded" here. We are feeding them and will leave them with medical supplies and our prayers. We shall be gone in two days, maybe three. So you can see they are in good hands.'

'We can supply a couple of men to provide protection if you wish. They are all specialists and probably worth three ordinary troopers.'

'Thank you, *non*. It won't be necessary; we are safe, and I do not think they will return.'

'Do you know where we can locate the headman of the village? We would like to find out a bit more about why and how this happened.'

Yes, I know where he sits and holds his council during the day. I will walk with you,' replied Marie Louise.

Michael, Marie Louise and Sergeant McBride moved slowly through the dust around the huts, scattering scrawny chickens in their path. Some of the huts were still blackened with ash where the straw from the hut roofs had been burnt. A few poles stood burnt and snarled in the roof supports. There were also bullet marks in the walls of some of the huts.

Amazing, thought Michael, *modern 7.62 ammunition had been fired from AK-47s, and yet the rounds did not penetrate through those mud walls*. The smell of death and blood had gone, but there were dark, almost black, patches on the ground where victims had fallen. *Some of the gooks as well*, thought Michael with satisfaction. *Bastards*.

At the centre of the village clearing was a large evergreen Garcinia tree. Squatting on their haunches at the base of the tree were the village elders, including the old man in the pinstriped suit and torn white shirt. He was the only one sitting, on a low wooden stool carved out of a single piece of timber. On his feet he wore what appeared to be sandals made of old tractor tyre rubber. Michael was pleased he had Marie Louise beside him to act as translator on his behalf. They all squatted in the dust facing the elders.

'*Bonjour*,' began Michael. 'I am saddened by your loss and sorry we could not have been here sooner.'

The elders just nodded and stared back at the three white people facing them. They were waiting for the headman to speak. Eventually, he nodded as well, then stared into the middle distance and clapped his hands sharply. Instantly, some women arrived, as if out of nowhere, carrying some cooked meat and two calabash containers of foul-smelling maize-fermented beer. The meal and beer was placed in the space between the two parties, and some of the elders shuffled through the dust to form a circle. The headman reached for the beer, took a long slurp and passed the calabash to Michael, who, like Marie Louise, was squatting on his haunches. He knew he could not refuse and took a small sip, the thick, fermented liquid almost sticking in his throat. The same sequence followed with the meat which was cooked over an open fire and to Michael's surprise tasted excellent. Marie Louise declined the beer offering but took some of the meat. The headman spoke in French and there was a pause each time while Marie Louise translated.

'I see you, soldier,' said the headman, staring deep into Michael's eyes.

'I see you too, sir,' replied Michael, head slightly bowed in deference to the headman.

'My people thank you and your men for saving the village. We are saddened by our loss, but joyed by the lives that have been saved, thank you.'

'We wish we could have done more, and done so more quickly,' Michael continued. 'Do you know why you were attacked? Are you from a different tribe or religion?'

'No, we are one tribe in this area.'

'Do you have something they want: foodstuff, cattle or land?'

'No, this is happening along the river at other villages. They take our young women, even young girls.'

'Why would they take your women? Why are they taking them? Do you know where they are taking them? Are they taking them to Matadi or Kinshasa?'

'We do not know why they are taking them or where they are going. We only know that these young women do not come back to the villages once they are gone.'

'My men saw some young women being dragged to what looked like army vehicles; they looked like the ones we drive in. They were over there by those trees.' Michael pointed to the treeline, some two hundred yards distant. 'Are these the young women you are telling us about, sir?'

'Yes, they are the same women.'

'Who are these men … the men in the vehicles like ours?'

'They are foreign soldiers, not from the DRC or from these dog bastard bandits who loot and rape the countryside.'

'Do you know what soldiers they are?'

'Aaah, for sure we do not know who they are.'

'Did they shoot at your people or attack the village?'

'No, they just sat and watched the killing and then they take the women.'

'And you do not know where they are taking these girls and women?'

'Aah, again I do not know this.'

'Thank you for talking to us, sir.'

The headman nodded again, then offered the calabash of beer to Michael, which he declined. Michael, Marie Louise and McBride rose. Michael turned to go, but then turned again to the headman.

'What is your name, sir? I will find your women and see what has happened to them. I will come back to see you myself and tell you what I have found.'

The words just came out. Michael was sure he would find them even though he had no way of knowing for sure what he would find and where and how he would then communicate this to the headman.

'My name is Patrice Muamba. My people are from the Luba tribe, and I am the headman of this village, which is in the Mbanza area. My youngest daughter, her name is Happiness. She is fifteen years old. They have taken her. Bring her home to me. May God go with you until we see you again, my son.'

Michael stared into the middle distance, as he did when in thought. You can believe I will hunt down these kidnappers and release the girls, if it takes months or even years to do so. He nodded to the chief, then briefly bowed his head in respect before turning on his heel.

Marie Louise walked back to the Land Rover with the two soldiers. She told them that her medical team would be moving back to Kinshasa inside of a week as their caring for those who were wounded was reaching a stage where the tribespeople could look after themselves. She told them medicines and bandages would be left for the use of the tribe.

'Michael, I ask that you do your best to keep your word and find those girls. Come and see us when you are in Kinshasa. À bientôt, Michael.'

'I will find them and punish those responsible,' he replied.

His look was one of calm determination, and Marie Louise was reassured by the way this tall, athletic man spoke, with quiet, firm confidence. 'I would not like to be an adversary of you, Monsieur.'

As McBride drove back to the mine, Michael sat in a deep, dark, brooding silence. He had missed the rape and killing of women from ethnic minorities in Bosnia and Serbia, but he had heard the tales of horror from older officers in his regiment. The frustration of having their hands tied by red tape still lived with all of those who had served. He felt that what he had seen at the village must have been at least the equal of some of those atrocities. This time there had been no red tape;

this time there had been justice.

The other half of the group that left the mine that morning – Edward, Mark Jones, Tim Abrahams and Robin Gibb – arrived at the Boma taxi stand in Matadi, just off the N1, having left Kobus and the Mercedes truck to continue on down to the port.

'Okay, look lively, lads. Keep your eyes open, as I'm sure our Land Rover will attract some inquisitive souls. Put your side arms into the waistband of your shorts and cover them up, leaving your shirts untucked. You certainly look the part of a tourist, Tim. Where did you get the Hawaiian shirt from? Oxfam, before we left the UK?'

'No, boss, my sister gave it to me when I told her we were taking a trip to Africa; she was sure we would be on a beach somewhere.'

'In your dreams, sunshine,' answered Robin.

'Hey boss, can we nip across the road to that general store, it seems to have everything. Maybe we can find some swimming trunks as the hotel has a pool,' asked Robin.

'Let's go. Stay focused and stick together,' answered Edward.

The group crossed the busy street and entered what appeared to be a bazaar, and there seemed to be everything one could need inside its cavernous interior. About the only things missing were designer label items of clothing; even the genuine fake clothing was missing. The bazaar had long, narrow walkways which criss-crossed the concrete floor area. Edward was reminded of some of the souks he had visited in Dubai – the ones not frequented by tourists. In each squared-off area, there were goods for sale piled high in stacks on the floor. There were areas for fresh food; cooking utensils; pots and pans; clothing; bicycles and dried foodstuffs. There was a strong smell of spices in the air – a Middle Eastern smell, the smell that permeates the bazaars of Marrakesh. There were also piles of not-so-fresh meat – *most likely elephant or chimpanzee*, thought Edward.

There were hessian bags of grain and flour piled up to the ceiling, all clearly stamped with 'property of UNESCO'. There were also large plastic cartons of sunflower oil with 'Red Cross aid to Africa' stamped on the bottles. It came as no surprise to Edward that food aid to Africa was being resold in the bazaar. He wondered just how the black market operated and how much food was lost in this way. Michael had once told him of a village in Zimbabwe near the Zambian border which was nicknamed 'Little Baghdad'. By enquiring locally, you could get an 'appointment' to visit the local warlord (Africa's mafia Michael called them) in his rooms at a shebeen in the makeshift shanty town. There, over many beers and by heated negotiation involving hard currency, mainly US dollars, you could order and pay for anything from a TV or a fridge, moving to a tractor or a luxury car in a specific colour and style. There were big-ticket items available: combine harvesters, 36-wheeler trucks, even helicopters – not to mention weapons. All stolen to order, much of it from projects funded by the United Nations or the World Bank.

Robin found a pile of underwear, and some swimming trunks which suited his shirt: gaudy, surfer-type swimming baggies. The group all bought a pair of surfer baggies and left the bazaar as quickly as possible. The smells were fast becoming nauseating.

The foyer of the hotel was clean and bright, and a helpful young lady in hotel uniform pointed out the pool table and games room, and showed them through to the poolside area where there was a lawn. The lads quickly changed in the men's toilet area and spread themselves out on plastic sun loungers, their side arms hidden in their towels. Tim hoped nobody in the group would ask about the gym bag that never left his side. Their pale skins stood out among the other hotel guests. Nobody had thought to bring suntan oil.

'Ah, this is the life, eh, boss?' called out Mark Jones. 'Who needs the French Riviera when you can have the pool in Matadi?'

'Knucklehead,' responded Robin, always the quick retort man. 'Next thing you will be telling us Lanzarote is on your bucket list.'

'Shut up, you prick,' responded Mark. 'You have probably never been further than Butlin's in Minehead.'

The others all laughed, Robin stood up, gave them all a look of disdain, stretched his muscled, toned body, then ran across the grass and dived into the pool.

They spent the afternoon relaxing and drinking the local Primus beer, which the lads thought had a similar taste to some European beers. Edward told them that this was not surprising as the major brewery in the DRC, called Bralima, was in fact owned by Heineken International. The lads were also surprised to learn that Guinness was very popular in Africa, but was served warm. In fact, the largest Guinness brewery in the world was in Nigeria.

The boss knows some weird stuff, thought Tim. *Either that, or he was once on* Mastermind – *chosen specialist subject: world beers!*

All too soon, the afternoon had slipped away, and the lads changed and made their way back through the foyer towards the front doors of the hotel and the car park in high spirits. A handwritten sign in the foyer caught Edward's eye. "The management apologises for the lack of running water in the rooms, we are working to fixing this". Strange he thought, a lovely pool and then no running water in the hotel. As they exited, Edward, Robin and Tim all caught sight of a Jackal armoured vehicle exiting onto the traffic circle further up the road. There were two uniformed men inside.

'Anybody recognise those uniforms?' called Edward.

'Boss, they looked pretty standard-issue camouflage to me – maybe NATO stuff,' said Tim. 'The guy driving had three pips on his shoulders – a captain, I reckon. Do you think those are the fuckers we ran into at that village, the soldiers that Matt saw in the Jackals in the trees?'

'Either that, or Supacat, the British manufacturer, has opened up a retail car sales outlet in Matadi. Buy one Jackal, get one free,' replied Robin.

'We don't have the firepower to back us up right now, and they have disappeared around the corner, giving them a five-minute start on us. We don't know the area, but this is good intel. Next time we are here we can have a quick recce around Matadi,' said Edward.

Tim kept quiet about his shotgun. It alone would still not give them the fire power they would need in a punch-up.

The lads all piled into the Jackal, and Robin started up and turned right onto the N1.

Edward reached for his radio.

'Charlie One, this is Charlie Two.'

Matt Birrell replied immediately: 'Charlie One, go.'

'Charlie Two, we are en route back to base. ETA 1800 hours, over.'

'Charlie One, roger that. All good?'

'Roger, all good. Interesting observation on the way out, will debrief when we get back.'

'Charlie One, sounds interesting. Will brief Sunray. See you in an hour or so. We will maintain comms in case of any problems.'

The late afternoon sun was behind them and heading towards the horizon as they travelled eastwards towards the turn-off to the mine. Robin broke into the song 'Homeward Bound' by Simon and Garfunkel. Robin was always trying to convince those around him that he looked like Richard Gere and had a voice like Bono. Tim shook his head, feeling relieved that he had brought his iPod nano with him. He rammed the earphones into his ears and settled back in the rear seat facing towards the sun, the wind in his hair.

The section ate in a circle around a basic barbeque fashioned out of a rusty old 44-gallon drum that had been cut lengthways down the middle and had a heavy iron mesh grid attached. The whole drum was welded onto two crossed steel bars, which supported it and gave it stability. This was the mine team's preferred option for eating.

The OP team took up position at last light, and the perimeter patrols started after a 'stand-to' sweep. Most attacks on enemy bases come at last and first light, so the section was all at the ready in what is known as a stand-to position at these times while a strengthened patrol swept the perimeter. After the sweep finished, the section would be stood down.

Having told Matt Birrell to signal an all-clear sitrep back to London, Michael and Edward found themselves sitting on a couple of canvas directors' chairs out in front of the admin building, not far from the barbeque, which was now deserted but where they could still see embers glowing.

Edward had managed to locate a half-decent bottle of South African Shiraz and a wine glass, and Michael had brought out, in his kit from England, a bottle of his favourite Macallan. For his part, he had found a glass somewhat resembling a whisky tumbler. The early evening sky was cloudless, and there was a slight breeze; a welcome relief after the heat of the day. The sky was a deep black but bursting with glittering stars, and the Southern Cross was clearly visible. The Milky Way was so bright it looked like a white sheet hanging in the sky. To the west, they saw a shooting star, which then disappeared down low on the horizon.

'Michael, what do you make of this Jackal business and the foreign troops?' asked Edward. 'It seems really odd that they were there, but that they took no part in the firefight and that they took young women away with them. Do you think they could be part of the UN contingent?'

'That doesn't make sense,' responded Michael. 'Firstly, there are no UN peacekeepers in British-made armoured Jackals. Also, if they were UN peacekeepers, why didn't they stop the massacre and why would they want the women?

'We need to get some answers from London about those vehicles. Having seen them again in Matadi, we should be able to carry out a little recce and see whose troops they are.'

'Agreed, Colonel Torrens has contacts at the MOD and the Foreign Office. It's not as though Supacat is a major player in the defence market. They have a single factory in Honiton. As far as I am aware, there aren't more than a couple of hundred Jackals out there in the field.'

Edward looked up into the night sky.

'Michael, you should have been there. We saw women and children literally hacked apart in front of us. Those gooks looked crazed; there was bloodlust in their eyes. They were gone, Michael; they were just gone. What on God's earth can turn a man like that? We need to find them and we need to kill them.'

'Remember, Ed, this is not supposed to be our war, but I agree: let's find them and find out if they were a part of it. If they were, let's slot them one at a time slowly. I made a promise to the old headman that I would find his girls, although right now I have no idea how I am going to keep that promise.

'We should be able to track the Jackals. It would be different if we were looking for a bunch of gooks who had AK-47s,' said Edward. 'Now there is a weapon of mass destruction, of human life. It's been around since World War II, and including all its improvements and updates, they reckon 75 million have been made. That's a lot of death and destruction. It's still the weapon of choice for drug lords and in wars, coups, terrorist attacks, tribal warfare – you name it. Mikhail Kalashnikov must be turning in his grave at the death and destruction his little rifle has rained down on Earth. One very nearly took you out, Michael!'

'Don't remind me, I still think of that day, and it's as though I can see it all in slow motion. I'm just so lucky it didn't hit a bone but went straight through the flesh. It's funny, Ed, you know the dangers and the risks, and yet you believe it will never happen to you – as though you are some sort of god. Perhaps the human mind simply cannot live with constant danger.'

'What, now you want a Purple Heart?' exclaimed Edward, trying to make light of Michael's bad, bad memories. He could see that Michael was going into an area he wasn't comfortable with.

'Wrong army, my friend, but I must say those marines deserved them. I have always marvelled at their total dedication to each other. To them, it was about watching out for each other, protection of the men, and the corps came first, second and last. The corps was foremost, a far greater priority than the conflict. Those marines never flinched from the task at hand. They are America's sons, and the best they have. I only hope those guys get a better homecoming reception than they did after returning from Vietnam.'

Michael stood up, looked towards the heavens and stretched his arms out above his head.

'The Yanks had mean firepower, too,' he said. 'No expense spared to equip them properly. Back to the task we have now. If they are out there, Ed, we will find them and kill the bastards. I am going to hit the sack and dream of Maria; she is quite a special lady.'

Edward looked at Michael and smiled. 'That's about

as far as you will get – in your dreams, Michael, in your dreams.'

Over the coming days, London came up with no answers to their enquiries as to how British-made armoured vehicles were operating in the DRC and who, in fact, were using them.

To Colonel Torrens' frustration, his enquiries at the Ministry of Defence (MOD) produced a firm response of 'the MOD has no record of Jackal-2 armoured vehicles being sold, seconded or even loaned to foreign forces'.

Torrens had also made discreet enquiries through personal contacts both at The Ministry of Defence and directly with high-ranking officers with whom he had served in the army, again with negative results. It was as though the Jackals had never existed.

Days ran into weeks, but the mine remained well protected and patrols continued to operate both thoroughly and professionally. There was no evidence of any hostile activity. The section were now all sporting good tans and had set up a makeshift gym under the canvas near the admin building. Fitness and focus were priorities – it's easy to slip into a laid-back routine in these sorts of situations, and that would invite catastrophe. The section was split into two teams, and Edward devised a series of challenges, including weapon stripping and cleaning, a temporary assault course and runs around the perimeter. Each team trying to set a faster combined time, these men were trained to the best of the best, proving it was good for morale. They all remained a fit, trained and lethal fighting unit.

For recreation, the group took turns to go in threes and fours into Matadi and to the pool at Hotel Ledya.

Here, too, they challenged one another, competing to do the fastest lap of the pool or the most laps in half an hour. When in a more relaxed mood, the lads also played pool and darts, normally for a six-pack of Primus beer. Robin Gibb had declared himself world champion at darts and pool, but had yet to win a solitary beer!

While in Matadi, both Michael and Edward had done some low-key reconnaissance in the two Land Rovers, cruising the streets through some of the outlying suburbs, trying to locate the Jackal armed vehicles and the soldiers who had been in them. So far, their efforts had not produced any results. They were only two weeks away from the end of their three-month stint, when they would rotate with another stick from Excalibur and relocate back to the UK.

Ten days from the end of their tour, Michael approached Edward with an idea that had been formulating in his mind.

'I've got an idea, Ed,' said Michael. 'Today, when we go into Matadi, I want to take along five of the lads in order to show some real force. They'll be kitted up, fully armed and looking for a fight. Full display, no skulking around back streets. Maybe this will get the bastards to come out to fight, or better still, to run, and then we can have a go.'

'Michael, that's fine, but we can't just open up on foreign troops in the DRC; we need a cause and a reason.'

'Of course, Ed, I agree. That's why I am hoping they will come out to play, we will encourage them to open fire and then to hit back.'

Edward, always the more cautious of the two,

reflected on Michael's plan for couple of minutes before responding.

'We can cope with five men here, so you taking five is not a problem. A word of caution and advice regarding your plan, Michael. I know I've said it already, but seriously, don't start a fight, and maybe before you get fully involved, call us here and we will relay the situation to Colonel Torrens to get his go-ahead. That way we are fully covered.'

'No problem, Ed. I agree; let's be careful, but let's try to wheedle them out from wherever they are hiding.'

'Good luck, call your big brother if you need him. I'll come running,' laughed Edward.

'Now there's a worrying thought: friendly fire, could blow us all up. Ed, you just sit back and relax and I will show you how it's done, son.'

Michael chose the long wheelbase Land Rover for its speed and mobility and had the LMG fitted on the roll bar. They also took the MAG machine gun and each of the men with him had their own personal weapons. He chose Tim Abrahams who also brought one of the sniper rifles, Mark Jones (plus first aid kit) and Robin Gibb, who was a solid soldier, although he had a mouth on him.

They set off at first light the following morning, as soon as the stand-to perimeter patrol was complete. The giant red orb of the rising sun gave way to an orange glow as the sun rose rapidly in the morning sky. Wood smoke from the village cooking fires was still clinging to the tree tops and Michael could smell the smoke.

Studying the maps of the Matadi area the previous evening, and the recces that had been carried out to date,

Michael decided to turn right off the N1 and towards the suburbs and surrounding areas of Bruxelles Nord and Fuka Fuka.

The Land Rover driven by Robin Gibb pulled over near the huge Catholic church which stood out amongst the repetitive mud- and rust-painted corrugated-iron-roofed houses.

'Where to, guv'nor?' asked Robin Gibb, in mock London cabbie-speak as they crested the small hill that led down to the athletic fields and the suburb beyond. The tar road had given way to gravel, and large rocks were sticking through it and the surrounding red soil.

'Pull over here, Rob. I want to do a radio check,' replied Michael.

As Rob brought the Land Rover to a sliding halt in the gravel, Michael pressed the send toggle on his radio.

'Charlie Two, this is Charlie One. Radio check, receiving, over?'

Matt Birrell's voice replied, almost immediately.

'Charlie Two, go.'

'Charlie One, we are commencing our run through Bruxelles Nord. All quiet, so far, will radio check again in about an hour.'

'Charlie Two, roger that.'

'Let's go, Robin. Nice and slowly, keep coming back on yourself so we cover each road.'

Tim, who was standing in the back of the Land Rover balancing against the rough terrain by holding the stock of the secured MAG, was tasked with looking over the hedgerows into the yards of each house.

There were large, green, leafy trees dotted up and down the roadside providing some cover from the sun, but still the temperature was rising rapidly. In Matadi, October was one of the hottest months. Michael observed that dark cumulus clouds were already gathering above the far hills. Heavy rain came in the late afternoon, often accompanied by violent thunder and lightning, which was almost stupendous in its force.

Another hour passed, and the patrol were beginning to feel both hot and thirsty. Michael thought of calling a rest break as Robin turned the Land Rover once again, left and up a side road to double back onto the road running parallel to the one they had just left. He had repeated this routine over twenty times in the previous hour.

'Hold it, skip,' called Tim. 'I can see two Jackal vehicles behind the house with the two trees either side of the wooden gates ahead. Seems they are in some sort of compound.'

'Drive slowly past, Rob. Listen up, lads. Weapons cocked, but safety catches on. Look sharp, and let anybody watching see you clearly,' instructed Michael.

Robin drove slowly past the front of the property, which seemed more upmarket than the surrounding houses. He did a quick observation, noticing that there was an electricity feed to the house, a TV aerial and some sort of satellite dish. He also saw a large, black Mercedes saloon with consular European Union numberplates. It was a neat driveway, which was very unusual; there was a big patch of lawn in front of the verandah where a sprinkler was rotating lazily, throwing water in spiralling circles over the mown grass. *Servants or gardener?* thought Michael. Despite the heat, the windows were closed and the curtains were drawn. *They must have air conditioning*, Robin thought. Then they were past the property.

'Robin, drive on a couple of hundred yards, and then we will go back again. Any observations?'

'Saw a fancy Merc in the front drive,' Tim replied and going on he said, 'the windows are closed and the curtains are drawn. They must have air con.'

'There was a satellite dish, boss, so they have TV,' Robin added.

'There was also a plaque on the wall to the right of the front door, but didn't pick up what it said, skip,' added Tim.

'I got most of that, Rob. When we go back past, check that plaque: it could mean something. Judging from the neat gardens, there are servants or gardeners, I reckon. Tim, Mark, look for any movement, concentrate on that back compound.'

Robin put the Land Rover through a three-point turn, which was harder than normal as the road was cambered away down from the centre on both sides. The tyres slipped on the hard protruding rock. They moved past the front of the house again.

As they went past, Robin called out, 'The sign has a UN logo; it reads: UNESCO with something else followed by teaching or something similar. Can't make it out.'

Mark cut in, 'The word is "sustainable", boss.'

How the hell does UNESCO sustainable teaching tie in with what are clearly Jackal armoured vehicles in the back compound, Michael asked himself.

'Skip, there are a couple of black guys in uniform near the Jackals. Can't make out the insignia or badges, but they look pretty smartly turned out. One of them is pointing at us now,' called Tim.

'Robin, drive on to the top of the hill and spin around under that big tree. There is a tin hut there that we can park behind. Let's watch to see whether they want to come out to play. On your toes, chaps,' instructed Michael.

All four men trained their binoculars on the house which could be seen clearly down in the dip of the road. Nothing moved away from the building, although they could make out troopers climbing around in the Jackals. No young girls appeared outside of the building. Another hour passed.

Even under the tree it was hot; the corrugated iron hut reflected the sun directly onto the Land Rover. On the hut was a sign with writing in flaking, red paint advertising mobile phones for sale on a network called Econet. The hut was empty.

After another hour, Michael reached for the radio and called the mine to update them: 'Charlie Two, this is Charlie One.'

'Charlie Two, go.'

'Charlie One, we have located the Jackals at the back of a house in Bruxelles Nord and seen a couple of troopers as well.'

'Copy that. Have you any sighting of the girls?'

'Negative, but the windows are closed and the curtains drawn so can't see in. There is a fancy Mercedes with consular European Union plates out the front of the house in the driveway.'

'You have about another two hours before the rain sets in, and then it will be getting dark. Do you want us to post a night observation team on the ground?'

'Charlie One, negative. We know where this place is now, we can call again. The mine is our first and main task. We will hang around for another hour or so... hang on, there's movement at the gates. Wait, One, stand by.'

The black Mercedes turned out of the gates and headed up the hill towards the hidden Land Rover. The car gathered speed but as it shot past, Michael saw a driver in uniform, and in the back passenger seat nearest the Land Rover, a man in similar uniform. In the back passenger seat on the far side sat a smartly-dressed, white person in a suit.

'I know the army guy in the back, or at least I have seen him before,' exclaimed Michael. 'I saw him in Zimbabwe and again in London. He is a captain in the Zimbabwean Army. Robin, get on to the tail of the Merc pronto, but hang back so they don't see us – and don't lose him, mate. Did anybody see the white guy clearly?'

'I saw him. He had a light suit, white shirt and striped tie. He looked so familiar, skip, somebody that I've seen on TV, or on the news, or similar. Yeah, I've definitely seen him before,' answered Tim.

Robin swung the Land Rover through 180 degrees, wheel-spinning the back tyres, which made the Land Rover snake out to the right. As he straightened up onto the hard-top gravel using opposite lock, he floored the accelerator and the rear tyres spun again, throwing gravel and stones up underneath the Land Rover. Tim muttered something about hanging on for dear life while Robin made a complete balls-up of his pursuit.

'Fuck off, Abrahams. Since when were you Lewis fucking Hamilton? I'm on it, boss; unless we hit the highway and the big fellow puts the pedal to the ground we won't lose them,' yelled Robin above the engine and tyre noise.

The Land Rover was racing through the gears, just keeping the Mercedes in view. The Mercedes headed back past the Catholic church and turned left, heading back towards the N1. A bus and a small utility vehicle entered into the road, which gave the Land Rover the cover it needed to follow at a closer range. At the N1, the Mercedes swung right. Michael wondered whether it might be heading for the Hotel Ledya, but it swept past and headed for the bridge crossing over the Congo River.

Robin had to swerve at speed to avoid a three-tonne diesel truck belching smoke from its exhaust, which was trying to enter the N1 from a minor road. Tim muttered again and received a silent 'bird' from Robin by way of reply. The two vehicles crossed the bridge at a moderate speed together with several other vehicles using the N1. As traffic built up progressively along the way, Robin kept the Mercedes in his view. Once over the bridge, the Mercedes built up some speed and started passing slower traffic. Robin found the Land Rover was struggling to keep up.

'Don't sweat it, Rob. We can drop back now that we are leaving the built-up area of the town. Traffic is thinning out as well, so keep a safe distance,' instructed Michael.

Suddenly, the Mercedes swung left off the main highway.

'Slow down, Rob. Take the turn, but let's not run up their arses. Hold back; there is no other traffic on the road.'

'Got it, boss. Hold on, Abrahams – would hate you to fall off and hurt yourself.'

'Shut up, Gibb, or you will get my boot up your arse when we stop,' replied Tim.

This road was narrower but still tarred. A mile down this road there was a rusty sign on top of two concrete and stone cairns which stated "Welcome to Tshimpi Airport, Matadi". Rob slowed the Land Rover down further as they were the only two vehicles on the road, and the gap widened to a quarter of a mile. Off to the left was a two-storey airport terminal with what barely passed as a control tower on the top. It appeared deserted.

'Rob, move off the tar and head for cover behind those buildings that look like some sort of garages. They're the ones with the rusty old fire engine,' said Michael. 'The maps and the intel show that this airfield is not in use; what are these guys doing here?'

As soon as the Land Rover came to a halt behind the low building, Michael, Mark Jones and Rob all grabbed their rifles and skirted around the side of the building, going in the direction that the Mercedes had driven in. Tim grabbed his sniper rifle and headed towards a brick and breeze block wall where he could hoist himself and his deadly weapon onto the roof of the single-storey garages. The roof looked like asbestos, but Tim made sure he moved up the beam struts marked by bolts through to the asbestos sheets.

Michael immediately noticed the airstrip was of compacted red earth, probably mixed with oil to harden the surface. A quick look around the apron and the airport terminal confirmed the area to be deserted, except for the Mercedes and the aircraft it had pulled alongside, a sleek Swiss-built silver Pilatus PC-12 single turboprop aircraft. Swiss-manufactured, ideal for unmade short runway bush-strip operations, usually carrying nine passengers and a pilot – although some aircraft carry two pilots.

The Zimbabwean Army captain and the civilian got out of the back of the Mercedes and walked over to the two pilots, who were dressed in dark trousers and short-sleeved, white shirts with pilot's epaulettes on their shoulders. The civilian was carrying what appeared to be, through Michael's binoculars, a very expensive, crocodile-skin briefcase – *money there*, thought Michael. The four men shook hands. The Zimbabwean officer kept sweeping the airfield with his eyes, at one point staring for several seconds at the roof where Tim Abrahams was now lying with his sniper rifle to his shoulder. Michael hoped he had not given away his position, but he doubted this was the case: Tim was the perfect sniper, unseen and deadly over long distances.

Michael looked over to see if there were any markings on the aircraft, but the plane was not painted. The original brushed-aluminium surface reflected the sunlight across the apron. There were no corporate logos or markings, but as with all aircraft, the alpha-numeric identification was painted on the rear fuselage in black lettering. The aircraft's identification was G-AXY: G denoted that the aircraft was registered in the United Kingdom or within the British Commonwealth. Michael committed the registration number to memory.

After a short discussion, the four men walked up the small stairs, which had been lowered from behind the cockpit windows towards the front of the plane. One of the pilots pulled the stairs into the locked position and the four men disappeared from sight. There was a low squawk from his personal radio and Tim's voice came softly over the air.

'Skip, I have clear visual. I can take out the engine from here.'

'Negative,' came back Michael. 'Let them go, I've got the plane's identification. Maybe we can trace it through London.'

'Roger that.'

The aircraft turboprop began turning, making a small whine which very quickly became a full roar as the pilot throttled forward and back to run up the engine. The flaps and ailerons were tested in turn and then as the engine increased in volume, the plane moved forward and began to run off the apron and down the earth runway. When the aircraft reached the end of the runway, the power could be heard again as the aircraft was turned and lined up on the runway. Seconds later, as the brakes were released, the aircraft appeared to do a little hop and started down the runway, rapidly increasing in speed. The intense whirring of the propeller, and the resulting air flow across the wings, made dust fly off both sides of the runway into the air. Suddenly, the aircraft rose quickly off the ground. The undercarriage was pulled up almost immediately and the aircraft turned towards the now setting sun, then climbed rapidly into the evening sky.

The Mercedes started up and turned in a hard circle, then sped off down the road towards the exit. Michael and the lads yomped back quickly to the Land Rover. Michael radioed the mine:

'Charlie Two, Charlie One.'

'Charlie Two, go.'

'We followed the Mercedes to Tshimpi airfield. The soldiers are Zimbabwean. I have a positive ID on a captain whom I saw in Africa and at Heathrow. They boarded a private aircraft, a Pilatus PC-12. The call sign is Golf Alpha X-ray Yankee. Get London to track the identification and see what they come up with.'

'Roger that, copied.'

'We will be setting off from the airfield now, so our ETA at your location is two hours – around 2000 hours.'

'Copied. All quiet here. Stand-to in fifteen.'

Over the next two weeks, the teams carried out daily observations of the house and its Zimbabwean occupants. No girls were observed either in the grounds, or coming or going from the property. The Captain did return, on his own, and was brought back to the house in the same Mercedes, which then drove away and was tracked heading down the N1 at speed in the direction of Kinshasa. The officer, NCOs and troopers kept their Jackals in the city environs. Edward and a couple of the lads bumped into them by coincidence, on one occasion, at the pool in the back of the Hotel Ledya. Neither side spoke to the other, and when the Zimbabweans got a little raucous after a couple of dozen beers, Edward and his lads discreetly withdrew.

London was being stonewalled on all their enquiries regarding the Jackals. Torrens' normal contacts appeared to know nothing, but it was established the aircraft was registered to an executive private leasing company based at Luton, a commercial international hub airport north of London. The company specialised in private charter and leasing aircraft with a high net worth. Michael suggested to Edward that they pay a visit to the company upon their return.

Michael and Edward discussed raiding the house, but decided it would amount to an attack by mercenaries on what appeared at face value to be Zimbabwean troops who were welcome guests in the DRC. As frustrating as this was, they decided against any action.

9

Firefight

The team started the task of getting ready to rotate home as the new team were due to arrive in 48 hours. Two more days at the mine and their three-month tour would be over.

Michael and Edward sat in their movie directors' canvas chairs in front of the admin building. Stand-to and stand-down had been completed and the first double sentry patrols were beginning to move towards the perimeter fence line. Their flak jackets and helmets with night vision goggles lay on the metal table in front of them. The whisky was long gone, but there was a good stock of cold Primus beer. Michael used his belt buckle to open a couple of beers and handed one to Edward.

'Except for that first skirmish and our run-in with the Zimbabweans, it's been pretty quiet, as operations go,' said Edward.

Michael looked up into the darkening sky, trying to calculate where was due south, looking for the first sighting of the Southern Cross.

'Yes, Ed, it has been, as always, 99% boredom, 1% sheer terror. And that 1% is when the training and experience kick in. I've been pretty disappointed by the lack of wild animals – only a couple of antelope and small wild cats like servals and civets. Plenty of birds, but you wouldn't visit for the wildlife, would you?'

'No, I guess not, but it would have been good to have found the time to travel north to the rainforests and seen the gorillas. It's supposed to be thick with wild stuff in those rainforests: there are elephants, buffalo and big cats, as well.'

The two officers relaxed, each lost in his own thoughts as the night sounds started around them in the dusk. Edward heard a dog barking in the distance.

Suddenly, all hell broke loose. Somebody yelled, 'Incoming,' from the OP on top of the admin building, and the unmistakable sound could be heard of a shoulder-fired RPG rocket launcher missile leaving its launcher with a 'whoosh' and homing in on the admin building; at the same time, small arms fire opened up from a line of trees further up the hill from the mine. A now disused quarry had hidden the attackers' approach. The trees lay beyond a natural fold in the earth's contours which had created a rocky ridge hidden by long grass and bush. From this direction, some 300 yards to the left of the mine entrance gates, muzzle flashes and a sound like high-pitched whip-cracking filled the air as rounds came in, seeking to kill or maim. The dark sky was suddenly filled with flashes and explosions.

Michael and Edward were already on their feet when the RPG round thundered into the admin building high on the second floor with an almighty thump, spraying bricks and plaster all around the area where they had been sitting. They sprinted to the cover of a caterpillar grader blade, which was closer to the entrance gates than their directors' chairs, and a whole lot safer.

The 50-cal heavy machine gun opened up from the rooftop, pouring return fire in the direction of the trees. There was a solid thump-thump sound from the rounds tearing apart tree trunks and branches, they disintegrated from the power of the shells hitting their mark in the treeline.

Somebody in the OP yelled, 'Watch my tracer.'

Each weapon had a combination of normal and tracer rounds. There was one tracer round for every seven normal rounds, and they lit up the night sky in the direction that the enemy fire was coming from. This gave anybody who did not have target location a point to aim at. Immediately the tracer got its target area, further firepower came into play: the heavier weaponry of the section pouring death and destruction down on the tree line and quarry. From the back of the compound began a steady whump-whump of the grenade MG, the rounds falling just behind the tree line and intended to cut off any would-be escapees. A vehicle exploded somewhere, probably in the quarry bed, and rose almost in slow motion into the air in a flaming arc, briefly bathing the killing field in light. Michael hoped all the guys had their night vision goggles on to reduce the effect of night blindness from the light.

Michael remembered that when the firing had started, one of the two men approaching the perimeter fence had been hit. Dust had flown off his flak jacket and he had spun sideways and dropped like a stone. He racked his mind to think of who the first two patrol troopers were, but in the heat of the moment, it remained blank.

A cry came across the open ground leading to the exit road and perimeter fence line: 'Man down, medic.'

Immediately, Mark Jones, who had been under the cover of the three-tonner near the mine stores shed, ceased firing and sprinted towards the two men who had been setting out on the evening patrol and who now lay exposed in the open road near the fence. In his left hand, he carried his medic pack; in his right hand, he gripped his rifle by the stock just behind the barrel.

Michael and Edward saw Mark jinking towards the fallen man, and opened up with their own rifles on full automatic in order to provide covering fire, although more to keep heads down in the dark near the trees than to seek out targets. The 50-cal started to take its toll along the ridge: there were screams from the trees and the amount of incoming fire from the quarry lessened.

From the OP on the admin building, the Minimis opened up as well, but when muzzle flashes and rounds started coming in from an older quarry sight further to the right of the treeline, they changed to a new field of fire. Another RPG passed overhead and thumped into the three-tonner which had been Mark Jones's cover. The truck became a fireball as the fuel tank exploded.

Sergeant McBride shouted from the top of the OP. 'Put some fucking fire power on the quarry with the Minimis. Watch my tracer.'

His rounds fell into the scrub grass just ahead of the quarry. Loose stones exploded and shrilled off into the dark, screeching like Chinese fireworks.

Edward and Michael leopard-crawled to within ten feet of the three men lying near the road, and Michael could make out Mark Jones kneeling over the fallen and wounded man. He switched magazines on his rifle, and both he and Edward switched to three-round bursts, now aiming more accurately. From the rooftop, increased amounts of covering fire whined overhead like angry bees laying down cover. When the air started to crack with the sound of incoming rounds, it was time to move – the rounds were close.

Michael's personal radio came to life and he heard the calm, quiet tones of Tim Abrahams.

'Skip, in position on the roof at the end of the admin block, and through my night-sight I can see a couple of Toyota Hilux pick-up trucks. Also the terr who fired the first RPG, terr at two o'clock, moving away from a large tree for his next sighting. Taking him out now.'

Michael couldn't hear Tim's single sniper round above all the other firing taking place, but within seconds his radio came alive again with the same calm, quiet voice.

'Man down, gone away, head shot. Moving position now, looking for the other RPG man.'

'Roger that. Can you see how many of these guys are out there?'

'Wait one, moving. There are two groups and three vehicles, skip. There were four, but one fucking exploded. Four to six guys moving closer towards the fence near the gates, using the end of the ridge for cover – your left, ten o'clock. Leaving them to you and looking for the other RPG man.'

'Copy that. We will move to close off the guys sweeping around the ridge; keep a look out for our moving forward.'

'McBride, you copy?'

'Copied. We are concentrating on the gooks in the tree line. Pretty sure we have knocked a few of them over.'

'Whoever is on the grenade MG put down some rounds on the end of the ridge to the right front of the gate.'

'Copied, firing.'

The distinctive sound of 'phoom, phoom, phoom' commenced at once. There was a delay of a few seconds, and then the grenades exploded in rapid succession behind the ridge.

Thank God the quality of radios has improved since Afghanistan, thought Edward. So often in Helmand, there were unnecessary casualties caused by useless personal radios.

Michael and Edward heard running from the rear of their exposed position as they crawled towards the relative safety of the low, two-feet-high, whitewashed concrete wall on either side of the entrance gates. A long burst of fire came off the ridge, snaking across the gravel, kicking up spurts of dust, only to lift inches above their heads as rounds whipped overhead from the AK on full automatic and kicking up high and right. The radio man, Matt Birrell, flung himself into the dirt next to them and opened up at once on the ridge.

'Figured you needed my help,' he shouted. 'Two officers together – an obvious weakness in our defence.'

He grinned at them both; they had now joined him in firing at the ridge. Michael raised himself just above the wall and found himself locked in eye contact with a man in dark fatigue overalls, who was turning, almost in slow motion, towards where the three men were lying behind the wall. He had an RPG rocket launcher propped firmly on his shoulder. As the man's finger closed on the trigger, Michael lifted himself up and realised that his elbows were no longer locked into the ground to steady his aim; he was going to be milliseconds too late. As his mind willed him to move, he saw the back of the man's head explode. The RPG fired skyward as the body fell backwards, and again he heard the quiet, calm voice from his radio.

'Head shot, gone away. RPG man on his way to another world.'

Michael fell back in relief and visualised Tim Abrahams inserting another cartridge into his sniper rifle whilst scoping out his next target.

The loss of the second RPG man seemed to take the wind out of the attackers' sails, and they broke into a ragged retreat, running and stumbling their way back to the remaining Hilux pick-up trucks. The engines sprang to life, the gears meshed, and the pick-ups bounced across the quarry road down away from the mine compound, engines screaming at maximum revs. They were now lost from the view of the men on the ground, but from the roof came the familiar 'whoomp, whoomp' of the grenade MG. The rounds fell and exploded in the bush and trees along the dirt road, showering the withdrawing trucks with debris.

Michael spoke quickly into his radio, 'Those of you on the ground, form up on me in a sweep line. McBride, get down here; check on the man down and see how he is doing. Jones is still with him. I want to know who it is and his condition. I can see a drip is being held up by one of the guys. Three guys stay on the roof OP – stay alert and watch for movement. The rest of you join the sweep line.'

He turned to Matt Birrell and issued a further order:

'Matt, check with McBride on how bad the wounded man is, then get on the radio, in the following order: chopper medevac stand by, or call it in if our man is bad. Call them through Médecins Sans Frontières in Kinshasa. Next, call London with a sitrep update and then raise the local police in Matadi and ask them to get out to the mine as we have been attacked.'

'On it, skip,' answered Matt and sprinted off to meet McBride, who was now kneeling next to the wounded soldier. There was a quick exchange of words and then Matt was off running again, this time to the radio room. He ducked under the camo netting as he went.

Michael, Edward and three troopers formed a single line, spreading themselves out until they could only just make out the next man. McBride joined the sweep line.

'Who is down, and how is he?' asked Michael of Sergeant McBride.

'It's Sean Ahearn, boss. He has taken a round in his hip region, just beneath his flak jacket. The round appears to have deflected off his web belt downward and has exited through his arse!'

'Literally?' asked Michael, taken aback.

'No, boss, through his right buttock – neat exit wound near his left lung. Fucking lucky it didn't hit any vital organs or any bones, it would have rattled around his rib cage like a pinball, tearing the bones apart. So, as it didn't hit any bones going through the body, he just has a good deal of muscle tearing. He has also lost a lot of blood, but with a casevac by chopper he should be fine. Jones has done a good job to stop the bleeding – or to slow it down, at least.'

'Good, now spread as far as you can and we will

sweep through the ridge in front of the gates, then sweep in a circle right up the hill to the quarries and the treeline beyond. I want to find one of these guys still breathing so we can ask him who the hell they were. Copy?'

The six men acknowledged the order, cocked their weapons' night sights on, took their safety catches off and set the fire rate to automatic, more for protection and cover than accuracy. As they exited the gate, they spread into an extended sweep line. The night seemed dark and quiet after the mayhem, but the smell of the firefight remained hanging in the air. During a sweep through the ridge, they found a body lying alongside of one of the RPGs. *Abrahams' sniper shot*, thought Michael. There were signs of somebody having been dragged towards the road. Whoever it was had been hit hard; there was a steady stream of fresh blood. The group moved slowly up towards the old quarries, each man responsible for his own field of night vision and also covering those on either side of him.

The vehicle that had received the grenade hit was now upside down in the quarry, a mangled blackened hulk with one of its tyres still burning. There was no sign of the driver, or any of the other occupants. There were further signs of wounding as McBride knelt and studied the blackened earth for trails of blood.

'Watch for booby traps. Tread carefully,' called Michael, although, in his own mind, he doubted that the enemy, while retreating, had had time to set any kind of effective ambush.

At the far end of the sweep line, Robin Gibb stopped and leant forward. His rifle was held at his waist, and he was pointing at something, or someone, on the ground.

He knelt down in the grass, then called out, 'Boss, I've got a live gook. Seems wounded in his left arm and concussed – maybe from the grenade launcher. Otherwise, he appears okay.'

Michael ran across the uneven ground to where Gibb was kneeling. The rest of the sweep went in a circle, 100 paces from the huddle, then got down into kneeling positions, facing outwards, their eyes seeking out movement, or any signs of a counterattack.

By the time Michael arrived, Robin had dragged the man into an upright position and propped him against a tree stump. He appeared dazed, and Michael noticed that his eyes were dilated and bloodshot. *Caused by either drugs or fear – or both*, mused Michael. The man was not in any kind of military uniform: he had on a dark green shirt covered in blood from the wound in his arm, and torn, long trousers, ripped open at the knee, probably more a result of age than the firefight. On his feet, he had sandals made from old tractor tyres. He was thin, and appeared much older than he actually was. His weapon, an AK-47, lay in the ditch near his good arm, and the magazine was missing.

'What is your name?' Michael asked in French.

The man stared back at the man standing over him. His eyes lifted slowly to meet Michael's own.

'My name is Olivier,' he replied. 'Please do not kill me.'

'I am not going to kill you. If I was going to kill you, I would have shot you already.'

'I have a wife and many children, and they need their father. I am the only one who can bring food and money to my family.'

'Why are you attacking this place? Who sent you here? Who do you work for?'

'His name is Rahul. He is a very rich man in Matadi, and he wanted us to steal the diamonds from this place. He told us to kill the soldiers and the mine people and we will get a big reward for this.'

'Rahul who?'

'Aaah, I don't know his other name. He is a very rich man; he owns many trucks and warehouses in Matadi. Please can you give me some water? Also, please fix my arm; it has much pain.'

'Rob, take this man back to the admin building. Find Matt, get him patched up, and then find somewhere we can lock him up. When the police arrive, we can hand him over. They will know who this Rahul character is.'

'Roger that, boss.'

Robin grabbed the man around his shirt collar and pulled him roughly to his feet. Fifteen minutes ago, this man had been trying to kill him.

'Come on, Olivier. Let's get your sorry arse fixed up. Your fighting days are over, and judging by the hole in your arm, that's probably finished as well.'

Robin had spoken in English, and so Olivier just stared blankly at him. He stumbled forward, being half-pushed and half-dragged towards the main gate.

Michael turned his attention to completing the sweep and collecting up evidence from the fight. He found spent cartridges and Olivier's AK, as well as another RPG which had been smashed by an incoming round that had passed through the hollow barrel and then through the person's head, who had the weapon on his shoulder – more evidence of Tim Abrahams' deadly ability. A further sweep revealed no further bodies or recognisable equipment. The bodies of five men were placed in a line and covered with a tarpaulin.

Back inside the compound, the damage was being cleared up by mine personnel. Smith had organised two working parties and a front end loader to clear the rubble.

Michael Edward and Sergeant McBride held a briefing on the rooftop while Abrahams and the rest of the team kept their night vision binoculars and the SUSAT night scopes on their rifles ranging over the open ground outside the gate.

Half an hour later, Matt Birrell joined the group, having carried out his various radio duties and sitreps, and made a distress casevac call. He answered the questions Michael was going to pose before he had a chance to do so.

'Skip, I raised Médecins Sans Frontières. They will have a medevac chopper and medical team in the air inside of two hours after daybreak; they won't fly in darkness. I checked with Jones and Ahearn is stable. He is now dealing with that wounded bad guy. Secondly, got through to Excalibur; neither Maria nor the colonel were in the building, but they have been given a full sitrep, which will be waiting for them in the morning. I will update it after this with the casualties and get David Smith's feedback for his people as well. I finally had to phone the cops in Matadi; they don't seem to be on radio comms. A Captain Bertrand will be on his way with troopers as soon as he has spoken to the man in charge – that's you, boss. I can get him on the line as soon as you are ready.'

'Good lad, Matt. How about our current alert status, Sandy?'

'I've got men in the OP and at all four corners of the OP. All are using night glasses and we have 360-degree visual covered. I don't expect those buggers to be back anytime soon. All our weapons and equipment are intact, although the mine lost a three-tonner. We have more than enough ammo, so we are tight, sir.'

'Thanks, Sandy. As usual, you have it all covered. I'm going to check on Ahearn, and then we can call our good captain of the constabulary. Matt, see if you can get him on the line in ten.'

'Copied, skip.'

Michael moved off to the admin building to check on Ahearn and the wounded bandit, where he also checked on how Mark Jones was coping with administering first aid.

'How are you coping, Mark? It's been some time since you have been in a battlefield situation. Is Ahearn conscious?'

'Yes, boss, he is comfortable. He's been complaining that I should be in a nurse's uniform, which tells me the bullet missed his brain, sadly!'

'What about the bandit? How is he doing?'

'I've stopped the bleeding, boss, but I wouldn't be surprised if he loses his arm. The bullet has shattered his humerus, and his arm is barely holding together. I've bandaged it as tightly as I can and cleaned the wound.'

'Good lad, Jonesy. I would put my faith in you anytime in the field.'

'Boss, don't get shot – that's your best bet. When I think back to Afghanistan, you used most of your nine lives taking that big smack. Anything to get out of walking from sangar to sangar...' laughed Jones.

They were interrupted by Mark Birrell coming through the front door with a field phone in his hand.

'Skip, I've got Captain Bertrand on the phone. Sounds pretty pissed off.'

Michael took the phone from Matt's hand.

'Major Michael Ashton, Excalibur Security, speaking. Who am I speaking to?'

He heard a deep voice speaking in broken English.

'This is Captain Bertrand from the National Police Force, Matadi. Why have you been attacking innocent Congolese citizens?'

Michael was caught on the wrong foot for just a second and then shot back, 'We have not been attacking anybody; we were hired by White Cliff Resources to guard the Mankula Mine. Our presence here has been sanctioned by your government. While carrying out our duties this evening, we were attacked by bandits. Their aim was to overrun the mine and steal the mined and stored diamonds. We were defending the assets of the mine and the diamonds, as stated.'

'You and your men are mercenaries. You are on DRC soil, and you have been waging a private war against our citizens!'

'I say again: we were cleared by your government to be here and protect this mine, which is what we have done. We also protected innocent citizens from some sort of massacre at Chief Muamba's village. We reported all this to you, including seeing foreign troops at the scene. It's strange that we have not had any further information or feedback from you. Do you have any follow-up information on them now?'

'That is another matter, major. We are concerned about your attack tonight, not some fabricated story of foreign troops and a massacre. This is just nonsense,' snorted Bertrand. 'When my police patrol arrives at the mine, we will arrest you and your men.'

'How many of you will there be?' asked Michael quietly.

He was speaking almost in a whisper, but the menace in his voice was still clear. There was another silence at the other end of the line.

Michael continued, his anger now starting to rise. 'Who is paying you, or pulling your strings, Captain? How can there be a cover regarding what we reported to you about the massacre at Chief Muamba's village? That in itself makes me very suspicious. Now you are accusing us of attacking bandits who attacked us. That's ridiculous. Who is putting you up to this nonsense? Not a certain individual called Rahul, by any chance?'

There was no response from the captain, just heavy measured breathing.

Michael continued, 'You say you are coming to arrest us, Captain. I caution you to make sure you bring many crack troopers with you!'

'What do you mean, major? When we arrive, we will arrest you.'

'Well let's hope your constables are very good at what they do. Any move to arrest anybody from my team, and you will have a fight on your hands.'

'I will call you back soon, major.' Bertrand was now breathing faster and more heavily. 'You cannot threaten me.'

'I am not threatening you; I am promising we will react to any hostile move on your part with whatever force is necessary. As I said, captain, just make sure you bring many highly trained troops.'

Michael slammed the phone back onto the cradle.

Almost to himself, he said in a calm voice, steady but firm: 'Fucking imbecile, obviously a puppet. Let's see whether or not he turns up. I'll reinforce the rooftop, in case he does.'

Michael stormed out of the room and called for Edward and McBride to join him to discuss the development that had taken place, and the measures they could take to remove the potential threat of a bunch of DRC police troopers running around the mine, intent on arresting everybody.

No policeman materialised during the night.

As dawn broke, Michael heard, coming in low over the treetops, the steady 'whup, whup, whup' of helicopter rotor blades chopping through the cold morning light. The helicopter was a French Alouette III, dark green in colour with large Red Cross decals on the sliding doors. This was a workhorse carrier in the DRC, carrying people, cargo, ammunition and troops, playing a similar role to that which the Bell Hueys had in Vietnam. The helicopter started hovering, and dust, leaves and small bits of wood and rock were thrown through the air for thirty metres around. The pilot flared out into the open area alongside the motor pool and workshops, where the burnt-out wreckage of the mine's three-tonne truck was still smouldering. The engine noise decreased as the rotors were shut down. Then, the large curved door slid back and a medical team was on the ground in seconds.

Michael recognised the lady doctor, Marie Louise, in the middle of a small group of medical personnel.

'*Bonjour*, Michael,' she called, waving her hand in the air.

'*Bonjour*, Marie Louise. Good to see you again. My trooper will be in good hands.'

'We were told there were two wounded, Michael?'

'Yes, one of the bandits has a serious upper arm wound; unfortunately the round hit his humerus and shattered it.'

'*Mon Dieu*, these terrible weapons, and all this human suffering. Michael, I am pleased you are safe. I remember being angry with your military attitude to death and war. I am sorry. In hindsight, it was not fair: it is what you know. I still abhor fighting and killing, but as I spend more time in the DRC, I understand more of the cruelty and lack of pride in being alive. Take me to the wounded men; we have a good team with us.'

Mark Jones met Marie Louise at the doorway of the makeshift medical casualty post and they disappeared inside. Michael turned away and went over to the chairs which he and Edward used as their evening recreation spot. He had to pick up the chairs that had been scattered by the RPG explosion, and while doing so, he noticed a shrapnel tear in the back of one chair. He flopped down as the high adrenaline levels fell away completely, replaced by a numbness of the mind. Around him clean-up operations were being carried out by the mine personnel and the soldiers under the stewardship of Sergeant McBride.

That evening, with the police still conspicuous by their absence, the team got together with the mine staff and medical team for a farewell barbeque. The South African Kobus, extolling his expertise in doing a real *braai*, as he called it, was guarding and patrolling the fire, pouring sauces and beer over the meat in equal quantities. The wounded bandit had been moved to a government hospital ICU unit in Matadi, where he had lost his arm. Sean Ahearn, drugged up on painkillers, complained at having to lie on his stomach on a medical trolley, hooked up to a drip in the medical room with his backside in the air. Despite having lost a lot of blood, he still wanted to be wheeled out on the trolley and to take part in the fun. This was firmly overruled by Marie Louise, who politely declined his offer of a kiss of gratitude, as that would have meant bending down into a vulnerable and compromising position to reach the trooper.

She is an old hand at this, thought Michael.

Edward, Tim Abrahams, Robin Gibb and Matt Birrell drew the short straws and were assigned to be on guard in the OP on the admin building roof. The beer flowed freely and the mood lightened. The replacement Excalibur team were in Kinshasa at the Matadi mine compound and would arrive tomorrow during the latter part of the afternoon.

Michael and Marie Louise wandered off to the edge of the firelight, Michael carrying the directors' chairs and a good bottle of claret extracted from David Smith's private collection. Marie Louise carried a couple of decent wine glasses, again courtesy of David Smith. They sat side by side in silence for a few minutes, taking in the bright stars, so bright in the night sky, and watching the fire, the flickering flames casting shadows which appeared to dance across the compound, reflecting off the building walls and among the leaves in the trees on the far side of the compound.

The pair sat in quiet reflection, shutting out the hubbub of voices and laughter behind them, until Michael's personal radio came to life and they heard Tim Abrahams telling him that all was quiet and there was no sign of anything untoward. Michael acknowledged him, sighed and turned to look at Marie Louise. 'Where is home for you, Marie Louise?'

She stared up at the stars for some time before turning to him. His question had obviously brought back some hard memories: her face looked sad and resigned.

'Sometimes, I feel as though I have been in Africa forever. It has become my home. First it was Ethiopia, then the Sudan and now the Congo. Home is wherever Médecins Sans Frontières asks me to be. The work is always voluntary. I go wherever I feel that by helping I am doing some good. Africa is a continent somehow forgotten by the rest of the world when it comes to economic development. Throwing money at the problem doesn't work, it makes the dictators richer. Africa still struggles with basic hygiene, overcrowding, bad sanitation and corrupt governments and political leaders. In the east, we see that there is massive poverty and no food, and we are told it's all caused by drought. It's not, Michael. It starts with internal wars, people abandoned by their own governments in the desert, caught in the crossfire between the feuds of rival murdering gangs who call themselves the opposition. The bandits steal the foodstuffs and aid sent by the West. Add to this that there is no birth control and that babies are born to no food or water, and you see why millions die. In the west of Africa we have good rainfall, but this brings its own medical problems: malaria kills two million people a year. West Africa is a breeding ground for disease. AIDS and other easily transmitted diseases such as Ebola move like wildfire through the population. We in the West make the right noises, but until it comes to our own countries, our own doorstep, there will be no real help.

'I read a saying once that has become a mantra for me. The saying goes: 'Your day should start with helping somebody who can never repay you'. That is what I try in my own small way to achieve each day. That probably sounds a little contrived to you as a soldier.'

'Not at all. I understand,' he replied quietly.

'Anyway, I do not wish to depress you. You asked where my home is. My actual home is in Provence in France, south of Avignon, near a market town called St Remy. Do you know Provence at all?'

'I have been to Avignon and did spend a couple of weeks one summer in a great little *gîte* on a cauliflower farm not too far from St Remy, but I don't know the area well. Do you have family there? Do you go home much?'

'My mother and father live in Paris, but my late husband's family are from the St Remy area. I still have a home there. It is looked after by my husband's family, and my parents use it in the summer. I do not go home often; it is now a lonely place for me. My husband and I were doctors. We were coming back from a dinner party with friends about six years ago in our car when we were hit by a pick-up truck driven by a drunk farmer.

My husband was killed.'

'I am very sorry for your loss. It must have been hard for you.'

'My life has moved on. My work drives me. The pain has eased, but the loneliness lives with me constantly. One day I will go home – not yet though.'

They sat in silence for a while, enjoying the peace, the wine, the darkness and the myriad stars in the heavens above.

'Michael, what about you? Where is your home?'

'I haven't lived at the family home for many years. For six years I was in the British Army and home was many places. Since leaving the army and starting work for Excalibur, I have bought my own apartment in Wimbledon Village, not too far from the Lawn Tennis Club. My parents' house – and mine, I guess – is in Cranleigh, down in the stockbroker commuter belt area of Surrey. Do you know it?'

'*Oui*, a little. It is not far from London, *non*?'

'About an hour or so if the traffic is good. Edward, my second-in-command is my flat mate at the Wimbledon apartment. Cranleigh is a straight run down the M3. My parents moved there when they left Africa around 1980 after Zimbabwe's independence. We had a petrol station and garage in Africa, but when my father arrived back in the UK, he and my mother went back to study. My father is now a director on the main board of a large financial services group and a complete Bob Dylan fanatic, knows every word of every song. My mum is an academic and chairs various charitable trusts. They were childhood sweethearts.'

'They sound interesting. And what about you,

Michael? Have you always been a soldier?'

'Pretty much. It is the only job I have had since my university days. After university, I went to Sandhurst and then into the light infantry. Growing up in Africa, I loved the outdoors and the bush. I guess the army in the UK provided the way of life that was closest to what I had in my younger years. It's not the war element that drives me, or the weapons – more the camaraderie and friendship.'

'Aaah, the male bonding thing that you men believe in so much,' she replied, smiling at him.

'I guess that is a part of it. In my own way, I feel that I too have tried to help others as well. I like the fitness, the outdoors, the leadership and the personal discipline that I have learned.'

'Do you have somebody, a young lady or a fiancée perhaps?'

'No, I guess I have never been the proud homeowner type with a little house in suburbia and 2.4 children! A girlfriend now and again, but usually they grow tired of my nomadic lifestyle. Excalibur operates wherever there is a need to guard or protect British assets or citizens. People, assets – even small countries,' laughed Michael. 'I am always away somewhere for lengthy stretches at a time, sometimes leaving at a moment's notice. Doesn't do much for a stable relationship.'

'Maybe one day you will settle down, grow up and get a real job,' said Marie Louise only half in jest.

'Maybe, but not yet – still too many places to visit, too much to see and do. Talking of which, when we leave for London tomorrow, I am going to establish what happened to those young girls that were abducted.

I know they were abducted in UK-built assets, a couple of Jackal armoured vehicles. I know there were Zimbabwean troops involved. Also, there could be some sort of UN involvement. Have you heard of UNESCO Sustainable Teaching?'

Marie Louise shook her head in response.

'Could well be linked to agriculture and farming teacher training. We spotted some European leaving an address in Matadi that could be linked to whatever is going on.'

Michael did not bring up the UK-registered private aircraft.

He continued, 'My enquiries through our London office have so far run into a brick wall. I promised Chief Muamba I would find his girls and bring them home. God knows how I will achieve it, but I have to find them; I always keep a promise. The reason for bringing this up is to ask whether it would be possible for you to keep your ear to the ground at this end – be my eyes and ears here, so to speak?'

'Yes, Michael, I will do that for you. I do not know how much I can find out, but what I do, I will pass on to you at Excalibur.'

'Thank you. If those girls have been harmed in any way, I will personally kill the bastards involved. That's another promise.'

They lapsed back into silence, each lost in their own thoughts. Behind them, people were leaving the barbeque and the fire had died down to glowing embers. The night sounds came to the fore: distant drumming and the soft whistle of bat wings sweeping through the trees, heard but not seen.

Marie Louise stirred in her chair then stood up, her skirt rustling as she rose.

'Michael, I will say à bientôt. I must check on your wounded soldier, and you, I'm sure, must start preparing to return home to England. I shall stay in touch with you regarding anything I hear about the young girls.'

Michael rose from his chair and lifted his arms above his head, stretching his tall, lithe body.

'You are a good man, Michael. I look forward to seeing you again. Michael, Merry Christmas, the time of rejoicing and thanksgiving, ironic don't you think?'

She rose up on tiptoes and kissed Michael lightly on both cheeks. He in turn held her for a brief moment in his arms.

'À bientôt, Marie Louise. Take care in your work. I had forgotten all about Christmas, sad really. I look forward to hearing from you – perhaps we will even meet up in London.'

'Perhaps, I will pray for you, Michael,' she called over her shoulder as she made her way across the parking area towards the temporary hospital room.

He returned to his chair, lowered himself into it and put his head back so that he was looking up at the myriad stars in the night sky. He closed his eyes slowly, and his mind drifted to mistletoe and wine, roaring log fires and the lights on the Christmas tree, always with an angel on the top.

10

Excalibur London

It was Monday morning, and the weather was typical for January. Grey, miserable and overcast, although there was no rain. A biting, but thankfully light, wind was swirling around their faces and ankles, the last remnants of the late autumn leaves building steadily on the damp pavement. Michael and Edward decided to get the train up from Wimbledon and walk over Hungerford Bridge from Waterloo, up through Trafalgar Square and down Pall Mall as far as St James's Square. From there, they cut up through Duke of York Street at a brisk pace and across Jermyn Street through to Piccadilly and the Burlington Arcade. The West End of London was fully awake, and taxis, buses and cars were jostling for position in the early morning rush hour. Surprisingly, there is always some order to the apparent chaos of London traffic, and if you are quick, somebody will always let you filter in.

They arrived at Excalibur's offices just as a light drizzle was starting to fall. Michael unconsciously turned his collar up to keep out the wet and to protect his face, then pressed the buzzer next to the black lacquered door. He heard the click of the Yale release, and the door gave way allowing them to enter. Maria was already behind her desk when they got inside. She gave them a genuine 'welcome home' smile and stood up to greet them both.

'Welcome home, you two. Things got a bit hairy, I gather, on the penultimate evening. I am pleased you are both back in one piece. Sorry to hear about Sean Ahearn. We have had word that his wound is healing nicely, and he is nagging all the nurses at the Burnside Clinic in Harley Street for a date, so he must be on the mend.'

'That's good to hear,' said Michael, hoping Maria would not notice how she managed to take his breath away just as she started to speak.

God, he thought, *she is just so beautiful, and she dresses so immaculately.* Edward nudged him out of his little trance.

'Yes, we were stonked hard on that evening, but the lads held fast and we turned the tide without too much of a mess.'

'As I said, it is good to see you in one piece. Go on up. Colonel Torrens isn't here yet, but your debriefing is set for 0900 hours and he will not be late, knowing him.'

'Are you coming into the meeting?' asked Michael, aware he sounded like an anxious schoolboy hoping to meet the girl he likes in the school corridor.

'The colonel will call me in if he thinks it's necessary, I'm sure.'

Michael and Edward bundled into the small lift, and as the doors closed, Edward gave Michael a punch on the arm.

'Are you coming to the meeting?' Edward mimicked

Michael. 'How obvious can you get, Michael? You're a great soldier, but lousy at chat-up lines! It's fairly obvious to me that you have a thing about the lass.'

'Don't be daft, Ed. Oh hell, was I that bad?' asked Michael, before continuing without waiting for Edward's answer, 'it's just that she is so good-looking and bright, and she dresses so immaculately. I would love to see her away from the office sometime, in a pair of jeans and a casual top.'

'Why don't you ask her out on a date instead of swooning every time you see her? Honestly, you look like a lovesick gorilla.'

'I guess it's not my style, Ed. I haven't been into dating for a couple of years. I'm also not into serious stuff.'

'You are running scared, my friend, just speak out. You certainly look serious enough to me.'

'Yeah, okay,' muttered Michael, in a tone that indicated the lesson on chat-up lines was over.

They entered the boardroom and made a beeline for the Nespresso machine. The two men were dressed in a similar manner, with blue denim jeans, button-down Oxford shirts, Michael's white and Edward's pale blue. Their shoes were all leather and from Jones Bootmaker, and their navy blazers were from DAKS in Bond Street. Michael flopped into a boardroom table chair and put one leg over the arm.

'What do you think the boss will want to know?' asked Edward, thumbing through an A4 pad covered with handwritten notes. 'I have a pretty good summary of all the events; should be able to bring him fully up to speed.'

'He will already be up to speed. He has a nose and mind for this stuff – not to mention that he will have our daily sitrep reports. Not only is he a brilliant military tactician and his military appreciation work is incredible, but he also seems to know our every move. He probably knows about us getting a little under the table on Saturday night; the walk down the high street home was a major task all on its own. He's a wily old devil.'

The boardroom door swung open and Colonel Donald Torrens headed for the top end of the table. Nine o'clock on the dot, Maria had said, and the clock on the wall said exactly that. He was in a tailored, blue pinstriped suit from Bond Street, a white shirt and a dark blue tie. As he pulled out his chair he looked at Michael.

'What wily old devil were you talking about as I came in, Major Ashton?'

'Oh nobody, sir. Just my uncle who came up to London this weekend,' shot back Michael.

Before he had time to pat himself on the back, Colonel Torrens continued, 'Wily, I like, Michael; the old devil bit keep to yourself, young man. Did your uncle join you and Edward on your high street booze parade on Saturday evening as well?' The question hung in the air. 'Never mind, let's get started. Welcome back, chaps. White Cliff Resources are very pleased we saved their mine and their diamonds and they have extended the mine security contract for a further six months beyond your replacement stick's arrival. That's good news for the firm and means bonuses for you two and your team. Ahearn is on the mend. We will pick up all his medical expenses and send him off to a nice sunny place to recuperate – the south of France, or something similar.

Reading through your summary of the time at the mine and the penultimate evening's punch-up, it appears that it was an isolated attack carried out by bandits rather than militia, and we have confirmation of this from our sources in the DRC. Our friends at MI6 are checking out your trader Rahul to see if we can prove that he was the ringleader, although I doubt he is the top man. We will teach him a small, but powerful, lesson, one big enough for his bandit cronies to pay attention: a reminder that British assets are just that and not to be attacked at will.

'Now, there has been an official complaint made to the Foreign Office by the DRC Consulate here. It seems some police chief has reported you to his superiors because he thinks you buggers were shooting up the locals for sport. We rejected the claim outright. The complaint was relayed to me over the phone by the Deputy Minister of State and not Sir Gary Jackson, the Minister of State, so no real fallout there. Sir Gary will receive a briefing on the matter from his own people. So other than your firefight, there doesn't seem to be any real information we need to dissect – it's all fairly routine. The stores return on weapons and ammunition will come through in the next day or two. Edward, you will need to sign off the checklists and account for the equipment, ammunition, etc, used on the contract. Oh yes, while I think of it, Michael: why did you choose to go out of Kinshasa Airport with all flags flying and not undercover, as instructed?'

'We – that is, I – felt that a show of strength might deter any would-be ambushers, sir. We didn't want to be taken on and then have to retrieve weapons that had been stashed away.'

'I agreed with Michael, sir,' interjected Edward.

'Yes I'm sure you did. You're always backing up young Major Ashton. Edward, be that as it may, our intel showed no perceived threat around Kinshasa Airport – your action could have started something.'

'Roger, sir – point taken,' Michael answered.

'Good, let's move on. The action you took in defending the local tribesmen in the village near the mine…'

Michael started to protest and justify the decision, but Colonel Torrens held up his hand to silence him.

He continued, 'I understand your rationale for taking the action you did: to protect the villagers. I would have done the same. I abhor the slaughter of defenceless civilians. I am also aware and remind you two that, strictly speaking, this is not Excalibur business. By that I mean it's not part of any contract, or any task we have been asked to carry out by a client or the government, or any government for that matter. We are, however, civilised men, and cannot sit by and do nothing. However, anything we do is not a company remit, or to be seen as such. Do you copy?'

They both nodded their understanding.

'So let's talk about what we know and what we think happened.'

Michael shifted forward in his chair, unhooked his leg and began speaking.

'We do not believe that it was any kind of ethnic cleansing. They are all from the same tribe in that area. Also, the chief told us that they did not steal livestock or food. These guys were on a mission to steal the young girls in the village. Women and children, as well as old and young men, were butchered, but the young girls were rounded up and removed.

'Agreed. So why do you think they were taken?'

'We don't know the answer to that yet, but they were being dragged to a couple of armoured Jackals manned by Zimbabwean troops who were observing rather than fighting. The killing and shooting was being carried out by bandits. No doubt someone had paid them to carry out the abductions.'

'Why do you say Zimbabwean?'

'We tracked the Jackals to a house in a Matadi suburb and also Edward saw them in Matadi itself on a couple of occasions. We recognised the Zimbo uniforms. When we were staking out the house in Matadi, a Mercedes-Benz came out of the house and in the back seat were a Zimbabwean army captain whom I had come across in Zimbabwe, and again briefly in Johannesburg and London. Also in the back seat was a familiar-looking white European. We followed the Mercedes to the airport and called that in to you back in London here as well. We did not observe any of the young girls at the house.'

'Doesn't mean they were not there.'

'Agreed, but my sixth sense told me that they were gone: there were no guards that we could see, no bars on the windows. They must have taken half a dozen girls at least, and that would make it harder to hide in a house without there being some sign of their presence.'

'That is pretty much as I read it and understand it. I just wanted to hear it directly from you.'

Colonel Torrens rose from his seat at the head of the boardroom table, picked up a buff-coloured file and opened it on the boardroom table. He walked over to the china board and pushed a buzzer which lowered a greaseproof screen, the type that allows writing and erasing. He picked up a black felt tip pen and turned to the two men sitting facing him.

'I've been through all your sitreps again, watched the video footage of your feedback to the Ops room and also heard from you both this morning. I have written down what you might call a list of clues. Gentlemen, I suggest we put down on the board what we have and what we know. Good idea?'

Both Michael and Edward nodded in agreement.

'Right. Don't take notes; commit what we discuss to memory,' said Torrens. 'Here goes. We know there were Zimbabwean troops involved. We know that they were driving British-made Jackals. So far, I have been stonewalled on that one – perhaps a little trip down to the factory might help.

'We know some girls were abducted by them, we don't know why. Could be for pleasure, in which case they will be dead by now; could be for profit, meaning they may have been sold to a brothel in Matadi; could be for forced terrorist training – if not as fighters then as carriers, first aid or cooking. We've got our friends in MI6 looking at that closely.

'We know there is some sort of connection with a UN-sponsored agricultural set-up called UNESCO Sustainable Teaching. It's probably a front for their activities, or maybe they are just using the building where the organisation were based. There was also a fancy Mercedes with EU plates involved; did you track the number, Michael? I don't have any recent updates regarding that in the file.'

'Yes, sir. The plates are diplomatic issue and we have tracked them to being a batch issued in Luxembourg, so I was wrong about them being standard EU plates. Again, it looks as though they may be linked to some quasi-EU governmental body there.

'We can add that to the knowns, then, Michael,' said Torrens, scribbling something onto a sheet in the file on the boardroom table.

'Right, let's continue. We know that the aircraft is a Pilatus, call sign Golf Alpha X-ray Yankee. It is UK-registered; no details on that as yet. We have, however, tracked the plane to one of those luxury private executive aircraft companies at Luton Airport. The company's name is Corporate Jet Solutions.'

'Very original,' quipped Michael. 'They must have had Saatchi & Saatchi on the case.'

Torrens continued, 'I doubt that they were involved, Michael, but a look at the logbooks and flight plans for the period in question might help. A Pilatus does not really fit with the company's fleet of small commercial jets. That tells me it's there as a favour to a friend.'

'Gentlemen, that's it from my side. Go over your own notes and try to recall what happened, and see what you come up with. I am sending you both off on a couple of months' leave, anyway; these investigations and subsequent actions are off the record and will not reflect in any Excalibur communication or documents. What you tell me, or feed back to me, is entirely up to you. Your salaries will be paid into your UK bank accounts as usual; all your expenses will be met from an unnumbered Jersey bank account. Maria has the details. You can operate credit cards on the account; they are ready for you. Good luck – stay out of trouble if you can, and try to stay alive.

'Ah, yes. With that in mind, I am attaching your talisman, Abrahams, and his sniper capabilities to you as well. I smell big money and power somewhere: that is always a dangerous combination. Once you know what we are facing, I will, if necessary, come on board with the full company resources, but for now, we will keep it off the radar. We have Ahearn in St Thomas' Hospital; no life-threatening injury, but nevertheless, having had an AK-47 round through his stomach, he is a very sick and sore lad. He is out of ICU and that's a good sign. His vital signs are strong, and his temperature is around normal. Keep me in the picture on all new intel coming through.'

With that, Torrens closed the file, tucked it under his arm and pushed the buzzer on the board again, which did two things: wiped the board clean and raised it back into its concealed position.

11

Picking up the Trail

Michael and Edward sat in silence in the boardroom, mulling over what they had just heard and discussed. Each was lost in his own thoughts. In the distance, a suppressed police siren only just broke the silence, managing to penetrate despite the triple glazing and soundproof walls. It was a reminder that the law was still on the streets of London, whether dealing with petty crime or a terrorist threat.

Where do we start? Michael asked himself. We have enough leads to choose to start in a number of directions, but what are we looking for? Yes, of course, for the girls, but for now the priority lay in establishing what the girls were part of. Human trafficking, prostitution, forced terrorist recruitment, child soldiers for some African warlord, or perhaps just pleasure in the DRC. If it was the latter, the girls would almost certainly be dead by now. There was the possibility of Rahul or his friends passing the girls to drug dealers and traffickers in the UK.

The newspapers and television were filled with news about slavery and articles about human trafficking rings and the police's occasional successes in dealing with the problem. Public awareness about this dark, violent underworld was currently heightened, but the human mind is strange; it does not take long for the old adage of 'if it doesn't affect me, then it's not really happening' to refocus the mind on more everyday and pressing things like trying to get a mortgage.

Michael's mind drifted and he started thinking about how he operated in two different worlds: one in the light that everyone sees and one in the darkness, a world of subterfuge, terror threats, spies, wars, power and double-crossing. People prefer the happy, mundane side of life, where there is nothing to fear: hurrying to a meeting, running for a cab or a train, shopping and coffee with the girls, school trips to museums and tourists photographing the Changing of the Guard. They are all oblivious to the parallel world that we operate in. Just as well really, people don't like living in an emotional state of constant fear. Only when a terror event occurs do they become more aware and focused. It reminds them that when the dark world crosses into the light, everyday people become part of the death and destruction.

For weeks after the London Underground bombings on 7/7, people were very scared, and this made them frightened and vigilant. A briefcase too far from its owner on a bus, a person dressed in Middle Eastern garb with earphones linked to an iPod hidden in the folds of their clothing, an extra-large backpack which its wearer kept on while standing on an underground train – all of these incidents led to a multitude of 999 calls. Why? Because now the fear was real, in your face, it was intruding into people's everyday lives. Nothing promotes awareness of the value of one's own life and the urge for self-preservation like the fear brought about by the thought that this could happen to me – it really is all around me. Two parallel worlds colliding in an instant, wreaking death and destruction amongst us.

'Michael, Michael.' Edward's voice penetrated Michael's thoughts. 'We have a good deal of stuff to go on – more than I first thought. By putting it all down in sequence we can come up with an allocation of tasks and action points, don't you think?'

'Yes, you are right. Sorry, my mind drifted away, thinking about all the evil that seems to be building up every day in our world.'

'Don't be too hard on yourself. We are in the business of protection and rooting out evil; it's bound to affect us. Working with conflict, being good at what we do puts us in the biggest business in the world: the business of war.'

'I was thinking more about those who don't live in our world day to day, or by choice, like you and I. Those who go about their everyday, normal, happy suburban lives: they are, through no choice of their own, entering the realm of terror. Anyway, that's a discussion for another time, probably over a pint of Guinness! I will give Tim Abrahams a call.

'Let's meet up tonight to look at what we have, to decide our priorities and draw up a plan of action. There is a pub I quite like called the Duke of Cumberland at the top end of Dean Street near Soho Square. It has cubicles where we can talk freely. How about we meet up there tonight, at say 1900 hours, and from there we can grab a bite to eat at Leonardo's, the little Italian around the corner from there?'

'Roger that, I can find the pub. I'll see you there; right now I am going to do all the mundane stuff you seem to be avoiding – the paperwork from our little tour in the DRC'.

'Good for you, mate. That's what makes you a great second-in-command. I was never much good at paperwork.'

Edward burst out laughing.

'Second-in-command? Piss off – you made major before me on age alone.' It was true Michael was only six months older than Edward. 'I think the army looked at you, and realised they needed to surround you with support from top soldiers and a batman to wipe your backside, old boy!'

Still laughing, Edward left the boardroom, closely followed by the black felt tip pen, thrown by Michael. Luckily, it missed his ear by an inch and bounced harmlessly off the wall.

Lost in his own thoughts, Michael walked through Piccadilly Circus towards the Duke of Cumberland. He hardly noticed the rain, which was more October evening drizzle than a downpour. Droplets formed in his hair and ran down the back of his nick. *Should have brought an umbrella*, he thought. The restyled Dickensian street lights reflected in a golden hue on the cobbled stones.

He arrived at the Duke of Cumberland slightly ahead of seven o'clock, wandered over to the bar and ordered a pint of Guinness. Looking around the pub, he saw a cubicle towards the back of the bar away from the foot traffic to the toilets. He liked the pub for its old-world-liness, and for the fact there was nothing distracting in the bar area like fruit machines, or noisy music; nothing to distract from getting a drink and enjoying a conversation. He made his way over to the cubicle and sat facing the main entrance. The last of the West End workers were finishing up their drinks before running for their trains to suburbia. As they left, the early night-out crowd started arriving to take their places.

Tim Abrahams was the first to arrive and indicated to Michael he was getting a drink from the bar on his way to the table. Did he want a refill? Michael shook his head, as he had only just started on the pint in front of him. Tim came over in his familiar laid-back shuffling way of walking and sat down facing Michael.

'Evening, boss. How are we then?'

'Good thanks, Tim. How about you? Good break so far?'

'Yeah, good to catch up with my folks and my mates, but very pleased that we are not going to be sitting around for the next month or two twiddling our thumbs. Good to have something constructive to do – maybe even a little excitement.'

'Did Colonel Torrens explain to you what was going on?'

'He gave me a brief outline, something to do with looking into those missing girls. His main concern is having somebody watching your back. He seems to think that if we ask the wrong people, or stick our oar in where we are not needed, we could stir things up a bit. He wants you in one piece, I gather – he who fights and runs away and all that.'

'Yes, the colonel seems to think we could do that – stir things up, I mean. Personally, I'm not even sure we will get to the bottom of it; it seems strange that the girls would be moved to London or the UK from the DRC, but either way, we are going to try to find out what happened. We will go where the trail leads, even if that means going back to the DRC.'

'Fine by me, boss. We could even have some fun along the way – always wanted to go back to that wonderful hotel in Matadi.'

Michael smiled and then broke eye contact with Tim as Edward came through the pub entrance. He stopped, turned and then held the door, and Maria entered ahead of him. *Bloody hell,* thought Michael. *What is she doing here? I didn't think she would be joining us.* He admired her slimline black jeans and stilettos, which she wore together with a simple, black, off-the-shoulder silk top and Irish shawl. She shook off a wet dripping umbrella before securing it in a closed position. Edward headed for the bar, and Maria walked across to the cubicle where the two men were sitting. Michael almost fell off his seat in surprise.

'Hi Michael, hi Tim. I met up with Edward as he was leaving and he explained that you were all meeting up and why. The welfare and whereabouts of those girls concerns me a lot. I can be an extra pair of hands; keep the home fires burning and collate all the intel if you guys are all over the place. Are you okay with that, Michael? It's your show, and Edward says it's your call.'

'Not sure that's exactly true; the colonel has the last say. Maria, we are not sure where we are going with this. It may be nothing, or it may turn out to be a nasty situation. That brings its own problems. I know you can handle yourself, but are you up for whatever happens, wherever this thing takes us?'

'I want to help if I can, and if we run into flak, so be it. I know where I am at. However, as I see it, while I am manning base, so to speak, I cannot see trouble coming to me.'

'I can see that point, but more importantly, how does the colonel feel about it? From my point of view, it's fine, Maria; you are more than capable of looking out for yourself.'

'As I said, I met Edward as he was leaving, so I have not seen the colonel to ask him. As I am only going to watch over what comes in and coordinate and provide logistics if needed, I shouldn't think he will mind.'

'No, I suppose not. Better run it past him, though.'

Edward arrived from the bar, carrying a pint of Guinness and a large Sauvignon Blanc for Maria. He cut across Michael's thoughts as he pulled out a chair and sat down.

'Good news, chaps. As you can see, I have managed to persuade Maria to join our little fishing and fact-finding mission.'

Edward winked at Michael and got a frown and sullen glare in return. This mischievous grin was missed by the others. Edward shrugged his shoulders and winked again.

Michael observed how at ease Edward was in the moment. *He has such natural charm and is so at ease with ladies; life would be so much simpler if I had the same*, he thought. *It's not that I haven't had relationships, it's just that I'm not very good at building something beyond first dates and messy relationships;*

*it becomes a blur of wine bars, beds and dinners, with
the odd party thrown in. Most of my relationships don't
go beyond the six-month stage at best,* Michael reflected.
*Probably women pick up on the fact that I am not yet in
the market for settling down, or it could just be that I'm
a waste of space.*

'Boss, all present and correct,' Tim said, breaking
into Michael's thoughts. 'Do you want to give us a
rundown on what we have?'

For the next half-hour, Michael outlined the facts
he had put together so far in discussion with Colonel
Torrens on the DRC encounter, including his thoughts
on the girls being sold off to warlords.

'If that is the case, boss, then, with respect, why are
we getting involved? It's probably a done deal and some
of the girls will be dead already,' said Tim.

Maria cut in: 'Tim, when you were in the DRC and
that terrible attack happened, Michael gave his word to
the village chief that he would look for, and find, the
girls.'

'Don't get me wrong, Maria,' Tim replied. 'I would
love to catch the bastards who abducted them; I just
don't see how we can effectively find them from here in
the UK. Maybe we need to get back on the ground in the
DRC – surely that would make more sense. Maybe we
can use that French lady doctor to sniff around.'

Michael joined the conversation.

'For now, we leave others out of what we are doing,
including Marie Louise; we have to keep this tight. You
may be right, Tim, but let's look at what we can put
together from London first. We have several leads we
can follow up.'

'Cool, boss, then point me in the right direction and let the fun begin.'

After further discussion, it was decided that they would start by trying to get at the flight plans and logbooks of the aircraft registered to Corporate Jet Solutions at Luton Airport. Tim was allocated the task of making enquiries at Luton. Edward was tasked with using his family and personal connections to once again follow up Colonel Torrens' Ministry of Defence enquiries and to use various army contacts to try to find out where the Jackal armoured vehicles they had seen in the DRC came from, while Michael would be taking a trip down to the West Country; to Honiton and the Supacat factory site.

Maria volunteered to fly out to Luxembourg and the European headquarters of the European Investment Bank to talk to a friend of hers, a bright young corporate lawyer who worked in the banking division. When Michael argued that she was deviating from her role of manning the fort, Maria responded that she would do it over the forthcoming weekend and that she would be perfectly safe in Luxembourg. Her friend might know how to run a check on the registration numbers and vehicles issued to bank senior employees; she might even know somebody in the UN agricultural division, which covers some parts of UNESCO. The group concluded that 'sustainable teaching' made it sound as though it might have its business goals linked to one of the agricultural divisions of the European Development Bank, which, in turn, was an offshoot of the European Investment Bank.

'All on a bloody gravy train, if you ask me – that EU lot,' said Michael. 'I've been over there a couple of times and the corporate business expense cards support the whole infrastructure of Luxembourg. I've never seen so many fancy wine bars and restaurants per square mile. It's not just the European Parliament whose MEPs earn twice that of a UK Member of Parliament, but also the banks and support agencies that go with the whole dream. The shareholders of the European Investment Bank are the member states of the European Union, and they have to pay an annual contribution to sustain the bank's lending and growth. That's taxpayers' money being used. Look at the wording in the mission statement of the European Investment Bank: "to help developing Third World countries and the Caribbean region to grow their economies through investment in their infrastructures and projects designed to help the growth and economic enhancement of their people". That's fine, until you read a little further, where they state many of the loans are not expected to be repaid, or words to that effect. A recipe for corruption and abuse of funds – not by the Europeans themselves, who probably really believe they are making a difference, but by the ruling elite and the dictators running the countries. Then look at the inward investment: you would not believe the money being spent in Luxembourg on things like the Opera House, superb new headquarters for the banks, various government offices, etc.'

'Whoa. Some lecture. I take it you are not fond of the whole EU concept, Michael?' asked Edward jokingly.

'No, Ed, you are wrong. I believe in the principle of European Union, but under a common economic trading platform, leaving each member state to run its own country. We don't need 500 members of the European

Parliament. Of course we should help the developing world, but there are not enough foot soldiers on the ground monitoring where the money actually goes in places like Africa. You cannot oversee a humanitarian, or economic development project with your base in Luxembourg and a couple of project managers on the ground.' Michael paused for a moment. 'Enough said, it's getting late and I have taken us off-topic. We know our tasks, so let's meet back here a week from today and see what we have come up with. Stay in touch with Maria if anything interesting turns up, or you need help.'

The group stood up and Michael and Tim carried the empty glasses back to the bar, a quirky thing people do in England to assist the barmen and waiters. Once out of the pub they could feel the night chill. There was a light, biting wind, but the rain had stopped. Tim walked off back towards Waterloo Station, while Maria, Edward and Michael headed in the direction of Ronnie Scott's jazz bar in Soho for a nightcap. None of them noticed the two men standing in the shadows using a small camera to record their faces.

12

Information Gathering

Tim caught the 9.30 am train from St Pancras to Luton to avoid the early morning rush hour and the sad, over-crowded people trying so hard to ignore one another even though their faces were inches apart. The journey time would be 45 minutes. As the train wound its way through the northern suburbs of London, the last of the early February morning mist – it was too thin to be called fog – started to lift, revealing row upon row of suburban houses for commuters. Terraced houses looking wet and dank; here and there, a light from a window, or a glimpse of somebody doing something around the house. Staring at row upon row of box terraced houses, he was reminded of a hit song by Manfred Mann, a band from the 1960s, who had a song called 'Semi-Detached Suburban Mr James'. In his carriage there were a group of young twenty-somethings. Their backpacks and cases were piled up at the carriage entrance, and they were laughing and chattering away the way people do when they are excited about going somewhere nice. *Probably somewhere warm, too*, thought Tim; *Ryanair, here come your loyal followers.*

Maximum hand luggage ten kilos, €50 for a case, so long as it weighs no more than fifteen kilos. No pre-assigned seats, no food, unless you are willing to pay a small fortune for a coffee and a sandwich on board, and the incessant messages from the cabin crew about lotto tickets, places to stay, cars to hire, all recommended by Ryanair and their travel partners. However, the great thing about the airline was that the planes were clean and up-to-date and very nearly always on time, for which the larger airlines deeply envied them. Tim had a sneaking admiration for Michael O'Leary, the chief executive. He had once read somewhere that, although he was a multi-millionaire, O'Leary was very careful with his own money as well as Ryanair's and did not like extravagant designer labels. *Like me, but in my case it's not because I'm a millionaire; I just can't afford the stuff*, Tim thought. Despite this, he had tried to dress like a gentleman who might be likely to hire a private jet, in his old but countryside Barbour jacket, pleated chinos and a button-down white Oxford shirt.

Upon arriving at Luton, he sought out a storage locker facility off the platform, which was in the entrance hall to the station. He locked away the duffel bag he was carrying, wandered out of the concourse and then started the short uphill walk to Corporate Jet Solutions' hangars and offices on the near side of the airfield behind easyJet's huge orange administrative buildings. The Corporate Jet Solutions building itself was a small, converted, corrugated-iron hangar, but once inside, things became very different; there were a couple of smart dark leather couches and plush, royal-blue carpeting. There was a coffee table between the two couches with fresh roses in a cut glass vase, surrounded by an assortment of aircraft magazines.

'Can I help you, sir?' a voice called from behind a reception desk. Tim wandered across to the counter and leant on the countertop. Seated behind the desk, almost hidden by the high counter, was a pleasant receptionist dressed in a standard dark blue airline uniform.

'I hope so. I am interested in hiring an aircraft to take about six to eight friends and me up to Scotland for a little salmon fishing.'

The lady flashed a smile at Tim.

'A bit of bonding with the boys,' she said.

'Something like that. Hopefully, it won't be too expensive – nothing too big, probably a turboprop aircraft, not a corporate jet type.'

'Our chief pilot will be happy to talk to you about what type of aircraft would be suitable once we have an idea of where you will be flying to and what airfield you would use. I take it that as it's a private charter, you won't be using one of the big commercial airfields?'

'Oh, I haven't got that far as yet. Just wanted to get an idea of what types of aircraft are available and an idea about the cost.'

'We have a brochure which details the types of aircraft we hire and their passenger and cargo capacities. I'll just get one for you,' she said.

Tim watched as she went through a door behind the desk into a back office. His eyes quickly scanned the office. There were two doors at the back: probably one went to the hangars and the other to an administration and back-office area. Both doors had Yale-type keys and deadlocks. The doors looked like they were made of solid but not heavy timber. On the walls around the office were a series of photographs of corporate jets and next to the door the woman had left through was an alarm control box. So that means the front door is alarmed. *What about the windows, are they on the system?* he asked himself. The windows appeared to have individual locks with small individual keys – nothing too sophisticated. The ceiling was false with bright aluminium surround downlights, about two-and-a-half metres above the floor. Being a hangar, it was obviously suspended, which meant there was a lot of space above the false ceiling. There were no strong lockable filing cabinets or safes in view; they were probably in the back administration area. The front of the building would be hidden by taller buildings at night, but even at this time, most airports were still well lit and as busy as during daylight hours. Must try and have a look around the rear of the building at the hangar area, probably large, heavily protected sliding doors, certain to be alarmed. Further thought was interrupted by the lady's return; she was carrying a glossy brochure. A label on her lapel told Tim her name was Ann – either that, or she had borrowed a colleague's. *Never second-guess, my boy*, Tim told himself.

She handed the brochure to Tim.

'Thank you, Ann. I see your name is on your lapel. Do you mind me calling you Ann?'

'Not at all, Mr…?'

'Oh, sorry. Clark, Paul Clark,' replied Tim.

'Well, Mr Clark, the brochure will describe our aircraft and under each of the gallery pictures you will find a technical section giving you information about seating, range, engine, load capacity, etc. Please go through that, and then we can chat further, and I will call our chief pilot to have a discussion with you.'

Shit, that's the last thing I want: a discussion on where I'm going, who with, weights and which airfield I will be using. No, thank you.

'No need to call him just yet, let me sit over on the couch and go through the brochure, Ann.'

'Certainly, if I can answer any questions, I will be happy to, Mr Clark.'

Tim made a show of studying all the various types of aircraft and their technical specs, turning each page slowly as he tried to look very impressed, glancing over at the counter every couple of minutes. Thankfully, Ann seemed to be wrapped up in something in front of her and was not watching him.

Damn, there was no Pilatus with the call sign GAXY in the photos.

Tim rose and went over to the counter, and as Ann looked up, he asked, 'Do you have any other aircraft other than those in the brochure?'

'Those are our own aircraft, Mr Clark, although we do also look after privately owned aircraft and these are leased out through ourselves from time to time.'

'Not being an expert, mind, I was thinking more along the lines of a ten-seater, say, single turboprop – something like a Pilatus?

Ann moved her mouse on her pad and clicked on something on her screen, which Tim could not see from where he was standing.

'Oh, yes, here we are. We do have a Pilatus here on site. We maintain the aircraft for a private corporation and supply pilots, but unfortunately they do not allow the aircraft to be leased out to our clients.'

'Any chance of looking over the plane to see whether something similar would suit?'

'No, Mr Clark, I'm afraid we cannot show you the aircraft; it's in our hangar in an area that is restricted to the public.'

That confirms the information I really wanted: the bloody plane is here on the ground at least, thought Tim.

'Perhaps you can give me the corporation's contact number, then I could enquire whether they might consider leasing the aircraft.'

Ann's body language became more formal and aloof. She looked at Tim in a more studied manner.

'Mr Clark, we cannot divulge our clients' details to members of the public. As I explained, our chief pilot can go through your requirements with you.'

Time to withdraw quickly; I'll have to pay an after-dark visit tonight, Tim thought, rising from the couch.

'Thank you, Ann. No need to bother anybody at this stage. I will give it some more thought and get back to you.'

Tim turned, and without waiting for any reply, left the building, waving casually over his shoulder as he went.

He walked down the hill to the station, collected his duffel bag and then returned the way he had come to the first traffic circle on the airport approach and checked into the Holiday Inn Express. Once in the room, he emptied the contents of the duffel bag, which contained dark blue overalls with 'Airport Maintenance' printed across the back in white lettering, leather gloves, a balaclava, a small electrician's tool kit, complete with a torch and a Glock 17 semi-automatic pistol. A tiny black Sony digital camera completed his kit. *Hope to hell I don't get caught on this lark: in a country deeply concerned about terrorism and hijacking, law-breaking around an airport would set fires alight, and the end result doesn't bear thinking about.*

Tim lay down on the queen-sized bed and started to flick through the TV channels before texting Michael, the boss.

'Arrived and in situ. The goods are there, but will avoid the rush and carry out a late night shop.'

His phone pinged immediately in return: 'Understood'.

At 10 p.m. Luton Airport was still in operational mode, with passengers, aircrew and airport staff coming and going as usual. Tim made his way out of the fire exit side door to the ground floor of the hotel, his duffel bag slung over his shoulder. He avoided making contact with any desk staff and guests, as they might later have recalled seeing a man in dark blue, airport maintenance overalls. He went slowly along the pavement, hanging back from the road, walking in the shadows. As he approached the terminal building, he turned sharply left and cut between the terminal and the bright orange easyJet office building, avoiding two armed police officers standing alongside their blue-and-yellow-checked police vehicle. *More a show of force than actual security*, Tim thought to himself: *the airport will have its own security teams as well, probably unarmed.*

He walked quickly past the front office door of Corporate Jet Solutions. A tall electricity pole with a bright sweeping bulb lit up the area around the offices;

there was too much artificial light to attempt entry. As Tim made his way around the side of the building, from the shadows on the terminal side of the building, a voice called out.

'Hey, hold up a minute.'

What the hell do I do now? Tim asked himself, before making a snap decision to pretend he had heard nothing and kept on walking.

'Hey, wait up,' came the voice again.

Well, at least he's not saying 'Stop, put your hands in the air' – perhaps it's not security, thought Tim. He stopped and turned towards the sound of the voice, at the same time gently pushing his right hand into the right pocket of his overalls and gently clasping the butt of the Glock. He gently eased the safety catch into the fire position.

'Sorry, mate, didn't see you. Thinking about other things. Can I help you?' he asked, sliding his duffel bag off his shoulder and placing it on the ground at his feet.

'Do you have a light, please, mate? I'm dying for a cigarette,' the voice asked, and a tall, thin man about six feet tall emerged from the shadow of the walkway wearing black overalls.

Tim half-smiled. *Be careful what you wish for*, he thought, easing his hand off the Glock.

'Sorry, I don't smoke, mate,' shrugged Tim, making to pick up his bag and move off.

'You probably know that we are not supposed to smoke anywhere near the apron, but there is no refuelling taking place in any of the slots at the moment, so no harm done. I'm sorry you don't have a light; I really could do with a cigarette right now. I could kill for one.'

There you go again, idiot. You have no idea of how close you came to, at the very least, getting my Glock slammed into the back of your head – that would have put you off smoking for a while. Tim started to turn away.

'Where are you going anyway?' the voice asked.

Tim looked across the tarmac apron and saw a Thomson Airways Boeing Dreamliner standing near a large hangar. He pointed towards the aircraft.

'We got a call at electrical maintenance. Some minor warning light keeps going off in the cockpit. It's probably nothing, but I'm just going to check it out anyway. The plane is scheduled to fly again in the morning. My supervisor will be here in a minute to check my findings.'

'I read somewhere that there has been a lot of electrical stuff with those Dreamliners.'

'That was last year, mate. All sorted now. You know what it's like with new airliners. Great aircraft to fly in, though; that's why I am sure there is no real problem. I'm on a time limit though – see you around, mate.'

Tim moved off towards the Dreamliner, hoping that the conversation was now over. His path to the rear steps of the Dreamliner would take him close to the back of Corporate Jet Solutions' hangar. He heard a muttered response or farewell from the man in the black overalls as he stopped to let a food truck and baggage tractor pulling empty luggage trolleys past. Good to have movement around the place.

He reached the hangar door without further mishap or intrusion and placed his duffel bag on the ground, in the shadow cast by the overhanging hangar roof. The large sliding doors had two very large industrial padlocks at the centre and bottom. The reason for their size was to deter anybody with bolt cutters. *Not a problem to pick the two locks; it's what happens when I slide the doors back that's the concern: there may be an alarm system, in which case I'll have about thirty seconds.*

Standard SAS training included breaking and entering into premises. Tim had enjoyed the sessions on blowing things open using explosives, but he was rusty on lock-picking. He pulled on his leather gloves and extracted the bunch of keyhole lock-pickers on a metal ring, then tried a couple of them for size. Having found the right one, he inserted it into the lock and gently twisted the pick until the lock mechanism gave way and the lock opened. The other lock was identical, so it was easier the second time around.

Here goes nothing, he thought, leaning against the door and easing it back enough to allow himself to slide through carrying his duffel bag, quickly pulling the doors to behind him. There was no tell-tale beep of an alarm being set off, no need to rush in and cut wires frantically, just an eerie silence. Not surprising; it's very hard to sneak an aircraft out of the hangar and spirit it away. *Probably the doors to the admin office are alarmed; hopefully I won't need to go in there*, as that would involve further lock-picking, silencing the alarm, opening cabinets, perhaps turning on computers. Maria was on standby to take remote control in the event of having to get into the computers themselves, not something Tim relished, definitely not his forte.

The hangar was not in complete darkness: there were windows high in the roof area and these let in beams of light from the airport's high-security lighting. There were five aircraft standing at various angles around the hangar floor, four corporate jets and, in the far corner, its aluminium body shining, stood Golf Alpha X-ray Yankee. Tim recalled having it in his sights on the roof of Matadi airfield. There were a number of large square tool boxes on wheels and heavy duty electrical leads snaking across the floor on the hangar. The hangar floor was spotless, not like some garages Tim had seen. At the rear of the hangar, where there was a door which led into the office administration area, there were a number of floor-to-ceiling industrial shelving units with high ladders on wheels alongside them. Down one wall were a number of tall, metal filing cabinets.

The whole scene appeared to Tim to resemble the flight deck of an aircraft carrier. *Where do I start?* he asked himself. Logic told him to approach the aircraft – *there's nothing like going for broke*, he thought. He approached the door to the rear of the Pilatus flight deck and gently pulled down on the cabin door mechanism. To his surprise, the air lock release gave a low hiss, and the door started to open towards Tim. He gently lowered the door. On the inside of the door there were steps and a holding rod to lock it in the down position. Tim moved quickly up the stairs into the passenger area. The configuration of seats inside was intended to create a luxurious atmosphere rather than maximise the seating capacity. There were four large wine-coloured leather seats facing each other, which created the effect of a lounge, and there was a large, shiny mahogany table between the seats, dividing the area. At the rear of the aircraft there was a toilet, which, judging from its size, housed both a toilet and shower facility. Tim noted that the runners in the floor onto which further seating could be fixed had a number of new scratches from screwdrivers, a sign that the seating had recently been increased, probably at the expense of the cocktail bar and fridge. There was also a small jump seat to the rear alongside the cocktail bar, probably for cabin crew.

He moved forward on the plush pile carpet to the cockpit area, which, unusually for this type of aircraft, had been sealed off from the cabin. Smaller executive aircraft normally were arranged in an open way, but this was probably for reasons of privacy. The cockpit door had no locking mechanism, just a standard handle. Tim found himself in the small cockpit behind the left-hand pilot seat, the seat the captain of the aircraft would sit in. His torch picked up a number of manuals stowed behind the seat in a pouch attached to the back of the seat. He pulled them out of the pouch and went back to the main cabin, then, sitting in one of the backwards-facing leather seats, spread the manuals out in front of him.

He immediately discarded the technical manuals, then started looking through the booklets. He found that one of them had the aircraft's registration details. Golf Alpha X-ray Yankee belonged to Moonshoot Technical Defence Systems Plc. He photographed this page, along with all the flight logs for the past twelve months. Tim noted the aircraft had made several trips from Luxembourg down through Europe and North Africa to the DRC.

He rose from the seat and moved forward to place all the manuals and logs back in their pouch. He shone his torch around the cockpit area and the cabin where he had been sitting, then made his way quietly and quickly down the steps, resealed the cabin door and headed for the large hangar doors. He slid these silently back into place and attached the large locks to them. He hugged the side of the building, retracing his steps slowly and deliberately, but saw no sign of the chain smoker. He came down to the main road and settled in behind a small group of arriving passengers pulling their cases down the pavement towards the train station. I just hope the information I have photographed is relevant to what's going on. Anyway, job done for now.

13

Luxembourg

The Luxair Dash 8 turboprop broke through the early
morning low cloud, making its final approach to
Luxembourg International Airport, approaching the
runway downwind west to east. As the pilot throttled
back the engines, there was a clump as the wheels
locked in the down position. Maria looked down on a
bright spring-like morning, a complete contrast to what
the weather had been like at London City Airport. She
had left behind awful winter weather; grey, low scud-
ding clouds, rain squalls and gusts of wind that had
made parking her Mercedes 350 SLK in the short-stay
parking difficult, given the limited space available. As
the aircraft flared out like a fat, squat, waddling duck,
from her window, she caught sight of the massive tax-
free Eurozone hangars and giant storage warehouses.
Row upon row of cargo jumbo 747s lined the apron. *I'll
bet there is a lot of stuff through that isn't quite kosher*,
she thought. The plane bumped hard onto the runway
surface: a textbook landing, making solid contact and
staying firmly on the ground. Immediately, the turboprop
engines screamed in reverse thrust. The aircraft, which
was only half full, slowed quickly and turned off the
runway towards the double-storey terminal buildings.

Maria cleared immigration with just a flash of her EU British passport. The customs man just waved her through with a half-smile. As she exited the passenger area, she found herself on the first floor, looking down on the milling passengers and visitors below. Down there, in the throng of people, she saw her friend, Susi Loxley. She waved a hand frantically and caught her eye.

They had been friends since meeting as first-year students at Trinity College, Dublin. Susi was always the bright one, at ease in a crowd and always the life and soul of the party while Maria was quieter, but was simply stunning with her dark hair, deep blue eyes and silky cream skin. But studious Maria was the perfect foil for her friend. The pair were nicknamed 'the dream team' and were always in great demand on social occasions. When their university days came to an end, it was the City of London and law for Susi. She was stunned when Maria announced she wanted to join the army and specialise in light infantry and, if possible, in a specialist unit. They went their separate ways but stayed in touch and met up whenever they had space in their diaries and a suitable meeting place.

They exited the car park in Susi's Mini Cooper, dodging all the barriers that were protecting the construction work on the never-ending airport expansion. Luxembourg was immune from economic downturn, and it was the home of the man who was a leading architect of European integration, Joseph Bech, a Luxembourgish politician. Today, big politics and big money mix with consummate ease. It was a land of plenty, as long as you were connected in some way to the EU. It seemed that the majority of Luxembourg's population were.

The Mini Cooper shot around the traffic circle. At the final exit, Susi narrowly avoided a large black Mercedes 500 saloon which had slowed suddenly in order to enter the Luxembourg Golf Club. Accompanied by a screech of tyres, a blaring horn and Susi yelling 'idiot', the Mini shot around the Mercedes and careered off down towards the Rue de Trèves in the Zens district of Luxembourg not far from the airport, where Susi had a fabulous three-terraced apartment on the second floor of a small block of apartments. Each floor had only two apartments, accessible by a pair of lifts which opened directly into each apartment and could only be accessed by inserting a code into a pad inside the lift.

Maria had visited Susi a number of times over the past two years and knew which was her bedroom. There were two guest rooms, but Susi used the second guest bedroom as a dumping ground for additional clothes and unwanted furnishings; it also doubled as a sort of laundry-cum-ironing room.

At 11.00 in the morning, Maria came out of her room and heard the pop of a champagne cork. Oh my God, here we go – well, at least it's Saturday. Susi appeared from the kitchen and headed towards the large terrace, which led off from the main lounge and dining area.

'Come on, darling,' she called over her shoulder. 'Come and tell me why you have made this surprising but welcome visit to us here in the land of the not-so-mighty euro.

The two women settled into leather recliners and wrapped themselves in two large travel blankets. Winter wasn't far away now; leaves were falling from the Canadian maple trees, and the light wind blew some of them onto the terrace, where they hissed across the terracotta tiles.

Maria looked across at her friend and smiled. Susi had been a young rising star in the London commercial law offices of an Antipodean banking group, where she rapidly rose to company secretary with responsibility for compliance matters. This was before a brief but unfulfilling affair with one of the married regional directors. He turned out to be a real dickhead – or at least, that was how she described him to her close friends. When she called it off, he became spiteful and petty in the workplace and started stalking her around the building, especially when she worked late. This had led to a couple of scuffles between them as he tried to 'reignite the fire', as he put it, culminating in an attempt at forced sex on a leather couch.

When he was put firmly in his place, not to mention having his ego dented, by receiving a hard slap to his face and a well-directed knee to his private parts, he tried unsuccessfully to implicate her in a compliance lapse related to money laundering, which he was directly responsible for. After a brief internal compliance hearing, at which she was fully exonerated, Susi resigned and the director was sent back to Australia on a sideways promotion. Then followed a year's sabbatical relaxing and enjoying her life around Europe. She was a very attractive girl and had a number of brief, discreet and steamy liaisons or trysts. One particular affair seemed to offer the promise it might grow beyond incredible sex to reach new frontiers of passion, but the guy, who was most definitely her kind of man, kept running back to his estranged wife. Susi ended up cutting him off and avoided contact, which was such a pity, she told friends: he was great in bed – the best – and very caring, but mentally screwed-up – *c'est la vie*. Susi then applied for, and was successful in securing, a commercial law position with the European Investment Bank, where she had responsibility for African and Caribbean contracts. She was once again a rising star, and she was happy in her job, if a little lonely at times, missing her friends and colleagues in London.

Susi handed a glass of bubbly to Maria.

'Come on, Maria. You sounded so secretive on the phone. What brings you to Lux? Is it your new top secret spy job? This is so exciting. Your secret job that you can't discuss even with your best friends. Are we going to spy on someone, perhaps even kidnap them?'

Maria laughed. 'Don't be so dramatic, Susi. My job is very dull and boring. I am a receptionist, not a spy, and, no, before you ask: I don't have a licence to kill.'

'So why the hush-hush conversation? And by the way, there is no way you could be a receptionist – that's just bullshit.'

Maria ignored Susi's comment. 'To be honest, it's a matter of the heart. I was at a drinks reception at the Dorchester and met a very charming man who obviously was somebody of importance, and to be honest, I felt quite charmed by the man. He was so courteous and well-mannered, but I never got his name as we were not officially introduced, but I followed him out of the reception in the hope we might strike up a conversation – pretty forward for me, I know. Anyway, he had a car waiting and drove off before I could collar him. I did notice the car he drove off in had special EU plates and was hoping you could try to find out who he was.'

'That's it? You could have just called me.'

'Yes, rather boring, but the real reason I came over was it was a great excuse to visit you, my best friend and party partner.'

'Cool, party we shall. Give me that number and I will speak to a friend who has some boring job looking after the motor pool for the EU bigwigs. He can track it down if it's a Lux EU car. Could be Brussels, and then we will need to think again.'

Maria delved into her handbag and handed a slip of paper to Susi.

'Thanks, Susi. I know it's all a bit silly, but I am interested in finding out more about him.'

The taxi arrived at Susi's apartment at exactly 8.00 pm and on the short drive to the Rue Notre Dame, the central square from where Luxembourg's nightlife spreads out, Maria watched idly out of the window as they drove past large houses set in even larger manicured gardens, many built in a classical Austrian villa style. On the driveways were a variety of large expensive limousines. *No shortage of cash around here*, mused Maria, recalling Michael's 'gravy train' speech in the pub. She closed her eyes and thought briefly about this man she worked closely with. He was a really great guy, she thought, handsome in a rugged sort of way, but a little clumsy and unsure around women; he was also fairly serious, even slightly aloof at times, but she could sense his inner strength. *Hmm, if we didn't work together, then maybe, just maybe*, she thought.

The taxi turned onto Avenue John F. Kennedy and passed the stunning new opera house, built at great expense by the EU, presumably for the EU elite. On either side of the dual carriageway were many grand steel-and-glass-clad buildings, each apparently attempting to outdo the previous one. Most had sweeping entrances with flags flying around the entrances. The new headquarters of the European Investment Bank towered over the other surrounding buildings. Large sculptures were scattered around the boulevards and parks, most made from metal that looked like bronze or steel to Maria. She caught a glimpse of the European Court of Justice and the famous large bronze sculpture of a pistol with its barrel twisted into a knot, representing peace over violence.

The girls poured out of the cab at the bus station end of the Rue Notre Dame. Susi set off at a steady pace secure in knowing exactly where she was heading. Maria followed and was surprised at the number of people wandering around the central square. The square was full of bars, fountains and restaurants, and in the centre was a large bandstand where a military-type band in full regalia was playing classical music. Many of the strollers looked local, immaculately turned out in the latest fashions, with small children and toddlers' prams. The mid-evening stroll was a traditional outing for Luxembourgish families, giving the central square a 'Sound of Music' feel.

The evening started with a couple of glasses of bubbly at the Zanzen Bar, which was crowded and buzzy, full of people, all of whom were trying to be heard over the crowd. From there, it was a short cab ride to Chez Bacano, a wonderful Portuguese restaurant in a nondescript concrete building, which was famous for garlic *gambas flambées* and *frites*: magnificent grilled king prawns in an exquisite garlic butter sauce with skinny French fries. A simple tomato and buffalo mozzarella salad infused with olive oil completed the signature dish. All washed down with a well-chilled bottle of Gavi. Over dinner, Maria returned her conversation to her curiosity about the EU.

'Susi, do you know anybody in the EU agricultural set-up – maybe under the UNESCO umbrella?'

'Let me guess. You were at this reception in London, and…'

'No, Susi, not linked to that,' cut in Maria. 'Just curious about how much aid is given to the developing countries via the EU. You know, things like training people to farm in a sustainable low-cost environment – or something along those lines.'

Susi frowned briefly and then responded, 'My side of African lending is linked to the legal documentation around funding capital projects which will assist and ensure sustainable growth within that particular country. Things like water storage dams or hydroelectricity schemes, sometimes green energy projects. In my opinion, we have, from time to time, funded non-essential stuff, like a new national airline aircraft fleet, for example. And recently we lent to a hotel consortium in the West Indies to pay for employment and training. I often wonder about some particular countries' ability to repay, but that doesn't rate high on the funding list. The ethos around the project funding is more about helping sustainable growth and development, a sort of self-reliance goal. Our mission statement states that we should not always expect to receive repayment in full, so we build in an allowance for a fair measure of non-repayment. Funny, really – wouldn't happen in the commercial banking environment, where repayment is always number one on the agenda.'

Maria smiled once again, remembering Michael's words in the pub; trust him to have read the European Investment Bank's mission statement. She decided against any further enquiry down this route so as to not arouse suspicion. *The various agricultural agencies within the EU must be documented somewhere*, she thought.

After a leisurely two-hour meal they got back into a cab and went back up the hill to Susi's favourite night-club, the Secret Garden, which was in Côte d'Eich. The club had the ambiance of a giant Middle Eastern Bedouin tent, and was split into a number of club rooms. There was a long, glitzy bar with blue lighting and mirrors. This was obviously the home of the moneyed euro set, definitely a playground for the wealthy young. Maria quickly cast an expert eye around and noticed a number of older men with younger women, sitting at tables or lounging on the multicoloured Bedouin cushions. *The hardships of being an MEP*, she thought.

The evening was laid-back and pleasant, as the two friends recalled old times together, laughing and sharing a bottle of Veuve Clicquot. They declined the attentions of two young Arab businessmen who had forsaken their traditional dish-dash robes in exchange for Versace or something similar. They offered to share their hookah or hubbly-bubbly water tobacco pipe with the girls, but they didn't take rejection easily, and Susi had to draw the attention of one of the many floor managers to the situation. After that, they laid back on their oversized Bedouin cushions, listening to the latest dance music. *Not my favourite kind of music*, thought Maria. As they were debating whether to have a nightcap – or, as Susi called it, 'an ABF' (absolute bloody final) – they once again received uninvited attention; this time, they had to fend off the harmless advances of a group of happily inebriated young men who announced they were in offshore financial services.

'Oh, that sounds so terribly important,' giggled Susi, as she ducked under one of the young men's outstretched arms.

'Oh, wait a minute. If you guys are interested there is a massive hen party at Henri's nightclub – gorgeous women everywhere. Do you know where it is?' she asked innocently. 'It's about four blocks from here. Keep going until this road runs into a cul-de-sac.' The young men all made a charge for the door.

Susi laughed out loud.

'Henri's?' asked Maria. 'Is somebody from the bank getting married?'

'No, silly, but it will make them happy for a few minutes – until they get there, that is. It's the best known gay bar in Luxembourg.'

The two girls hailed a cab across the road, quickly climbed in and beat a hasty retreat to Susi's apartment.

Sunday morning was spent lounging around the apartment in their gowns drinking copious amounts of Colombian coffee, chased down by Buck's Fizz and energy bars. Susi dropped Maria off at the airport in good time for her late afternoon flight back to London. They hugged at the terminal entrance and Susi promised to get back as soon as she could about the car registration, muttering that the guy was probably married and had a couple of mistresses in tow. Maria laughed and thanked her for her positive attitude.

14

Man from the Ministry

Edward's attempts to progress matters at the MOD proved fruitless at first: none of his normal sources and contacts could throw any light on why a couple of Jackals would be in the DRC, let alone in the hands of a Zimbabwean army unit. He got the breakthrough he was looking for after yet another meeting at the Ministry of Defence building in Whitehall. On that occasion, he was meeting a captain he knew, although not well, who was on secondment to the ministry. He found himself sitting in a small, eight-feet-by-ten office with 'Logistics' painted on the door. The captain told him that a close scrutiny of records had shown that all Jackals were under British command. Edward couldn't help but wonder how accurate those records were, given that the annual budget was £36 billion. *They probably don't know where all the Challenger tanks are, never mind the armoured Jackals.*

After this, Edward thanked the captain and left the building, passing through the cylindrical body scanners for a second time. On the outside of the building, at the south entrance, was a large brass plaque announcing to the world this building was the Ministry of Defence. *Why do we feel the need to tell the whole world exactly where it is housed?* Edward wondered.

As he turned sharply back towards Whitehall, he nearly walked into a man coming the other way.

'Sorry,' Edward said, looking up at the person he had just missed.

'Edward, fancy meeting you here, old chap.'

Edward immediately recognised one of the battalion majors from the last tour of Afghanistan. He had been at Bastion with Edward and Michael on re-training before going out on operations.

'Hello Jack, how are you?'

'Pretty good, actually. Picked up a little shrapnel in my calf muscle in Helmand. Not life-threatening, but enough to give me some problems getting back up to operational fitness. So they have got me pushing a pen at the ministry for now. How about you, Edward? I heard you have left the Guards.'

'Yes, I am a civilian now, Jack, still doing stuff to do with the military. In fact, I have just come from the ministry and a rather unfruitful meeting.'

'Got time for a coffee? We can catch up?'

Edward hesitated, and then he thought: *What do I have to lose?*

'Why not? That will be good.'

The pair set off down Whitehall towards Parliament Square, on the opposite side of the road to Downing Street. There was a small café near the HM Revenue and Customs building which did very good fresh sandwiches as well as coffee and tea.

They ordered Americano coffees at the counter upon entry, then settled into a booth and waited for the coffee to arrive.

'So, Edward. What brings you to the ministry?'

'Well, as I explained, I left the Blues and Royals together with Michael Ashton, and we decided to join a private security company set up after 9/11 by Colonel Donald Torrens. We supply protection and intel to UK companies and their assets worldwide. You may recall Colonel Torrens.'

'I think most officers know Colonel Torrens by reputation if not personally. I have heard stories from when he ran the SAS. He was brilliant and successful, led from the front. Lot of covert ops stuff in Afghanistan. He took out a number of al-Qaeda commanders, I heard through the grapevine. Also picked up a couple of gongs, though, as always with the SAS, not much info was given away. Good boss to work for, Edward.'

'Yes, he is, and working alongside Michael makes it even more of a complete unit.'

'I envy you, with the cuts and infighting we very soon won't have much of an army left – certainly not one that can take the offensive, at any rate. Even within the battalions there are "watch your back" types just waiting for the chop. The Americans, due to their mantle of "protectors of the free world", know how to keep their capability up to speed. Still, I digress, what were you looking into at the ministry?'

'A curiosity question, really, based on an on-the-ground incident in Africa,' answered Edward, weighing up in his own mind just how much to say.

'Not sure I could help. Africa is not my area, really – I'm more about control of assets, pen-pushing stuff.'

'Are you on the logistics side then?'

'No, not the sock and jam stealers, more on where

assets are at any one time on the ground.'

'Good, then you may be able to look into something for me.'

'Well, as long as it's not official secrets stuff, and in no way compromises anything the MOD may be up to, then happy to help, old boy.'

'Well, we were out in Africa protecting UK assets – a mining complex actually, and we came across an incident which involved Zimbabwean soldiers operating Jackals. I was surprised to see UK equipment in use by a military sanctioned list and was trying to find out what they were doing there and who gave them to the Zimbabweans.'

'Did you get into some sort of punch-up with these guys?' asked Jack.

'No, nothing like that. Just we saw them in use by Zimbabwean troops,' replied Edward, playing down the incident. It was, in fact, the truth that at no time had the Jackals engaged Edward's men.

'Anyway, I decided to enquire about how the Jackals could be in Africa under the control of these guys. So far, I have run into a brick wall – either there is a cover-up or somebody is hiding something, or perhaps some private arms dealer has been able to source and buy to order for the Zimbabweans.'

'Well, I can tell you that we certainly would not have supplied the Jackals – that would be a no-way situation. There is a complete ban on supplying the regime in Zimbabwe; the same applies to arms sales to private dealers. It's common knowledge that one of the biggest private arms dealers is based in Wokingham, so we keep close tabs on what they buy and sell on. Perhaps you saw South African Ratel armoured carriers. They're very similar to Jackals, and we know that their military hardware sales into Africa are booming.'

'No, they were definitely Jackals. My enquiries have not progressed beyond being told that all the Jackals were safely under army control.'

'Well, that's probably correct then,' responded Jack. He frowned, then continued, speaking more slowly. 'But something did come across my desk the other day. We have loaned a few Jackals to one of our big defence contractors. They are adding more firepower on the Jackals – something along the lines of the new Gatlings the Yanks have. Firepower of over 3,000 rounds per minute. Their Humvee armoured vehicles have been adapted to take six-barrel guns, so our contractors are developing their own version to increase the Jackals' firepower to achieve the same rapid fire capability– well, that's the aim. The tests are being carried out at their own firing range and facilities in Norfolk though, nowhere near Africa.'

Edward sat back, sipped his coffee and pondered the possibility that the Jackals he had seen were the same as those being used in Norfolk.

He was brought back to the moment when Jack continued, 'The reason I know about this is that I have to schedule a site visit to check on progress and, of course, our vehicles. We have five out on loan to the contractor.'

'What about other Jackals? Have we any more on loan, or sold to third parties, or even foreign govern-ments and their armed forces?'

'No, nothing like that. These are our only Jackals

I am aware of that are out of the control of our military at this moment.'

'You are right, Jack. It does seem as though this is another dead end. Thanks for the intel, though; it's obviously not a military secret. Who is the contractor? Have their tests been successful?'

Edward was careful to ask two questions so as to avoid Jack focusing on what he really wanted to know.

'As far as I know, the tests on the firing range are proving very successful. The contractor is one of the biggest we have in the UK: it's Rapier Systems Plc. They supply a lot of weaponry to the MOD.'

Edward sat through the next half hour, politely exchanging stories of past battalion efforts and achievements in the more recent conflict – big boys' war stories. The pair called for their coffees to be topped up. He glanced at his watch and said, 'Jack, I never realised the time. We have a meeting at the office to discuss a new client take-on. Thank you very much for the discussion. It was really good to see you again. I'll get the coffees on the way out. Thanks again.'

Jack called out to Edward as he left the café, 'Good to catch up with you as well. Who did you say you were with again?'

Edward pretended not to hear and waved back as he exited the café and set off in the direction of the Horse Guards' sand parade ground – used more recently for the Olympic women's beach volleyball.

15

Debrief

As soon as Edward was a short distance away from the café, he stopped and dialled Michael's mobile number.

Michael answered on the second ring.

'Speak to me, Ed. How did it go?'

'Have you left for the West Country yet?'

'No, in about an hour. Have you finished up what you were doing? Why don't you come down with me?'

'I think I may have saved you a trip. There is something we should talk about.'

'Let's do that.'

Michael confirmed that Maria had also received answers to her enquiries and that Tim had developed the photos of the aircraft logbooks. The two men agreed to meet up at Gordon's Wine Bar in Villiers Street alongside Charing Cross Station and near the Embankment. The wine bar was a London favourite; it had a cavern-like atmosphere, sawdust on the floors and had been unchanged for many years. There was room to speak in private in one of the caves. Michael told Edward that he was going to call the rest of the team, and they agreed to meet in two hours.

Maria was the last to arrive, just after 6.00 pm, as she had been manning the front office at Excalibur.

The bar was a little more crowded than Michael would have liked, but he knew that the constant buzz of people talking would make their discussion easier.

'Well, team, what have we got that might help us?' asked Michael as soon as everybody had a drink and was sitting comfortably around one of the long pine tables set well back from the flow of people to the bar. Nobody around the table was carrying any paperwork; everything was committed to memory – it was safer that way. Tim had left the photos in the safe at Excalibur, but could recall all the necessary information.

He was the first to speak.

'The aircraft we saw at Matadi Tshimpi Airport that day was a Pilatus, call sign Golf Alpha X-ray Yankee. It is registered in the UK and is kept in a hangar at Luton belonging to Corporate Jet Solutions. Most of this we knew already. I managed to get into the aircraft and get a good look at the logbook and other documents, all of which I have photographed. The aircraft is registered to a company called Moonshoot Technical Defence Systems and the aircraft has done several trips down through Europe to the DRC. It seems the aircraft always flies out from Luton to Luxembourg and comes back the same way. I have done some checking with our own accountants and with Companies House, and it seems that Moonshoot is a subsidiary of a massive defence contractor, Rapier Systems Plc.'

'That's a big coincidence then,' cut in Edward. 'That name came up during my MOD enquiries about the missing Jackals.'

Maria also joined the discussion.

'Seems Luxembourg may well be a common thread

running through this thing. Think about the vehicle details as well.'

Michael held up his hand.

'Whoa, guys, it's all coming out in a rush. Let's get one fact established at a time.'

He went on, 'Anything more from your side, Tim?'

'No, boss, that's it. Oh yeah, one interesting thing I discovered is the plane is fitted out in exec style and the cockpit area is sealed off from the passenger area; that's unusual in this type of aircraft. I have done a little more checking, and with very little effort, the plane can be reconfigured to take up to eight or nine passengers by the quick removal of the exec layout.'

Michael nodded, taking in the information carefully.

'Let's look at the board of Rapier Systems and see whether there are directors or major shareholders in common.'

'I am waiting for that information as we speak,' responded Tim, 'but I do know the Chairman is Lord Thackett. I will look a little closer at his personal interests and connections.'

Michael nodded, and then turned towards Maria.

'Right, let's see what you have found out for us, Maria.'

'Well, my girlfriend has an admirer in some sort of motor pool that looks after the EU bigwigs and their transport. The registration plate was allocated to an S-class Mercedes-Benz. I'm not much of a car buff, but I gather that's a big fancy saloon. The car was indeed black, as you guys saw in Matadi, but here's the thing: the car was allocated to one of the UK's top EU commissioners, Simon Jones. He used to be an MEP for

Kent. He is now the EU Commissioner for Agriculture and Rural Development.'

However, Mr Jones informed the motor pool people that the car had been stolen in Brussels some eight months ago. What is unusual is that when the car is allocated to an EU Commissioner it comes with a chauffeur, but it seems that, for some reason, he was not driving Jones on that day as he was not on EU business. My friend's admirer recalls there was a bit of a fuss as Jones was not very forthcoming as to what he was up to exactly on the day in question and rather vague as to whom he was meeting. Anyway, nothing official went missing, nothing like classified documents or a laptop with sensitive stuff, so it all died down after a while. So, now it appears that the car was stolen and has somehow appeared in the DRC.'

'Not necessarily. It could have been sent there by Jones himself, if he is linked to this thing, or he could have arranged for it to be stolen. A long shot, I know, but we should not discount it,' responded Michael.

Edward, always the quiet and thoughtful one in the group, came in at this point.

'I had another fruitless meeting at the MOD, but then, as I was leaving, I ran into Major Jack Wells from Bastion. You may remember him, Michael. Anyway, he was slightly wounded in Afghanistan and is seeing out the time until he is fighting fit again at the MOD. He told me over coffee that there are several Jackals out on loan to a defence contractor, who is testing a higher firepower platform for them. The contractor is the same name that Tim came up with earlier: Rapier Systems Plc.'

'Maybe our different pieces of information all seem

related and I am beginning to sense a common theme, although we have yet to find out exactly what it is.'

'It certainly feels that we are on to something,' responded Maria, and the others nodded in agreement.

'Well, we need to move things up a notch and speed up our enquiries to build on what we have discovered so far,' said Michael. 'Let's investigate the Lord Thackett connection as well as putting a tail on his movements to see whether he has any association with the likes of Jones. Let's look at Rapier's testing ground areas and ranges in Norfolk and see how many Jackals we can find. I will contact Dr Marie Louise Ancelet in Kinshasa. It's a long shot, I know, but maybe she might spot our Mercedes around and about.'

Michael didn't notice the quizzical glance Maria gave him, and continued, 'It would be nice to know when our Mr Jones will be back in the UK. Maria, see whether your friend has any connection with immigration in Luxembourg; in the meantime, we will look into getting the info to our people at the London airports about picking him up should he pop over.'

'We had better include Manston as well,' responded Edward. 'He is a Kent resident. Let's get info to the guys on the ground at Luton to watch out for our Pilatus as well.'

Tim and Edward headed for the bar to get another round of drinks in for the group, leaving Michael and Maria alone at the table. Gordon's Wine Bar was slowing down a little as the commuters gathered up their personal belongings and started to head towards Waterloo or Charing Cross for the daily trudge back to suburbia and the country.

'How are things back at Excalibur?' asked Michael.

'Busy. We have two groups of security operatives out of the country at the moment, as well as your relief section out at Mankula. It's all quiet there, I am pleased to say. Colonel Torrens keeps a watching brief on you guys. He is very fond of you, Michael.'

'Not really, he is a tough disciplinarian. He probably just wants to make sure we are not crossing the line or ruffling any feathers.'

'Not at all. He is genuinely interested in what's going on. Those girls going missing upset him. He wants you to succeed in finding out where they are and if they are safe.'

'I made a promise to Chief Muamba that I would find his daughter and bring her home. If I can, that is what I will do.'

'You are a good man, Michael. I know you will give it all you have.'

'Maria, I was wondering whether, well, I know we work together, but I was thinking it might be nice to have dinner somewhere in town one evening, get to know one another outside of the workplace.'

Maria looked carefully at Michael's face and saw him half-frown, obviously wondering whether he had overstepped the mark. He had a strong rugged face, tanned and good-looking; it was a kind face, she thought, with deep, penetrating green eyes. He was handsome, but not in a pin-up way. *He also has impeccable manners and yet he is so awkward and shy around women*, she thought. *What about working together,* she asked herself: *surely that is a possible problem?*

Michael interrupted her thoughts: 'Sorry, I have

obviously put you in an awkward position,' mumbled Michael. 'We should probably leave it.'

'No, Michael. Sorry I didn't answer straight away. My mind was briefly elsewhere. I would like to have dinner, very much. Let me know where and when, and if I can make it, I shall.'

'Thank you. Leave the arrangements to me.'

Further conversation was brought to a halt by Tim and Edward returning to the table. The team discussed what more could be done to collect information more quickly, and it was agreed that they would meet up again after Michael and Edward had been to Norfolk and placed the tail on Lord Thackett and Simon Jones. This would involve seeking favours from friends in the Border Agency and the use of sleepers who did surveillance for Excalibur from time to time.

It was agreed they would meet within a week in the Excalibur boardroom and request Colonel Torrens attend to be brought up to speed. The four left in a group before splitting up outside Charing Cross Station and heading home. Once again, probably because they were not aware of having aroused any interest, they missed the two men who followed at a distance and took photos of the group from the arches in front of the station.

16

Waking the Serpent

The first week of that November in London was an announcement that winter was arriving. The bright blue sky created a biting cold, increased more than twofold by the wind-chill factor. There were small globules of ice on the railings, the cobbles on the surrounding streets were treacherous and slippery. The hurrying commuters wrapped up in winter coats, scarves and gloves, blew small clouds of warm air from their mouths as they silently scurried to their offices.

Michael and Edward took the twenty-minute journey from Wimbledon to Waterloo on the overground rail system, and then walked at a brisk pace to Excalibur's Bond Street offices. The front desk was not manned, as no official visitors were expected and their offices were not the sort of place people wandered into. Maria was upstairs in the boardroom, setting up the facilities they would use for gathering the latest information and feedback. When they walked into the boardroom, the projectors were running on idle, the whiteboard was down and locked in place, as were the screen blinds on the windows. Tim and Maria were sitting at the far end of the boardroom table in quiet conversation, two fresh cups of coffee in front of them. Edward and Michael went to the sideboard and each grabbed a black coffee before joining the others at the table. Michael and Maria had not spoken or arranged to meet up since the team had met at Gordon's Wine Bar. They had both been too busy with their own investigations and follow-ups. They exchanged 'for your eyes only' smiles as he sat down.

Michael leant back in his chair and stretched his arms above his head.

'Good morning, chaps. What time does this show get on the road? I thought it was at 0900 hours.'

'It is,' replied Maria. 'The time now, Michael, is 08.59.'

No sooner had she spoken than the boardroom door opened and in walked Colonel Donald Torrens, wearing the usual tailored navy pinstriped suit from Bond Street, a white shirt and a Guards tie.

'Gentlemen, young lady, good to see you all here. I believe we have made much progress on our enquiries, but as yet there has been no hint of any shenanigans or wrongdoing?'

'That's right, colonel,' replied Michael, thinking that he was the only person who could get away with addressing Maria as 'young lady' – there was a close bond between the two. Torrens was a leader who brought all those close to him onside. He continued, 'We have made good progress, but as yet nothing we can point a stick at, other than a long series of coincidences, and the fact that the same names keep cropping up. I've prepared some slides – mainly photographs we have taken – and put together a synopsis of where we are.'

'Go ahead, Michael, let's have a look at what we have got so far. Let's brainstorm these things as well.

If anybody has a question, ask it as we go, and let's see what we come up with.'

Michael moved to the overhead projector and picked up the remote control. The first slide was a photograph of the Pilatus in its hangar at Luton.

'We know the aircraft is registered to Moonshoot Technical Defence Systems, itself a subsidiary of the massive Rapier Systems Plc, a public company quoted on the London and New York Stock Exchanges. Rapier is probably this country's largest defence contractor. This is our first link to Lord Thackett, but he comes up again.'

'I've met him socially,' broke in Colonel Torrens, 'some junket at his country estate Moonrise Farm in Kent, beautiful scenery all along the white cliffs, several houses on the estate, well managed – cattle and wheat, as far as I remember. The man is very self-assured and confident, a good orator, and a very powerful man in government circles.'

Michael said, 'Perhaps we should recce his farm to see if anything comes up?'

'Hold that thought. I remember thinking at the time he doesn't like unannounced visitors: there were large metal signs on both sides of the entrance proclaiming 'Private Property. Keep Out'. We may come back to it,' responded Torrens.

Michael continued speaking as the next slide came up on the screen, a series of photos of the logbooks of the Pilatus: 'From the entries in the logs we can see the aircraft often goes down to Africa, most often the DRC, and always seems to route in and out of the UK via Luxembourg.'

Edward added, 'We agree that doesn't prove anything. Our enquiries have revealed that Lord Thackett has mining interests throughout Africa, through another public company: African Resource Contractors, or ARC, as it is called. The mining operations are diversified: it mines for several minerals, mainly platinum, gold, coltan and copper. There is a small oil interest as well, somewhere in Nigeria near the coast. So the trips could be linked to his interests there, especially to the coltan in the DRC.

Michael took up the theme again.

'Agreed, but here is the interesting thing: we have established that one of the Pilatus's most frequent passengers out of Luxembourg is our friend, the EU commissioner Simon Jones. While he is the EU commissioner responsible for agriculture and rural development, and so being in Africa would be within his remit, he is also the man who claimed his Mercedes was stolen in Brussels – the same Mercedes we saw coming out of the house in Matadi; the house that had a plaque with something about UNESCO farming on it. Although that too has reference to agriculture, let's not forget it was the same house where one of our mystery Jackals was parked in the backyard and where there were Zimbabwean troops in the house. To my mind, that puts him firmly in the frame somewhere.'

The next slide Michael put up on the screen was of Simon Jones.

'Strong possibility, I agree,' replied Torrens.

Tim broke into the conversation.

'I'm sure that is the guy I saw in the back of the Mercedes. I thought I recognised him at the time. He was on TV shortly before we left for the DRC, on our local TV station opening an urban farm for underprivileged kids. I remember thinking what a great idea it was. He made a speech about farming, saying that all kids should have the opportunity to see and touch animals. I saw him again at Tshimpi airfield through my telescopic sights.'

'Now, that makes his presence both interesting and relevant,' said Torrens.

Michael then put up a series of slides showing bleak, windswept Norfolk beaches, a lot of vehicle tracks in the sand and gorse, and a gunnery range. There were low, grey, concrete single-storey buildings scattered around the dunes. He also put up two slides showing photographs taken from a distance of a Jackal armoured vehicle firing a heavy machine gun at targets several hundred yards down the range.

'We have confirmed that the machine gun mounted on the Jackal appears to be a prototype spin-off of the American Gatling machine gun. Its fire power when we were lying in the gorse was stupendous. The British Army does not currently have this sort of heavy machine gun. This confirms that Rapier Systems are indeed testing a new, heavier gun platform. Edward and I scouted the entire range over two nights; we inspected all the buildings that could possibly house vehicles and at no point were we able to establish the whereabouts of all five of the Jackals. We reached the conclusion that since there were only three Jackals at the firing range facility, it seemed logical that the missing two were those we saw in the DRC.'

'Bloody hell,' exclaimed Torrens. 'Somebody high

up at Rapier must know that two of the Jackals are out of the country. I'll look into who I know there and make some subtle enquiries.'

'With respect, sir, we don't want to alert anybody to what we are looking into,' said Michael.

'Understood, Michael, but I have one or two close friends that can be relied on at Rapier. I will be careful. Would be interesting to find out how they got shipped out there.'

Maria joined in. 'Sir, if I were to guess, there are probably fifty jumbo jets a day that go through the giant free trade zone at Luxembourg Airport. I will ask my girlfriend if she knows anybody there with links to the Freeport complex or shipping.'

'Well, it's 99% certain we know where they are right now,' said Edward. 'Although knowing who got them there would be useful, I don't know if it's that important at the moment.'

Colonel Torrens turned to Michael.

'Any luck with your lady doctor friend in Kinshasa? Has she heard or seen anything Michael?'

'No, sir, I spoke to Marie Louise yesterday evening. She has not seen the Mercedes – that was a bit of a long shot really, but she did confirm that there have been no further atrocities or reports of abductions along the Congo River area around Matadi. It seemed so odd for something like that to happen in what is a relatively quiet area in the first place. The big hitmen and their gangs along with their boy soldiers are all to the far north-west, around the diamond and gold fields in the Goma area. That's where the ethnic cleansing is as well. What the hell really happened, I wonder? That's what we need to find out.'

Michael returned to the slides and continued, 'We have had tabs on Jones for the past two weeks. Yesterday afternoon he flew into London City Airport on a commercial flight from Luxembourg and proceeded to the British and Middle Eastern Sporting and Dining Club in Pall Mall, where he checked in. At about 1900 hours he was joined at the bar by none other than Lord Thackett, who comes back into the frame again. The coincidences are becoming too frequent to be real coincidences.'

'Yes it seems obvious that these two know each other well, so that brings Thackett more into the frame; we have to acknowledge that. Simon Jones riding around in Thackett's plane, his being in Matadi, us seeing Jones there and the missing Mercedes – still no proof of wrongdoing, but it's all bloody suspicious. There is still information missing, however; we have to remember that we did not see any of the young girls in the house in Matadi or at the Tshimpi Airport outside of Matadi.'

'Agreed,' replied Michael. 'But let's not forget the link as we progress.' He returned to the slides. 'Now, this next slide is interesting. At around 2100 hours the pair were joined by none other than the Shadow Chancellor, Kenneth Smythe.'

'Well, now the plot thickens,' said Torrens. 'What would Smythe be doing meeting those two, I wonder?'

'There could be a party tie-up. Perhaps Thackett is a big contributor to the party?' asked Maria.

'Hmm, again, maybe. We should pursue that avenue of enquiry, Maria,' said Torrens. 'That would be a logical explanation, but it could be there is something else. Michael, you are building up a formidable and extremely influential bunch of people here. How sure are you that they don't have surveillance on you by now? Is anybody looking at you?'

Michael appeared somewhat surprised by the question, 'I… we hadn't really thought about it, sir.'

'Cover your tracks, double back, check 360 degrees at all times. One of the first rules in basic counter-terrorism training, Michael, is that your friend can just as easily be your enemy. Just because you are in London doesn't mean you are undetectable. If there is something going on you can bet that by now your adversaries know about you and, to an extent, what you are doing. They will be watching you.'

'To be fair, sir,' came in Edward, 'we don't seem to be that far into anything as yet so none of us felt the need to check our backs.'

Maria and Tim nodded in agreement.

'All's fair in love and war, they say, Edward, but terrorism or espionage of whatever kind is never fair: it's based on domination by fear and knowledge of the enemy. Just watch out for yourselves – that's all I'm saying. Let's move on.'

Michael took up the discussion once again: 'Noted, colonel. We will start watching our backs. I think we need to increase surveillance on these three, check out their homes. I know Thackett has a pad in Knightsbridge. We need to find what the significance is of those three hanging around together.'

'Michael, what do you think is going on?' asked Colonel Torrens. 'Actually, not just Michael – does anybody else have an opinion?'

Michael spoke first.

'I think these guys are up to no good and are in some way connected to the disappearance of the young girls. Whether Kenneth Smythe is a part of it all is conjecture at this stage. We will only find out by carefully watching his relationship with the other two. What I am not sure of is where the girls are: whether still in the DRC; moved north and sold; dead; prostitutes – that I can't figure out. I personally think we should go back to Matadi, enlist some help and start from there.'

Edward and Tim agreed with Michael's rationale, and both concurred that the girls had been taken and either used as prostitutes or sold to the rebels in the north.

Maria shook her head in disagreement.

'Why would such powerful men be involved in a prostitution ring, and the capturing and selling of young girls in Africa? The profit from such an operation would be a pittance compared to what Thackett makes from his mining interests and his defence companies. It doesn't make any sense. I believe there is a personal angle to this.'

Torrens listened carefully to what Maria was saying.

'I agree it doesn't stack up that two or three powerful men based in Europe would be involved in sordid trafficking within the DRC or central Africa. You have got the likes of Boko Haram kidnapping young girls by the hundreds in Nigeria, probably for prostitution or self-gratification. It doesn't add up. We know the trail starts in the DRC; we witnessed the abductions by the Zimbabwean troops. We need to go back to where this all began. You could well be right, Maria; maybe this is not about money. That leaves two alternatives, personal gratification or trafficking the girls in Europe. The second alternative is also flawed – assuming our three friends are involved, why would they put themselves up against the Russians or Croatians, or the mafia from other Eastern European states? These Eastern European mafia thugs completely dominate sex trafficking in Europe. The more we think about it, the more the motivation does appear to be self-gratification. If that is so, we need to establish where this is happening.'

'How about in that house in Matadi?' asked Tim.

'You didn't see any sign of the girls – also Thackett and Smythe were not there at the time, although that doesn't mean they haven't been,' replied Colonel Torrens. 'I will get the boys who are currently at the mine to put a 24/7 observation post on the place for the next couple of weeks. Michael, how do you think the Zimbabweans are involved? Are they part of the group, or hired help? What are the chances that the girls have been shipped to Zimbabwe?'

'That would mean our band of brothers travelling to Zimbabwe. Don't see how Thackett could allow himself to be seen there, being in the arms business – or the Shadow Chancellor, for that matter.'

'So we assume they are hired help, although you did see the Zimbabwean army captain arrive in London. I'll get somebody to watch who comes and goes out of their embassy in the Strand for a while as well to see if he pitches up at some point. I doubt very much there is official Zimbabwean involvement, but let's keep eyes on the place.'

The group talked back and forth for another fifteen

minutes before Colonel Torrens and Michael finalised the surveillance details and assigned tasks. After that, the colonel left and the others started to make their way back to their own office areas. Maria stayed on to close down the boardroom. The door opened, and Michael appeared around the open door.

'I was wondering what you were doing on Friday evening, and whether you might be free to have dinner with me?' he asked.

'That would be nice. Thank you, Michael,' Maria replied.

'How about around 1930 hours? I thought we could have a drink at the Fire Stables and then from there go on to eat in the village. My spies tell me you are in Putney, which is not a million miles from Wimbledon Village. I will come and pick you up.'

'There is no need. I will get a cab and meet you at the Fire Stables. I know where it is, just off the high street.'

'Of course, good. See you Friday evening, then.'

Michael walked off down the passage with a sloppy grin on his face. *That is the hardest part over with*, he thought: *building up the courage to ask and not being knocked back. Roll on Friday.*

17

The Work of the Devil

The three men sat back in leather chairs, each with a large Scotch whisky in a crystal tumbler glass, smoking cigars and in silence. Each man was engrossed in his own thoughts. The mahogany panelling in the study reflected the glow from the open fire in the hearth in front of where the three men sat. One of the men stood up slowly, then placed his glass on the side table and left the room without talking to the others. He slowly made his way up the staircase to the room he had grown to know well over the past year. As he entered the room, he noted, with satisfaction, that everything was as it should be: the lights low and the heavy curtains firmly shut. In the middle of the bed, lying face down on white satin sheets over a white surgical sheet was the gleaming body of a young, dark-skinned girl. Draped halfway across her face were white pure satin panties. Her body had been bathed in an aromatic oil to produce a glowing sheen over her body. She lay still blindfolded, her face turned to the right. Her wrists were bound to the headboard and she whimpered quietly as she sensed the presence of somebody in the room. She heard the floorboards creak under the plush tartan carpeting. On the side table next to the bed was a small, white Egyptian cotton facecloth with a bottle of especially prepared aromatic oil placed on it. The oil was to be breathed in just prior to ejaculation, as it increased the size of the penis. The small table lamp light reflected off an evil-looking, nine-inch steel knife with a serrated edge, which was also laid out on the facecloth. He walked to the side of the bed and ran his index finger down her back, making a small indentation in the body oil. She whimpered again, and he reached up to her head, grabbed a fistful of short dark hair and pulled her head back in a violent twist. She opened her mouth to scream, but he cut her off by ramming the silk panties into her mouth with his free hand. He slowly removed his white bath robe, remaining behind her so that she could not see his face. He climbed slowly onto the base of the bed, carrying two pillows in white Egyptian cotton lace pillow slips. He lifted her around her waist and placed the pillows under her small hips. He then knelt on either side of her legs, which were flailing around the bed. By kneeling down, he pushed her legs together. He slapped her hard across her backside, which made her arch her back in pain, and her legs ceased jerking around the bed. He forced open her cheeks, and lifting the oil from the sideboard, poured a droplet directly onto her tight anus. He knew the oil would sting. With his middle finger on his right hand he penetrated her anus ring in a small rhythmic movement. The result was that his penis rose in anticipation, throbbing and angry. Her shoulders rose and fell, he could hear through her muffled cries that she was now sobbing. Suddenly, he lifted his body forward, and in one savage movement rammed his penis up her anus. He felt her split open as he commenced pounding into her body. This only served to heighten his lust. He felt nothing else. Very soon he felt his ejaculation building, and he reached for the bottle of oil and breathed in deeply, feeling his erection grow in size and width. As he started to reach his climax, he pulled her head back with one hand until he heard the neck crack, and with the other hand he reached for the knife and drew it across her exposed throat making a single deep incision, as he had been carefully taught; the victim must die as the climax was reached. He thrust one final time and exploded in the dying girl's anus, letting out a deep guttural roar. He slid off the inert lifeless body, then quickly wrapped his robe around himself, careful to avoid the blood which was now spattered on the sheets and growing in a pool beneath her body. He turned and left the room. Others would arrive to take care of the mess and aftermath. They would dispose of the body.

18

The Calm Before the Storm

Michael arrived at the Fire Stables just before 1930 hours on Friday evening. He was dressed in light tan chinos, a pair of dark brown dock shoes, a pale blue Oxford shirt and a navy blazer. He made his way to the bar and ordered a pint of bitter. Noting the couch by the open fire was free, he made his way over and lowered his powerful frame into the plush old leather. A couple of women at the next table gave him an admiring once-over and smiled, which he returned.

Maria arrived ten minutes later. She looked stunning dressed all in black. She was wearing stiletto high heels, bootleg jeans and a silk black top, which in the light showed off the outline of her breasts in a sensual rather than sexy way. She carried a black, light Irish shawl looped over her black handbag. Michael rose quickly to his feet as she made her way over to him.

'Hi, you look really fantastic,' Michael said.

'Why, thank you, Michael. You scrub up pretty well yourself,' Maria responded with a totally disarming smile.

Michael knew all the men in the bar would be staring at this beautiful woman that he was lucky enough to be with. The two women at the next table looked a little crestfallen that their possible entertainment for the evening was spoken for.

'May I get you something to drink?'

'Yes, please. If they have a good cold New Zealand Sauvignon Blanc that would be fine, thanks.'

He walked over to the bar and returned with a cold bottle of white wine and two glasses. He pushed the remains of his bitter across the coffee table.

'Thought I would join you,' he said.

'Great, I would hate to drink an entire bottle on my own,' she joked. 'I might think you had evil intentions,' she said as she smiled across the couch at Michael.

The evening passed in a happy and pleasant way. Although they worked together, this was the first time they had been out on their own socially. They talked about their schooling, and their university and army careers.

A little later, they went on to Michael's favourite little Italian restaurant in the high street, where they relaxed over dinner and the conversation moved on to more personal topics: old boyfriends and girlfriends, families, holidays and all the other topics which couples getting to know one another talk about. All too soon, they were leaving behind a wonderful evening having had a nightcap at the refurbished Dog & Fox lounge bar.

'I live just around the corner from here,' Michael said. 'I would offer to drive you home, but I think I would be somewhat over the drink-driving limit. We could go back to my place for coffee, but there is always the risk of Edward subjecting us both to the Spanish Inquisition as to how we got on. Edward likes to think he has my best interests at heart when it comes to the fairer sex.'

'I don't think that would be a great end to the evening, so perhaps you could just call me a cab.'

'Of course. Tell you what, why don't I come along for the ride? Make sure you are home safe and sound. It will be easy enough to hail a cab back.'

'That would be nice, if you don't mind.'

'Not at all.'

Michael hailed a black cab, and Maria gave the cabbie the address. As he pulled away from the kerb, Maria lifted Michael's left arm and snuggled in under his arm, resting her head on his chest.

'Thank you for a wonderful evening, Michael. I really enjoyed myself.'

'I had a great time as well, Maria, we must do this again soon.'

His heart was pounding so loudly as she lay against his chest that he feared she would hear it.

'I would love to. Perhaps when we have got to the bottom of this business with the girls, we can take some time off and relax a little more.'

They sat in silence, comfortable in each other's company and close proximity as the cab made the short journey to Maria's apartment. She lived in one of the many new chic apartment blocks alongside the Thames, all darkened glass and aluminium. There was a well-lit foyer with a concierge desk which was not manned as far as Michael could see. When the cab pulled up outside her entrance she sat upright and stared straight into Michael's eyes.

'Keep the cab, Michael. No need to see me to my door. It's been great.'

She leaned over and took his face in her hands.

'My knight in shining armour. You will get to the bottom of this thing, Michael, and we will all be there to back you up.'

With her hands holding his face, she leant over, and kissed him slowly and full on his lips. He responded by pulling Maria towards himself and returned her kiss, holding her tightly in his arms for what seemed too short a moment. She eased herself gently away from his embrace.

'Good night, Michael. I will see you on Monday.'

And with that, Maria was out of the cab and heading to the entrance foyer of the apartment block. Michael asked the cabbie to wait until she was inside the foyer. As the cab pulled away, he thought he saw a figure move back into the shadows on the corner of the apartment block.

'Wait just a moment,' he called. He bundled out of the cab and ran to the corner, but when he got there the street was empty. He looked slowly around and then returned to the cab.

'Sorry, thought I saw somebody I knew,' he explained to the driver. 'Let's go.'

He sat back, reflecting on his reaction to the shadowy figure. Maybe it was just an illusion, caused by the fact that after his discussion with Colonel Torrens he had the idea that people might be following him in his head. Shadows don't make me jumpy, normally I wouldn't react to them and I don't get it wrong. Could be that the person spotted me getting out of the cab and ducked into an alley. I am pretty sure there was somebody; we must all keep a keener eye on our surroundings and movements. I'll talk to Edward about it in the morning;

perhaps we should start to cover each other's backs a little more, splitting up and trailing one another. He sent a quick text to Maria, alerting her to what he thought he had seen. She replied immediately that she would watch from her window for a while.

'Not quite the text I was expecting, Michael,' she added, followed by a single 'x'.

Saturday morning found Michael wrapped up warmly heading down the A3 in his restored 1954 MG TF with the hood down. He loved the car, having restored it from bolts upwards. It was painted in Guards' red, and he had added a few mod cons: an extra gear for touring, unleaded fuel and better brakes than the original model. The upgrades created a classic that was enjoyable, safe and comfortable, although not *Concours d'Elégance* standard. He drove around the back of Guildford town, taking the cathedral slip road onto the A281 and passing the large Debenhams department store on the edge of town. Forty-five minutes after leaving Wimbledon Village, he drove through the entrance gates of Milkwood, his parents' home. His mum, Susan, came out to greet him, followed by his father, Geoff, who was smoking one of his signature small cigarillos. Michael often wondered why they were called cigarillos – they were clearly cigars, so why refer to them by the Spanish word for 'cigarette'?

His mum gave him a kiss on each cheek and suggested they all move inside out of the cold. His dad gave Michael one of his bear-hug embraces and said it was great to see him. The kitchen had been extended to make it a rumpus lounge and home entertainment centre, where his dad could put his wide-screen TV and

Bob Dylan collection. They settled into old comfortable couches around the open fire, and coffee and a variety of small cakes from local farm stalls appeared from the kitchen. As usual, none of his sisters were home; they were all adult and independent and were busy with their careers. One was an army doctor, one a civilian doctor and the third was a barrister. Their parents were very proud of the children's achievements and each had a special demarcated area on the lounge wall where a visitor could observe their achievements and awards together with photographs. Michael always found it a little embarrassing seeing himself in full dress uniform on the lounge wall. He always teased his mother about leaving space for RIP under his photograph; she was not amused by the joke.

After a wonderful roast which was spread over a couple of hours, Michael and his father walked to the local pub for a pint and a catch-up. This was a ritual whenever Michael was home on a Sunday. They always enjoyed their pleasant sojourns in the pub. Their conversation would always follow a pattern: Michael's father would invariably ask Michael questions about his work, and he would answer without actually ever giving any detail of his work away. His father knew this and always took pleasure in attempting to grill Michael. He always countered by moving to his father's favourite fantasy: having a torrid affair with a beautiful, dark-skinned Caribbean lady. The whole family knew about it, and it was always a great topic of teasing conversation. In fact, Sue had been Geoff's childhood sweetheart, and he still loved her very deeply.

'Wouldn't stop me, though,' he would mumble with

a naughty grin on his face after a few pints of Guinness.

Their walk back to Milkwood was relaxed and pleasant, the damp autumn leaves on the roadside rustling under their shoes.

Michael stayed on another hour before leaving for London. He hugged his mother and shook his father's hand and drove off down the lane towards the village and the main road. He was back in Wimbledon Village by 1900 hours on Saturday evening. He collected his gym bag and jogged down the hill to his health club. He spent a couple of hours working out and swimming; his fitness and keeping his body in shape was always an important part of his daily routine. When he let himself in, Edward was not at home, so Michael flicked through the TV channels and wandered off to his bedroom for an early night.

When both Michael and Edward were in residence on any Sunday they followed the same routine. This Sunday was no different: breakfast at Le Pain in the village reading the Sunday papers. Michael would order scrambled eggs, bruschetta and mushrooms, while Edward would order boiled eggs and salad; each always also ordered large coffees and then sat back to enjoy the Sunday papers. Edward liked to split the national papers into their component sections: news, sport, finance, property, motoring and the magazines – that way he could start with the bits he liked. Michael was not bothered by the order, or what he read first. Normally, they would sit on the pavement and watch the world go by. Wimbledon Village ladies in their finery were always a pleasure to behold, spending their husband's City bonuses on the finest in fashion.

However, this Sunday, the wind was sharp and cold, so the pavement chairs and tables remained empty, except for a couple deep in conversation, wrapped up in winter coats, gloves and scarves, their gloved hands wrapped around their warm coffees. Michael liked the sounds and the smells of the village: the cars going by, the hustle and bustle, not to mention the perfume of the ladies out for their Sunday strolls. He was definitely a city boy. He reflected on his upbringing, so different from his current environment: a small village with a quirky colonial lifestyle and a fair share of quirky colonial characters. The wonderful bush, hundreds of miles of nothing but large open spaces. The wild animals and the beauty and cruelty of nature; all of them combined to create an idyllic lifestyle for a young boy. He loved the smell of the Bushveld after the first rains, the explosion of births in the spring of all the young wild animals, but most of all, he loved the mighty rivers, the lifeblood of central Africa – especially the Zambezi. Yet he was equally at home in the city: he wasn't fazed by the traffic, the commuting, or even the underground. Like a chameleon, he learned quickly to blend into his environment, to fit in, to be invisible; although with his rugged looks and excellent physique, he was not an easy person to ignore.

The pair were sitting in the window and the glass enhanced the weak sun to create a feeling of warmth on Michael's face. He sat back, eyes almost closed, enjoying the moment. He was snapped out of his reverie by Edward.

'Bloody hell, what do you make of this?' exclaimed Edward.

'What do I make of what, Ed?'

'There is an article here in the *Sunday Times* about a body found in the Thames. I'll read it to you. The headline is "Murdered Girl Found in the Thames". It goes on: "On Friday in London, the police recovered the body of a young girl from the River Thames. The body has not yet been identified, but appears to be that of a young black girl in her early teens. The police have not revealed how she died, but are treating the death as murder. This means that her body must show signs of some form of attack that couldn't be self-inflicted. They go on to say that, unlike the recent recovery of two bodies showing signs of 'muti', mutilation for medicine, no organs had been removed in this latest discovery. Police are calling for witnesses, or any persons who were in the East India Docks area next to the Thames on Friday evening to come forward if they saw anything out of the ordinary or suspicious."'

'I am surprised they mentioned that much, Ed – about the recent mutilation cases, I mean. It could be totally unrelated, but we should find out as much as we can as quickly as possible.'

'Shall I text "reveille" to the team?'

This code word meant that all those available should assemble at Excalibur as soon as possible.

'No, it's Sunday. Not much we can do today. It can wait until tomorrow morning. Just tell the colonel, Maria and Tim what we have read in the *Sunday Times* in case any of them have missed it; that will give every-body time to think about what to do next. Knowing the colonel, he will immediately call a couple of people. The body has been recovered; there will be an autopsy next week for sure. We need to get in touch with any contacts we have at the Met Police to find out what the hell this is all about.

'Just text the team to be there first thing tomorrow. The colonel has excellent contacts; he is chums with the commissioner, Sir Bob Caldwell. He can give us a heads-up, or get us into the right area so that we can follow up quickly.'

'What are the chances this is one of the girls, do you think?'

Before Michael could answer, Edward continued.

'If this is one of them, we are now dealing with a different scenario. This is murder, Michael.'

'Hold on, Ed. Let's see what happens tomorrow. All will become a lot clearer then. The chances are 50/50 that it's one of the girls – no more than that at this moment. If the body is one of them, it's a bad mistake on the part of the murderer, because they should have dumped the body miles from where the attack took place.'

'It may well have been dumped miles away, Michael. They could have transported the body to London to throw people off the scent. The attack could have taken place miles away.'

'No, something tells me it's a careless mistake on their part. The crime took place in London. Anyway, as I said, it's speculation at the moment, Ed. We can't assume it's one of our girls.'

Despite his response, Michael was troubled and concerned about the direction their investigation might be taking. The breakfast didn't seem the same after Edward's discovery in the paper; they finished in silence, each thinking his own thoughts.

19

Someone to Talk to

It was Monday morning at 0900 hours, and the team were all gathered in the boardroom when they were joined by Ginger Hill. Michael recalled he was a member of the IT team, specialising in hacking computers, a necessary part of Excalibur's operations.

'Right, let's get up to speed on what we know.'

As usual, Colonel Torrens brought them all to attention immediately; there was no more idle chatter.

'A young black girl has been found dead in the Thames. The police have already stated it's a murder inquiry, so we can assume the body has signs of trauma. I made a call last night to Bob Caldwell to note our potential interest and he will keep me up to speed.'

Michael smiled across at Edward.

The colonel continued, 'Your Zimbabwean captain has turned up.'

Colonel Torrens nodded at Ginger, who came in on cue.

'We picked him up coming out of the Zimbabwean Embassy on the Strand last Thursday. He was not in uniform, but we recognised him from the photo we lifted off your mobile phone. His name is Moses Tekere; he is the son of a former high-ranking Zanu general, although he doesn't appear to be as patriotic as his late father. He has his fingers in a few pies, including illicit dealing in so-called blood diamonds. He attended the School of Infantry in Zimbabwe and is in light infantry. He has the rank of captain. He was, until recently, an intelligence officer with the Zimbabwean military detachment in the Democratic Republic of the Congo.'

'That's two oxymorons in a short space of time, Ginger,' cut in Colonel Torrens with a chuckle. 'First, your use of the word "intelligence" in an army context, and then "democratic" and "the Congo". Sorry, chaps, I digress. Carry on.'

Ginger hesitated, as if searching what he was about to say for any more oxymorons he could drop, then continued.

'While in the DRC, he was involved in a number of deals which earned him far more than his army salary, and, as far as we are aware, without the knowledge of his superiors. Bit of a loose cannon.

'On Thursday afternoon at 1500 hours, he made his way from the embassy to NatWest Bank on the Strand, where it turns out he has a current account registered to a London address. We have checked out the property details: it's in Tekere's sister's name; there is a moderate-sized mortgage on it with Birmingham Midshires. Looking into their records tells us that his sister is a legal secretary in the City. We have a surveillance team on site near the house and Tekere was there over the weekend so we know he stays there when in London. We also had a look at the bank systems after he was observed paying in a cheque at an ATM machine inside the bank. We matched the time of the deposit with the transaction records we hacked, and his name and account number came up. The cheque was for £30,000, and the cheque was issued by Moonshoot Technical Defence Systems. As we all know, that is a subsidiary of Rapier Systems, so it links our captain to Lord Thackett's companies.'

Ginger shrugged, giving an 'over to you, guys' look around the boardroom table.

'Thank you, Ginger,' began the colonel. 'Well the coincidences continue to build. We have enough, I think, to put at least Tekere and Thackett in some kind of mutual arrangement. I don't think the Zimbabwean government are involved. Bring in the Jackal vehicles and the plane, and we can include our friend Simon Jones, the EU commissioner, as well. Still not sure about the Shadow Chancellor – that could be nothing more than campaign funding. Maria has established that Thackett is a major contributor to the party. It's time we had a chat to somebody in that group.'

'We have Tekere's London address. Let's pick him up for a little chat,' said Michael.

Colonel Torrens seemed deep in thought, but after a few moments he replied, 'Agreed, but it's got to be done in such a way that there is no comeback on us or the firm. To remind you all, we are not a fully accredited security service in government terms, so the laws around kidnap and temporary imprisonment still apply to us.

Make sure Tekere cannot identify any one of you or your team and he must not pick up that any one of you is following him. When you have had your chat, leave him a little way from his sister's home. I will give the boys at MI6 the heads-up. They understand these things and also they owe us a few favours. For now, we leave the police out of it, at least at this stage. They are the upholders of the law and, as such, their hands are far more tied. Let's wait and see what their autopsy brings out and their attempts to find who the victim is before we meet them. Since there is a murder linked to our investigation, this makes it a police matter, and they will probably pick up the ball and run with it.'

The team said nothing, but Michael remembered the promise he had made to the old chief. *I will be there once we know for sure what's going on – you can count on it*, he thought.

The meeting came to an end at that point. Michael, Edward and Tim went back to the office that Edward and Michael shared. After a brief discussion, Edward called through to the motor pool to requisition one of the vehicles used for undercover surveillance.

That same evening, after the commuter rush hour, and with far less traffic than during the early evening, Michael, Tim and Edward parked one of Excalibur's nondescript pale grey, Ford Mondeo, four-door saloon cars in the shadows of a large maple tree on Vernon Road in Mortlake, a small commuter suburb of London. It was very popular with up-and-coming City types, an area of growth. The suburb was named Mortlake after the events that took place during the Great Plague of London, or the black plague, as it was known in 1665. Infected corpses were carried out to Mortlake in horse-drawn carts and buried in mass graves in marshland near the River Thames.

It was late evening, around 2200 hours. There was a chill in the air and a slight misty fog blowing in the street reflected in the yellow glow from the street lamp on the opposite side of the road. The maple tree had lost most of its leaves but was still able to hide the car from view of the doorway of 17A Rose Cottage. A two-man surveillance team had noted Tekere's arrival earlier in the evening at his sister's modest two-up-two-down terraced cottage. Michael, Edward and Tim, who had been sitting inside the Plough, a warm friendly pub in Christchurch Road, East Sheen, some five minutes away, nursing three pints of beer, left as soon as the signal came through and within five minutes they were all in position. They all wore black trousers, dark shirts and black parka jackets with no labels or identifying marks.

None of them wore watches or jewellery and each had a balaclava on the seat beside them. The car had false registration plates as well.

Michael sat staring at the cottage. The curtains were closed in the front room, which was common at this time of the year to keep in the warmth. The house was silent, but, as far as they could tell, all the downstairs lights were on and Tekere was still inside. At times like these, Michael switched off to everything that was happening around him, concentrating only on the task in hand. He was not a violent man by nature, preferring negotiation to confrontation. The exception was when there was any danger to colleagues, or if there was an individual suffering from injustice at the hands of perpetrators, somebody who was unable to defend themselves. In those cases, he would step up without hesitation.

At six feet three inches, he was a very big man, and he was also very fit, so he was more than able to hold his own. Michael was well-liked by those in his team, and he was respected for his leadership skills and good judgement. He was often teased by his peers as being 'England's upmarket answer to Jack Reacher', a fictional hard, ex-military character who never looked for trouble, although it found him. Michael, in turn, reminded those around him that he owned more than a toothbrush, unlike his fictional counterpart, and had a university degree. Despite this, he secretly liked the label.

He was certainly in a Jack Reacher mood that night as he sat in silence. *Never walk away from wrongdoing*, he thought. He focused his thoughts on the man inside the cottage, Tekere. *If you are involved in harming any of those young girls, you will regret it for the rest of your life, short as that may be*, he thought. Tim nudged him and offered him a Thermos flask cup containing hot, black coffee. Michael shook his head silently, and the cup was passed over to Edward, who was sitting in the rear seat of the car. It had been agreed Tim would cross the road at the first sign of any movement at the entrance to Rose Cottage and loiter in a mildly antagonistic manner under the lamppost. This would hopefully cause Tekere to cross the road onto the opposite pavement, the side the Ford was parked on. Edward would get out of the back seat of the car and approach Tekere from behind and ask him to step over to the car for a chat. Tim would close in, and Michael would climb out of the front seat to help bustle Tekere into the car as quickly and quietly as possible.

At 2315 hours, the door opened and Tekere and his sister were exposed in a beam of light from the ceiling lamp at the front entrance. Tim was immediately, and silently, out of the car and across the road whilst Edward moved slightly forward in a crouch. He would let Tekere pass by before rising up behind him. Michael tensed all his muscles, ready to burst from the car. Tekere hugged his sister and turned towards Mortlake overground station. His sister closed the front door and the hallway light went off. Seeing a shadowy figure loitering under the light of the street lamp, Tekere crossed the road. He looked over his shoulder at the person under the street-lamp; then, satisfied that the person was not coming towards him, he turned back and continued walking. This backward glance caused him to miss Edward who now rose up behind him.

Edward, balaclava in place, placed his hand firmly on Tekere's right shoulder and said, 'Excuse me, sir, may I have a word?'

Tekere reacted immediately, trying to break from the shoulder hold and pull away. He almost succeeded, but Michael was quickly out of the car, face covered up, and grabbed Tekere by the lapels of his winter coat. Edward immediately switched his grip, bear-hugging Tekere from behind, making it easier to bundle him into the car. Time was of the essence; all it needed was some watchful eyes from a window, a 999 call and the sound of sirens, and the team would be forced to back off.

Tekere was not going to give up without a struggle. He pulled violently away from the two men, stamping hard on Edward's right instep as he did so. Edward grimaced in pain and loosened his grip. Tekere managed to loosen one arm and pulled back to direct a punch at Michael. Michael stepped into Tekere, cutting off the swing of the punch and lifted his knee hard into Tekere's groin. Tekere started to double up in pain and Michael pushed through a short jab to his stomach. The combination of the two blows made Tekere slump against Michael so that they were able to push him into the back seat, where Tim was waiting. Once he was inside, they handcuffed the now subdued Tekere. Michael leapt into the driver's seat and Edward, nursing his painful instep, dragged himself into the passenger seat and slammed the passenger door. The whole thing had taken less than 30 seconds. Michael drove away slowly, checking the windows of the houses around that had lights on and curtains open. But there was no movement inside the houses – all was quiet.

Five minutes later, Michael pulled the car up 200 yards away from the Ship Pub on Thames Bank Road, a favourite late-night area for courting couples. He stopped under some oak trees, away from any street lamps, just before the Clifford Road Bridge over the Thames.

Tekere, still groaning, slowly lifted himself into a sitting position, where he was confronted by three men in balaclavas. He spoke, the pain he was feeling reflected in his hoarse, angry voice.

'Who are you people? What do you want? Do you realise I am a foreign consular official and that you are all in a lot of trouble for abducting somebody who has diplomatic immunity? I do not have any money on my person, so release me at once.'

Michael smiled under his balaclava. It had been decided that Edward would do the talking as he spoke with an upper class accent, and, as Tim put it, the interrogation would have more weight if it was carried out by someone who 'spoke like a toff'. Edward, who was still in some discomfort, turned in the front seat and began speaking.

'Firstly, old chap, sorry about the rough stuff – not normally our style. Secondly, you are a soldier, not a politician, so the immunity bit is a bit tricky for you. However, as you are a soldier, we will do our best to abide by the Geneva Convention in our discussions with you; although how closely we stick to it depends on your cooperation, sir. Finally, we will be asking the questions, so please refrain from asking any yourself.'

'Who are you people? I demand to know.'

For his trouble, Tekere received a sharp blow to his ribs from Tim's elbow. He winced and yelped in pain from the sudden blow to his midriff, still smarting from Michael's blow.

'Sir, please abide by my rules: no questions from you. I apologise for my friend's sudden slip of his elbow. The car is very cramped. He will try not to do that again. Not asking questions will help, I'm sure.'

Tekere tried to scowl at Edward in the darkness.

'Tell us about being in the DRC in Zimbabwean camouflage uniform in a British manufactured armed vehicle you were seen commanding around early November last year.'

Tekere thought briefly of blurting out his name, rank and serial number; his ribs and midriff were still aching. Instead, he remained silent and just stared straight ahead.

'Sir, not answering is not an option. Please answer my question.'

'I was part of the Zimbabwean army three-brigade

task force whose mission was to provide security and support to President Laurent Kabila, an ally of my country. His government requested the support of a friendly neighbour and we stood with him.'

'I believe that to be true, as it is an open secret that the Zimbabwean army and air force are providing military support to the Kabila regime, no doubt in return for a share of the country's diamonds, oil and other mineral riches.

'That is not the case. We are there purely as support to a neighbouring state on a humanitarian basis. A friend has requested our help in stopping the overthrow of a legitimate and elected government.'

Feigning a cough, Michael muttered 'bullshit' but stayed out of the direct interrogation.

'Sir, you have not answered my question concerning your own particular actions. Why were you in command of a British armoured vehicle in the Matadi area of the DRC in November last year? To help your memory a little, you were seen on the perimeter of an attack by local bandits on a village near the Congo River.'

Although Tekere was not actually seen at the attack, Edward had decided to include him in the hope of flushing him out.

Tekere sat staring straight ahead, but as he felt Tim move his body closer towards Tekere, he remembered the pain Tim's elbow had caused him and answered immediately.

'I recall that terrible attack. We were tipped off by the DRC army that an attack was going to take place, and we were sent to protect the villagers.'

'If that is the case, why did you not carry out your

orders and protect the villagers? You took no part in the attack, but you were seen pulling young women onto the vehicles and driving off. Several young girls from the village were missing after the attack.'

'We were providing protection to those young women; we assisted in taking them away from the attack and to safety.'

'You and I both know that's bullshit. Excuse the language, but I am tiring of your evasive and untrue answers. I am going to tell you what I believe you were doing, and if your answers are not what I want to hear, I will ask my colleague to break your neck quickly and quietly and throw your miserable body in the Thames.'

Tekere started to sweat, but as he was handcuffed, he could not stop the droplets from running down his forehead and into his eyes. The sweat stung his eyes and he blinked rapidly.

Edward continued, 'I believe you were acting outside of your orders. Your unit was outside of its remit, and this action was not sanctioned by your bosses either in the army, or the government. In other words, you were not providing either military, or humanitarian support. This makes life difficult for you. One word in the right ear and your military career is over. You will be court-martialled by your own military, if you are lucky. Otherwise, you might just disappear and then who knows what they will do. I believe you were involved in the kidnap of young, innocent girls and the Jackal armoured carriers were some sort of a gift, or cover, provided to you. Now to use good Queen's English, stop fucking around and answer my questions, or you are a dead man. Answer them truthfully, and we will have no further use for you and will take no further action.'

Then Michael started speaking from the front seat. He spoke quietly, but with deadly conviction: 'Unless we find you have had a hand in the torture, rape or killing of any of these young girls, that is; in which case, I will kill you myself.'

Tekere was now openly shaking and he was sweating so profusely Tim had to open the window slightly to allow the stale air to escape and allow the ice-cold outside air in.

'It's true – we received the trucks from an unnamed source. We were also involved in covering up the girls' kidnap, but we did not harm them, I swear. We took them to a safe house in Matadi, and from there we handed them over to an unknown European man. That is all I know'.

Edward stared hard at Tekere for nearly 30 seconds.

'I think not. You see, we have proof that you received a personal payment of £30,000 from an English company. Why don't you elaborate on this payment a little?'

'It is true: I was paid for this work, but I did not know the company involved, please believe me. I dealt with a man from the EU Agricultural Commission who said he had friends in Europe who would give these young girls good homes, an education and a new life. Females have little worth in the Congo: they are often raped and abused. To offer them a better life was a good thing. We took the girls to the airport at Matadi and they were flown from there.'

'Not even a fool like you would think these girls were going to a place of safety. If they were, they would have been given a choice about going, a recruitment programme would have been set up. We are not stupid, Tekere. You must think we are if you would have us believe that.'

Tekere sat bolt upright at the mention of his name.

'We know you had further contact with this man. You were seen at Matadi Airport. My friend sat next to you. He could have taken you out at any time; he is one of the best marksmen in the world. You flew out of Matadi with this man, why?'

'It was agreed I would go to Luxembourg to where the girls were to be housed, and that I would receive payment for my work on the matter there. I saw the girls with my own eyes. They were well clothed, had their own rooms and were well fed. They all looked fine, and some were smiling and talking. That is all I know.'

'Did you know the company that paid you? Were there any other persons present at this house?'

'No, I did not know the company, but I assumed it was to do with the man I had been dealing with. The cheque was made out in sterling at my request, as I have a bank account in London. Yes, there was a European woman in the house – a sort of house mother. We did not speak.'

'When you left Luxembourg, the girls were still there?'

'Yes, they were and they had not been harmed.'

'So you say. Why did you then come on to London?'

'My next posting is going to be as the Zimbabwean military attaché in London. I came to meet the people I will be working with and to visit my sister who lives in London.'

Edward glanced at Michael who nodded.

Tim reached into his pocket and undid the handcuffs. He leant across Tekere and opened the back door. Michael turned and addressed Tekere in a low voice, not bothering to disguise the threat.

'Remember my words: if those girls are harmed in any way you will wish you had never been born, and if you go to the police or report this meeting to your people at the embassy, we will blow the whistle on you, and your career, such as it is, will be over. We also know where your sister lives, and although she is probably innocent, don't push us.'

Before Tekere could answer, Michael nodded again and Tim used his foot to push Tekere roughly out of the back door onto the towpath. He landed heavily on his back. The car started up immediately and had vanished around the bend back towards the high street before Tekere had sat up.

Half an hour later found the three men back in The Plough at a small table by the open fire in the bar lounge.

Michael had been recapping.

'So, we know now that the girls were definitely kidnapped and that they are no longer in the DRC. I will let Marie Louise know, but I will ask her to keep an eye out for the Jackals and continue listening out for any useful information.'

'Good-looking lass, boss, and bright too – a doctor in the DRC, so add brave to that description as well,' cut in Tim.

'Yes, I dare say, and your point is, Tim? I can assure you, Marie Louise and I are strictly business, no other interest.'

'Good to hear it, boss, because Maria was asking me

whether the two of you were still in touch,' smiled Tim.

'Yes, well back to the task,' Michael answered, avoiding Edward's wry smile.

'We now know that Mr Simon Jones is in this thing up to his neck: his stolen car is in Matadi, he flew the girls out to Luxembourg, and Tekere is dealing with him as the link person in the kidnapping transaction. We can also assume that Lord Thackett, or somebody very high up in his organisation, shipped those Jackals out to the DRC and paid Tekere through Moonshoot Technical Defence Systems. My money is on Thackett. Do you remember his name coming up in that child pornography inquiry some time back? A dossier was handed over containing names of people in parliament and Whitehall, but then mysteriously disappeared.'

'I reckon they were covering each other's arses,' cut in Tim.

'Well put, Tim. Very appropriate – a succinct summary of the situation, in my opinion,' Edward responded straight-faced.

The three men all smiled before Michael brought them back to the subject at hand.

'We know Jones and Thackett are known to one another. Jones flew in from Luxembourg and stayed over at the British and Middle Eastern Sporting and Dining Club. We should take a deeper look at their backgrounds and the circles they move in. They were probably at public school together: Eton, Harrow or another of the schools reserved for the social elite. Not sure about the Shadow Chancellor yet; we will need to put a close tail on him. Not easy, as I think he has always got a plain-clothes police officer hanging around. We will have to be careful, although he tends to be high-profile – always big on photo opportunities with the press; he plays Commons football; he's in the House of Commons cricket team, and so on.'

Edward said, 'I'm sure he gave a big speech a while back about how when they win the next election a top priority would be to stamp out sex trafficking into the UK. Mind you, we have yet to find out where the girls are. If they are in some sort of safe house in Luxembourg we will need to find it and consider whether we should cut across borders to be involved.'

'We leave that sort of decision to the colonel,' replied Michael. 'We do need to find those girls fast. They are in grave danger. I have a gut feeling things are going to go bad.'

They finished up their drinks and, leaving the pub, slipped off into the night.

20

High and Mighty

Maria's investigation into the Shadow Chancellor Kenneth Smythe's background did not at first discover any direct link between him and Lord Thackett. They went to very different schools: Thackett went to Eton whilst Smythe went to a nondescript comprehensive in the Midlands. University again gave no further clues, as Thackett went to Oxford and Smythe went to Leeds: two universities separated not only by many miles but also in age of establishment and also the social make-up of students. Both men were in politics, but came to government by very different routes: Thackett via his family seat at Arran Castle and thus his hereditary peerage in the House of Lords, Smythe after years in local government, before taking to the hustings to win a by-election caused by the untimely death of a sitting Member of Parliament.

Just when it seemed there was no link, Maria picked up on the fact that Smythe had been, in his day, a very good cricketer – almost county standard and had played for a top amateur league team in Leeds. Although Thackett was a lover of the game, a long-standing member of the MCC, he was a very average player. Money helps buy favours and Thackett always hosted a two-day warm-up match at Arran Castle for visiting touring sides from all the major Test cricket-playing nations of the world. On one such occasion, Smythe had been picked in the Lord Thackett XI to play against Australia and, although out of his depth, acquitted himself more than adequately, both keeping wicket and as a middle-order batsman. The two men got on extremely well, by all accounts, and a personal friendship developed between the two. There were rumours of riotous after-match parties, at which Smythe never failed to supply a bevy of beautiful young women. So now, far more than a contact in raising party funds, Smythe had ensured he was added to the small number of the powerful lobby of men involved in shaping both industry and politics some way or another.

A few days later, Colonel Torrens called Michael and Edward into his office. He shut the door and invited the two young men to sit in the two wine-coloured Chesterfield leather couches. He remained standing.

'Bad news, I'm afraid, chaps,' he began. 'I've just got off the phone from speaking to the Met Police Commissioner, Sir Bob Caldwell. The teenage girl whose body was recovered from the Thames was from the DRC. She had been brutally sexually abused, and her throat had been cut either during, or shortly after, having enforced sex. I am sorry, Michael; not what you wanted to hear, I know – nor you, Edward. The girl is from the Luba tribe, which indicates she either comes from the area around the Congo River where your contact took place, or from further north. The police do not have a name, as yet, and the investigation is ongoing. The Met are working through the DRC Embassy in London and the police in Kinshasa and Matadi are furthering their enquiries.'

'That lot are bloody useless,' muttered Michael,

recalling his run-in with Captain Bertrand of the Matadi Police, who had called Michael's team 'mercenaries'.

'Be that as it may, Michael, we have to work through the right channels. It's now an inquiry into the murder of a foreign national on British soil.'

Colonel Torrens could see anger flare in Michael's eyes.

'Something else you are not going to like is that, as it is now a murder inquiry, Sir Bob Caldwell has requested we hand over all our files to the murder investigation team, who have been put together to investigate.'

'Does he know whom we have in the frame, or how high up in government and industry they are, sir?' asked Edward.

'Not completely. The Commissioner and I had a brief overview conversation. Edward, you two can fill in the Met team on all our work to date. I'm sure it will go straight up to Sir Bob and all the top brass at the Met Police. The investigation is being led by a Detective Superintendent Brownlee and a Detective Sergeant Cutler; they are expecting your call.'

Michael sat quietly, deep in thought. He felt his neck muscles tensing to near spasm. He could feel his anger rising and he struggled to focus on the conversation.

'Sir, I am not one to question your judgement or query your decisions, but is there no way we can continue to push forward this investigation? We have enough infor-mation on the suspects. We are pretty sure we know who these despicable bastards are, and I, for one, want to confront them.'

'Michael, I feel as you do, but this is murder and my hands are tied. You can, I'm sure, keep a watching brief from a distance and offer help, but I doubt the police will accept your offer.'

Edward, who had been sitting quietly, mulling over what Colonel Torrens was saying, said, 'We don't know for sure whether all the girls are in Britain or not, sir. The majority of them could still be in Luxembourg. Can we follow up that line of enquiry ourselves with help from Maria's contacts?'

'No, Edward, if there is a connection and it is confirmed that these are the girls we have been tracking, then I am sure the Met Police will involve the Luxembourgish police and work with them. Gentlemen, I am not in the habit of repeating myself, but we cannot stay involved, so I suggest you get all the information you have together and set up a meeting with Superintendent Brownlee. That's all, chaps; as soon as you have had your meeting, report back to me. There are a couple of new contracts to discuss and we need to decide which we will deploy to the assignments.'

With that, the colonel sat down behind his desk and started shuffling some files in front of him. It was obvious from the body language that the meeting was over and Michael and Edward stood up, nodded to the colonel and returned to their shared office down the passage. Colonel Torrens stared out of the window and sighed angrily, not because his two young operatives were questioning him, but because he understood their feelings of frustration and outrage.

Michael slammed the door of their office shut and sat down at his desk.

'I just can't believe it, Ed. We are starting to close in on this bunch of depraved individuals; we are so close, and now we hand it over to the police. I, for one, don't intend to sit back and give up. If I can prove that any of these girls have been raped and murdered by any of our suspects, I will hand out the punishment they deserve. It certainly won't be a prison sentence in some soft-arse open prison.'

'Torrens knows how you feel, Michael, but as he said, it's now a murder inquiry and his hands are tied. I believe he would back us all the way if he could.'

'His hands are tied maybe, but I will not sit back and watch these individuals get away with murder and use their power and positions to escape.'

'Michael, I am with you, but we will have to make bloody sure that we ourselves are not caught up in murder.'

Michael appeared to fade out from the conversation as he moved his eyes to the window and shrugged. He was clearly deep in thought. The picture was clearer now: young girls, many under age, kidnapped under the pretence of ethnic cleansing, a common practice by jihadists such as Boko Haram. The girls are taken to a safe house and the grooming starts. After a while, they are spirited out of the DRC to Luxembourg, and from there sold into sex slavery in the EU. Sex slavery with a disgusting macabre twist – being murdered whilst being raped. *What sick bastards do these things*? Michael asked himself; it seemed to be invariably those who were in positions of power or trust. These girls were not being brought in from the back streets of Bolton by Pakistani gangs for their own pleasure; these girls were being kidnapped for sex slavery of the most horrific kind – death sex. Worse still, people at the highest levels of the EU were involved – people elected to protect. *I will stop this by cutting off the snake's head, with or without Colonel Torrens' blessing*, Michael thought.

Just then, there was a quiet knock on the office door. Michael was about to yell 'piss off' when it opened, and Maria looked around it.

'Hi, Michael, I have just heard about the murder inquiry. I'm really sorry, especially as you were there at the time and made that promise to the chief.'

'Yes, well, looks as though my promise is not going to add up to much – for all we know, the dead girl could be Chief Muamba's daughter, Happiness. I am guessing you are in the picture on us now handing it to the Met Police as a murder inquiry?'

Michael tensed all his muscles from his toes up in an attempt to control his urge to slam his fist into the desktop.

Maria came into the room and sat down in a visitor's chair, facing Michael.

'Yes, Colonel Torrens has briefed me. Believe me, Michael, he would love to stay in on the investigation.

'Michael, we have worked together for more than two years now. We have grown in this company together. You are a man of your word and a man of integrity, which is unusual considering you're a fighting man, and some might even refer to you as a mercenary. We... I... know you will see this through somehow and you will keep your promise.'

She resisted an urge to reach out and hold his hand. He looked so low and vulnerable at that moment, a big, strong soldier and an honourable man, but both frustrated and helpless. But she was aware of Edward sitting at the opposite desk, and so she just leant forward and smiled into his eyes. She held his eyes for a moment and then thought: *What the hell, they are best friends*, so stood up and said softly, 'Michael, come round to dinner at my place tonight – around 1930 hours. See you then.'

Maria did not wait for a reply. She opened the door, walked through it and then shut it quietly behind her.

'What are you smiling at, Ed?' he asked once she had gone.

'Actually, Michael, I'm not smiling at your situation, and neither am I about to make a stupid remark. I was just thinking how lucky you are. Maria is probably the nicest woman and the most suitable female you have met since we became friends. I believe the two of you are really suited to one another. I hope all goes well for you both. You, my friend, certainly deserve a good woman in your life.'

Michael sat reflecting on his friend's words.

'I'm not sure this is going the right way right now. It could be that she is just feeling sorry for me because of the situation.'

He was not used to being with somebody caring and it left him feeling slightly unsettled and vulnerable.

'Rubbish, Michael. Thank God you don't have the same self-doubt about your soldiering as you do about your love life, or we would have all had our backsides shot off a long time ago – with respect to Sean Ahearn and his wounds,' laughed Edward.

'Thanks, Ed, not sure where we are going with this thing, though. In our line of work, it's never clever to be involved with somebody you work closely with. There is always the possibility that, in a tight situation, one's feelings could cloud one's judgement, causing bad split decisions.'

'Well, we are not in any fight or flight situation right now, so don't dwell on it. Just go with the flow, Michael. You have a couple of phone calls to make, which should lead to you attending a murder inquiry with the Met Police. I'll tag along and fill in the gaps if necessary.'

'Thanks, Ed. I know we have to stay inside of the law, but just thinking about what these bastards are doing and the abject fear and desperation those young girls must be feeling leaves me seething with anger, I will somehow be there at the end and if I can deliver retribution befitting the crime, I bloody well will. I am reminded of the old adage: don't get angry, get even. For those girls I shall do just that.'

Edward pushed back his chair, walked over to his friend and squeezed his shoulder.

'You hang in there, mate. The team will be right behind you. I will go along with your call, whatever it is, you know that. Let me know what Superintendent Brownlee says and when we will be meeting them. I am going to see what contracts are lined up for the team and say 'hi' to some of the guys. Sergeant McBride, Mark Jones and Matt Birrell are all in today. Oh yes, and Maria tells me that Sean Ahearn is out of hospital and home on light duty leave.'

'Yes, good news. I called in and spent a little time with him on Monday evening last week. He told me then that he was on his way home. He has already proposed to half the nurses on the ward. Lucky that round didn't touch anything, he seems to have it all together, but he will need to rebuild a lot of torn internal muscle in the gym.'

21

Maria

Michael arrived home earlier than usual that evening to give himself some time to freshen up before his dinner with Maria. While he showered, he turned the shower head so that the jets of water were at their highest setting. They stung like hundreds of small bees, which always left him with a warm sense of having been revitalised.

He dressed in jeans with a black polo crew-neck sweater and grey slacks, as well as a navy blazer to take some of the coldness out of the night air. At 1915 hours, he walked down the stairs to the foyer of his apartment block to the waiting cab. The journey from Grosvenor Hill to the waterside at Putney took just fifteen minutes and he arrived at Maria's apartment with a bottle of cold Veuve Clicquot La Grande Dame and half a dozen Dublin Bay deep red roses at exactly 1930 hours. The concierge called Maria's apartment from a phone behind his desk, and after nodding and answering, 'Righto, Miss, I shall send him up,' he replaced the receiver and pointed to the elevators, he said, 'Twelfth floor apartment – 5C, sir. Ms Mulvihill is expecting you.'

Michael thanked him, crossed to the lift and pushed twelve on the lift panel. As the lift came to a standstill it opened and to Michael's surprise, he stepped directly into the apartment. Maria stood facing him in the open plan entrance area. She was wearing a simple long, black flowing skirt with a black sequined blouse slightly off one shoulder. She was not wearing shoes. He could see her bare feet and noticed her toenails were painted with deep red nail varnish. They were small, but strong feet.

Maria, seeing his reaction to exiting straight into the apartment, smiled and said, 'Don't worry, Michael, unless I have seen the person's face on the CCTV as they enter the lift I am able to lock the lift doors so that they won't open.'

'Does this mean you have the entire floor of this building?'

'Yes, it's called a penthouse, although there are two more floors above me. I think it's estate agent-speak for all-round terraces.'

'Maria, this must have set you back a small fortune. The colonel must value your services very highly.'

Maria laughed with that open throaty laugh that Michael was so fond of.

'This has nothing to do with the colonel or Excalibur. About five years ago, my grandfather passed away in Ireland. I have two sisters and one brother. One of my sisters is a dentist in Dublin married to an Irish Member of Parliament supposedly destined for great things and my other sister is a leading oncologist. She has several hospital consultant positions in Cork and Tralee in Kerry. My brother, Josh, helps my dad on his farm.

Sorry, I digress: you asked about the apartment. My grandfather sold up his dairy farm just a couple of years before he died. His two brothers left Ireland and are now Catholic priests in the United States; rumour had it that they sent back funds from their good works. There is an old Irish saying: "Make Jack a priest and the money will look after itself" – not sure that's still true today. Anyway, that is how Grandad's farm grew to become one of the larger dairies in Kerry. Oh gosh, I'm off again, but I will get to your question about the apartment.

'Normally, because of Irish traditions and a few helpful European Union rules about capital gains, a farm will pass to the eldest son. So if my grandad had not sold the farm, it would have passed to my father when he died. However, as my father already has his own farm, my grandfather left a tidy sum to each of the girls instead. I suppose he felt my brother would inherit my father's farm one day. Anyway, we were all close to my grandfather and we were well looked after in his will. That's a long explanation to a short question about how I managed to buy this beautiful apartment. Come and have a look at the view.'

They moved onto the main terrace through bi-fold doors which ran the full length of the lounge. Below them ran the River Thames. There were a few working boats and barges moving downstream towards the City itself. There was also what Maria referred to as a party boat; it was lit up by flashing strobe lights, filled with revellers, and music was booming out, spoiling the tranquillity of the scene.

Looking at the party boat and the river, Michael's thoughts drifted back to a tragic event that had happened on this same stretch of river. On a balmy, clear evening many years earlier, a party boat, similar to the one that Maria had pointed out, was struck by a working dredger.

The force of the collision caused the dredger, named the *Bowbelle*, to rise up over the party boat named the *Marchioness* and within seconds it was at the bottom of the river. The lives of over fifty young revellers came to a sudden and shocking end. Michael gave an inadvertent shudder as he recalled the disaster.

Tonight, the water was almost pitch-black due to cloud cover, which only heightened the sense of tragedy, as it appeared to be moving downstream at high speed as well, probably because of the Thames Barrier gates being up.

The undercurrent was shown by waves several feet high, which curled back against the support buttresses of Putney Bridge as the water passed underneath.

Maria, unaware of Michael's thoughts, sighed and turned towards him.

'Michael,' she called softly, sensing he was not listening. 'Hey, Michael. I've lost you. Where are you?'

'Sorry, my mind was on other things. You were saying…?'

'Don't you love the way the ripples on the surface reflect the multitude of lights from the surrounding apartment blocks? They look like twinkling stars?'

Michael refocused on Maria and her happier thoughts about the river. He did not mention his sombre thoughts.

'Yes, the lights are stunning – not only the ones on the water either, but also those coming from all the apartment blocks as well. You could be looking down on the Hudson River in New York.'

Maria pointed out several landmarks further downstream: Big Ben, the Houses of Parliament, the spires of Westminster Cathedral, and the London Eye – now a permanent landmark. Some of the iconic City of London buildings were lit up in the distance, including the Gherkin, so called because of its shape, and the Lloyds of London building, whose quirk was that all the plumbing and ducting had been placed on the outside of the building in stainless steel piping. Maria pointed out St Paul's Cathedral in the background, still standing despite heavy bombing during World War II and at the time of the Blitz. Michael caught sight of the nearly completed Shard, reaching high into the night sky, its long, pointed shape making it appear like a shard of glass.

'Let's go inside. It's a bit nippy out here,' said Maria.

'I asked Tim what your favourite meal was and he said, "He's African, so he loves meat." I've prepared a couple of sirloin steaks and a salad, nice and healthy.'

'That's fine, thank you. Shall I open the champagne?'

'Thank you so much for the champagne, my favourite. Why don't we save it for a special occasion? I have some red wine open and breathing over on the sideboard; it's a lovely South African Shiraz. Hope that is to your liking.'

'That is splendid; it will go well with the steak. Shall I pour us each a glass?'

'That will be nice, thank you.'

Although the conversation was polite, it was relaxed at the same time, and Michael was feeling more relaxed already. Maria seemed to have a way of putting people at ease in her company. He poured two glasses of wine and joined Maria on the couch. She had tucked her bare feet underneath her long black skirt. Her skirt and top gave away nothing, but her relaxed position confirmed she was totally comfortable with herself and her surroundings.

'Why thank you, sir,' she teased as she reached up to receive her glass.

Michael smiled back at her.

Her hair was full and thick and seemed to have a flicked out shape all of its own. Hidden highlights accentuated this impression. *I bet she doesn't use any kind of tongs or curlers*, he thought. Her blue eyes shone in the low lighting of the room and she smiled back at Michael, taking his breath away. *My God, she is beautiful*, he thought.

'Penny for your thoughts?'

'Aah, that would be telling, madam.'

She smiled again lowering her eyes slightly at his gaze.

'Do you want to talk about the abductions before dinner?' asked Maria. 'I know it must be on your mind constantly.'

'I would like to avoid that, if possible, tonight. You are right, they stay at the forefront of my mind. I would really like the police to take swift action to resolve the situation and bring all the bad guys to book. More importantly, I would like those girls rescued before any more murders take place. We know that we can put Lord Thackett clearly in the frame along with the EU Commissioner Jones, and I am convinced that Zimbabwean army captain, Tekere, is involved. I suspect he is acting alone, without any official blessing.'

Maria nodded in agreement knowing Michael needed to talk despite what he had just said, then said, 'We have also got enough information on Thackett's friendship with Kenneth Smythe to put him in the frame as well. They are close, not just acquaintances. By tracing calls, hacking emails and doing a sweep of their computers, we have found that there are several other big business and industry names in the frame as well.

We have done some background stuff on Thackett's various residences. I have a number of addresses and GPS coordinates of Thackett's various homes as well as phone records on them all. There are also a number of badly disguised coded conversations we have picked up. Aside from Arran Castle, which I doubt he would use for any illegal sex crimes or murders, as his wife and family live there most of the time along with many estate employees, there is an apartment in Mayfair and a large country estate down on the Kent coast on top of the cliffs – that's far enough out of the way to be a possibility. The murder site indicates London activity but we should keep an eye on his Kent estate. The Kent police have drones nowadays – supposedly used in looking for illegal immigrants and possible terror activity along the Channel coast. Maybe the colonel can call in a favour or two and we could piggy-back their flights. Kent is away from prying eyes, so my bet is that he is operating from there.'

Michael replied, 'I agree with your assumptions but London is also a probable base for activities. I think Thackett would have been pretty pissed off at the dumping of a body in the Thames – that was a big mistake on their part. He will have moved his activities elsewhere by now. We should have a look at Kent. We have Thackett and his close associates directly in the frame; we just need to persuade the police to act on our intel. We have some huge and powerful names here, and you say there are others: politicians, big business people and the like. It will all come out, but for now, I just want the main guys in my sights. Edward and I have an appointment at New Scotland Yard in the morning with Superintendent Brownlee and Sergeant Cutler – they are heading the murder inquiry. Whether they like it or not, rest assured I will be right alongside them every bloody step of the way. Any hesitation or pussy-footing and we will move, with or without the colonel's consent.

Michael saw the frown on Maria's face, as going over the colonel's head was not the brightest move to make at any time.

He quickly continued, 'Let's see what tomorrow brings. Tonight I would like to spend a pleasant evening with you.'

'Let's do that. I'll get the steaks done. Perhaps you can toss the salad for me; there is some basil-infused olive oil on the sideboard along with a bottle of balsamic vinegar. Let's eat, relax and enjoy our wine.'

Dinner was eaten in silence. The sirloin steak was medium-rare and had a wonderful flavour. Fresh salad and Shiraz wine were the perfect accompaniments. Michael realised he was really hungry.

Michael helped clear the table and they moved to the couch with two glasses of Campbells Rutherglen Muscat dessert wine. Once again, Maria tucked her feet up beneath her and lay back against the cushions. The lights were turned down low, which made the flames of the tealight candles sparkle and dance around the room. The mood was completed by the latest Barbra Streisand CD whispering through Bose speakers.

They sat in silence enjoying the moment, two people comfortable in each other's company. Maria slid over the couch and snuggled up under Michael's arm that he placed behind her along the top of the couch. He used the fingers of this arm to gently stroke her temple, making small circles. Maria sighed and snuggled a little closer and placed her arm around Michael's waist.

Michael awoke with a start and realised he had fallen asleep. He looked down guiltily at Maria and was about to apologise when he realised she too was fast asleep. Her head had slipped slightly down his chest. The room was silent; the CD had reached its last track sometime previously. Michael's slight movement woke Maria, who looked upward at Michael's face.

'Hey, cowboy, what time is it?' she whispered softly.

'A little after midnight. We fell asleep, sorry.'

'Don't be, we both obviously needed to relax, and besides you felt very cuddly – warm and protective.'

'Cuddly, are you suggesting I am a little overweight?' asked Michael, with a laugh.

'Not at all, on the contrary I can feel your six-pack and hard stomach against my head. Might have been a little more comfortable if you were carrying a little spare padding,' she teased.

They both rose from the couch, and Michael did his normal long stretch, extending his arms above his head. He gazed down at Maria; her face flickered in the shadows thrown by the candlelight from the coffee table.

'Maria, I guess you probably know that I like you very much, and for the first time in a long time I have felt completely at ease in your company and being around you. At work there is little time to relax and play, and although it is not company policy to discourage relations between staff I'm not sure what the colonel would have to say about our friendship. I don't want our work to be a stumbling block, and at the same time, I know emotions can affect decisions and judgements. Not sure where I'm going with this but can we see where it goes between us?'

'Michael, we both have military backgrounds and understand both the art and the horror of warfare. We are now more than ever in hostile unpleasant situations. The world is no longer a great place for peace and tranquillity. Your role takes you all over the world, often into dangerous situations, even more than mine does. You are a bit of a loner as a result – as am I, in many ways. That said, I feel really good being around you: I know you are a good person in your heart, and you make me feel calm, happy and safe. Colonel Torrens is like a father to me. He knows everything that goes on around him, and I'm sure he knows that you and I are close. He would say something if he felt we were in any way compromising the firm. I care about you very much but I am sure we both can keep a perspective on work and being together. Hang in there, cowboy, I am not going anywhere.'

Maria stepped towards Michael and raised her arms around his neck. She stood on tiptoe and held him close. He bent his head forward and kissed Maria gently on the lips. He held her at arm's length and looked deeply into her eyes, and for a moment, time stood still.

'You are a princess, Maria, and I would very much like to be your knight in shining armour.'

He smiled and kissed her forehead.

'Thank you, Michael. Now, knights in shining armour need their wits about them – and their rest. This princess is going to bed, on her own, for now.'

Michael strode quickly to the lift door, not trusting himself to refrain from screwing up the moment.

The lift doors opened and he entered and turned towards Maria.

'Goodnight, Maria. Thank you for a wonderful evening.'

'Goodnight to you too. Sleep well, and good luck with the Met Police in the morning, my hero.'

As the doors silently closed, Maria blew Michael a soft kiss, which stayed in his thoughts all the way home.

22

The Metropolitan Police

New Scotland Yard is on a triangle of streets in Victoria, not far from the Thames Embankment, and half a mile from Parliament Square. The address is 8–10 Broadway, Victoria, London. The building itself is not any architectural masterpiece, although the use of blue glass and aluminium have had a softening effect on the outline, probably added as an afterthought in an effort to improve the look of the building. Plans have been drawn up to move the police headquarters to a new, larger state-of-the-art building, fitted with all the spy kit and computers designed to cope with the rising threat of terrorist activity. The existing building houses the Specialist Crime & Operations unit known as 'SC&O'. It also houses the Gangs and Organised Crime Unit and the head of the Metropolitan Police Force.

As Michael and Edward entered the building with its grey felt carpet tiles and myriad lookalike offices with glass walls, Michael wondered what the new building would be called: New New Scotland Yard, perhaps?

At reception, a uniformed officer checked his computer and confirmed they were expected, then they were photographed, probably for the twentieth time that morning as London has more CCTV surveillance cameras per square mile than any other major world city. They were issued with photo visitor passes, to be worn at all times, the officer stated, and shown down a long corridor to a glass office, which looked like every other around it.

'Sergeant Cutler and Constable Hogan will be with you shortly,' the escorting officer said.

'I was told we were seeing Superintendent Brownlee and Sergeant Cutler?' asked Edward, removing a small disc from his tweed jacket and placing it on the table in front of him.

'Sorry, sir, my meeting confirmation states that Detective Sergeant Cutler and Detective Constable Hogan are the two officers you will be meeting. Can I get you any refreshments – coffee, tea?'

'No, thank you,' Edward and Michael replied together.

'Righto. The officers will be with you shortly. I must request you do not leave this office until they arrive, or move to any other part of the building.'

'Understood,' replied Michael.

As soon as the escorting officer left the room, Edward turned to Michael.

'Why the change of investigating officers? We've been downgraded from having an interview with a superintendent to a sergeant and a constable.'

'Does seem odd. I'm sure when they hear us out they will bring in Brownlee and the rest of the bigwigs.'

'Let's check in with the colonel, Michael.'

Michael pointed to a sign stuck on the office window which warned that the use of mobile phones was strictly prohibited, then shrugged. Both men sat in silence, but they did not have long to wait. The door opened behind them and two plain-clothes officers came quickly around the other side of the desk and went up to Michael and Edward.

'Good morning, gentlemen. My name is Detective Sergeant Cutler, and this is Detective Constable Hogan.'

Michael studied both men briefly but thoroughly. Cutler looked every inch a copper – a long-termer – in his nondescript ill-fitting brown suit, white shirt and gaudy multicoloured tie. Thick-set, he had obviously been a force to be reckoned with in his prime. He had short grey hair in the crewcut style favoured by the American military. He had on a pair of rimless round glasses. He was the kind of man you would notice in a bar based on his size and presence. Hogan, by contrast, was a short man of slight build, with jet-black hair, thin lips and small, close-set eyes. He wore a grey suit; an off-white, almost grey shirt and a plain grey tie. A real nowhere man.

'My name is Major Michael Ashton, and this is Captain Edward Hunt,' Michael answered.

As the two policemen sat down, Cutler opened a plain brown file, which contained a couple of typed A4 pages and some handwritten notes.

'You said you are Major Ashton, but my notes show you have left the army and that you work for a private security firm now. Excalibur Securities, is that correct?'

'Yes, that's right.'

'Then I think we should address you as Mr Ashton, as your army rank has been handed back to Her Majesty. Do you agree?'

'No problem – I suppose because we are largely

ex-military, we tend to use our old ranks.'

'Hmmmm.'

Cutler held Michael's eyes in a steady gaze. Michael stared back without blinking. *We are off to a bad start here*, he thought. *He's an officious prick.*

'Let's continue. It says here you may have information concerning an ongoing Met Police investigation into a murder that took place in the East India Docks area of the Thames?'

'That's right, sergeant.'

Michael placed emphasis on the word 'sergeant' to get his subtle message about rank over. Cutler gave a shrug and looked down at his notes but the message had been received.

'So what is it that you think you have for us then,' he replied.

Edward put his hand on the disc and started to push it across the desk, but Michael placed a light restraining hand on his arm.

'We go back a long time before your murder investigation, over six months. Our own enquiries and investigation have unearthed what we believe is a major kidnap and sex exploitation ring. It's very well organised, and some of the people involved are from the very top of British society, sergeant,' Michael said, again referring to Cutler's rank. 'They move young women out of Africa across Europe and into Britain to be used for self-gratification, or sold into sex slavery. Obviously, with the discovery of the body in the Thames, the stakes have moved up – as well as sex slavery, we now have murder.'

Cutler made rapid notes in the file. When he finished, he looked up and addressed Michael and Edward.

'That's a hell of a statement. We are in the business of solving murders here, not plotting Hollywood fantasies. Assuming any of this is true, how high do you allege this thing goes?'

'To the top of government and industry. Believe me, there are some very big players here.'

'Do you have any proof to back up what you say about the alleged perpetrators?'

'Well, it started as circumstantial; however, as we have delved deeper, so the coincidences have built up and grown to a point where the evidence is pretty damned overwhelming.'

'Do you have what we call on our side of things 'hard evidence': photos, phone calls, witnesses or the like?'

'Some conversations about payments and meetings. We have built up some pretty damned good telephone intel, but no direct confession as yet, if that is what you are looking for. We do, however, have evidence about individuals receiving payments, being seen with others. It all links up – meetings, times, places, etc. We have evidence of aircraft movements between Africa and Europe as well. We have witnessed first-hand the kidnapping of young girls, as well as having observed individuals named in our investigation on the ground in the DRC. From what we have found out about the people named in the intel, they were definitely involved. They have been in the wrong place at the right time too many times, so to speak.'

'Hmmmm... is that disc a complete summary of all you have?'

Edward did not push the disc forward this time; instead, he answered Cutler directly.

'Yes, this contains both a timeline and full informa-tion about all the evidence we have put together, which leads us to believe there is a major sex ring involved. There are some photographs as well, which will give you the names we have in the frame. Our boss, Colonel Torrens, has asked us to cooperate fully with the police in their enquiries. He has said as much to Sir Bob Caldwell, the Met Commissioner.'

'I know who Sir Bob Caldwell is, Mr Hunt. Why don't you let us have a look through your file and then get back to you?'

Michael gave a small nod, and Edward pushed the disc across the table.

'Is this the only record of your allegations?' asked Cutler.

'Sergeant, we hold many copies, together with hard copy and computer images, photos and other intel. Of course it's not the only file.'

'I am sure I do not need to remind you that this is now a police matter and, as such, your independent investigation activities should cease. We may require all the documentation, digital or otherwise, in due course. We will come over to your offices if we need these.'

'We understand, Sergeant Cutler, but I should caution you we operate under special licence directly under MI6 and the Ministers of State. It would require a lot more than you two dropping in. An approval that goes a damned sight higher than you are capable of requesting, or seeking, to obtain.'

'We will see about that, Mr Ashton; we represent the law of the land, not some shadowy MI6 offshoot.'

'So do we, sergeant, so do we. Putting aside what

authority, or level we both operate under, we are fundamentally both trying to keep the peace and provide homeland stability. We therefore formally request that, as we have been involved in this investigation from the beginning, since the original kidnap in fact, we be allowed to tag along and assist wherever we can, or help when needed,' replied Edward.

Cutler looked hard at Edward, and then turned to Michael.

'You will understand that this is now a police murder investigation, Mr Ashton, and as such, we don't need the assistance of some ex-army types playing at private detectives. Once we have looked at your files and information, we will, or may, call upon you to explain further or answer any queries we may have. Gentlemen, I cannot see we would require your services beyond that.'

Before Edward could respond, Michael pushed back his chair so hard that it crashed against the small office wall. He looked down directly into Cutler's face.

'People's lives are at stake here, sergeant. Let's hope you're not as inept as you are sarcastic; you need to act fast to prevent further murders. Our intel is sound and solid; we expect to hear from you within 24 hours regarding what you read into the information we have given you. Otherwise, I assure you, we will back here again. Let's go, Edward; there is nothing further to be gained from continuing this meeting. Remember: 24 hours, and we expect to hear from you.'

As they turned to leave, Cutler looked up from his desk closing the file slowly. He spoke with a dismissive look on his face.

'You will hear from us, major; I can assure you that

you will hear from us.'

Michael and Edward made the short journey back to the reception desk quickly and in silence, slowing only to throw their visitors' tags on the desk.

They walked back to the Excalibur offices in silence. Michael was visibly angered by Cutler's dismissive and aggressive attitude. His training led him to look behind the man's words to his attitude, but just now nothing jumped out red-flagging the antagonism of the policeman. *Perhaps he is just a class A prick*, thought Michael, but he was still troubled by the man's open hostility.

Their walk took them along Birdcage Walk and through Green Park. If it had been summer the multi-coloured deck chairs would already have been out in neat rows, but this early spring morning, the air was refreshing and the bright blue sky belied the last of the winter chill. It had both a refreshing and calming effect on both men. The first daffodils were breaking through the neat green lawns and the green buds on the trees was just enough to take away the harsh outline of the winter branches. A homeless man with long, greasy hair in an oversized coat and half gloves, tattered where the knitting had unwound, shuffled towards the pair, but seeing the speed they were walking at, and the look of single-minded determination on their faces, backed off. As they swept past, they missed the small digital camera in his hand, with which he took a series of close-up photos of the pair.

When they reached Burlington Arcade on Piccadilly, the pair slowed and wandered through the arcade, glanc-ing abstractedly at the designer shops and jewellery stores offering old timepieces and jewellery from a bygone era.

Edward spoke first: 'What on earth was that all about? For God's sake; anyone would have thought we were the KGB – or the FSB, as it is now. Either that or if we are not perceived as a threat then at the very least we are no more than an irrelevant irritation.'

'Yes, it was very strange, Ed, almost bizarre. Although on reflection it's becoming clear the man doesn't want us involved, I have always found when somebody goes on the attack like that they have some-thing to hide – or maybe they have far more information than they are letting on and feel that the best way to cover it up is to bluster and push us off guard.'

'Did you notice Hogan said very little?'

'Yes, a real lightweight. Just learning the trade, you might assume. Although, the blue Masons' ring on his wedding finger tells me that he is one of the chosen ones.'

'Does that stuff still exist? It's hard to believe in a brotherhood in this modern era of policing.'

'Oh yes, alive and well. Forever bound to the frater-nity and greater brotherhood.'

'So, somebody with clout, or soon to have it.'

'Yes. Cutler, on the other hand, is old school, no sign of the Masons there – a hard copper, seen it all. I can't work him out. What is hiding behind that verbal attack? I'll work it out, but for now he needs to be watched. I am going to ask our tag team to follow him.'

The conversation brought them to the door into Excalibur's offices. Maria was at her desk behind reception with a coffee, piping hot, judging by the steam rising from the Wedgwood cup. She glanced up at the sound of the buzzer and reached below the reception desktop. There was an audible click, and Michael pushed the door open.

'Good morning, you two. How did it go with the detectives at Scotland Yard? Did they welcome all our evidence? What did they have to say about it all?'

'They had a say, all right. They were rude, dismissive and not particularly interested in our assistance. How did that sergeant put it? "A couple of ex-army types playing at private detectives".'

Maria appeared taken aback by what Michael had said, but recovered quickly and smiled wryly instead.

'The colonel is in and has asked you to let him know how it all went as soon as you get in. He has visitors in the boardroom just at the moment. Some English and Chinese partners involved in a joint venture space exploration company, looking for 24/7 protection of their top people and also their intellectual property. I have a feeling that it's bigger than that, goes to design, rockets, etc. Could be a huge contract. I will buzz you as soon as he is free.'

'Thanks, Maria. Oh yes, can you get our computer spooks to run a background check on Sergeant Cutler – a long-time Met copper – and his sidekick; a DC Hogan, new, but probably with connections. Let's put a tag on Cutler as well – where he goes and what he does. Let's look at his known associates as well, that kind of background. He has a major chip on his shoulder about us. Also, let's check out Superintendent Brownlee. Ask the lads to use our top encryption stuff and stay invisible. I don't want the Met, or the Scotland Yard computer guys to know we are looking. I sure as hell don't want Cutler to know we are following him.'

'I will get on to it straight away. I often wonder when we use this stuff whether GCHQ can see what we are up to.'

'Probably – in fact, almost certainly – but I am sure that when they see where it's coming from and our clearance level they just keep a watching brief. Let's not forget the colonel is a personal friend of the boss man at GCHQ, so it gives the boffins a heads-up. So when they trace it back to us rather than be suspicious they, too, might want to have a look at what we are looking at. Big Brother watching Big Brother – quite clever, really.'

'Let's hope you are right. I will ask Ginger and his team to stay below the radar.'

Michael and Edward sat in their shared office, trying to analyse just what had caused Cutler to adopt the negative and belligerent attitude that he had. They recounted their meeting, and passed their thoughts and ideas back and forth. Edward felt that perhaps it was just an old policeman who had seen it all before being sceptical and cautious. Michael thought there was more to it.

'He took us on from the word "go", Ed. That ex-officer bullshit right from the start. No, there is something more to it. Perhaps we are stepping on their toes in an investigation they already have under way and Cutler was just trying to warn us not to cock it up.'

Within two hours there was a light tap on the door and Maria entered.

'We have got some stuff on your policemen. Superintendent Brownlee is a graduate from Durham University. After his two years on the beat, which I never knew every policeman had to do, he went on to specialise in forensics and became a rising star in the Serious Crime Unit. He has been involved in breaking up a couple of very nasty drug and prostitution rings, mostly from Eastern Europe and the Far East, Hong Kong being where he has achieved considerable success. He is tipped to become Met Police Commissioner one day and has a shining and clean record. Cutler is a career policeman, mentioned in dispatches, very keen and a real ball-breaker in his early career. Then he seemed to slow down, a messy divorce, some drink issues that appear to have gone away. He has had a couple of run-ins with superior officers. It was as though he felt that he was not getting the credit he deserved. The last few years he has been off the boil; he's not likely to advance much further and there was recently an internal inquiry into some of his underworld and organised crime associations. He came through the inquiry clean, claiming his contacts supplied information, snitches ratting out other criminals. He did not, however, come out completely above suspicion. Our young detective constable is the son-in-law of the Chief Constable of West Yorkshire Police; he seems to have had a bit of a hand-up in becoming a junior detective at this early stage of his career.'

'That and the Freemasons connection,' retorted Michael.

'Not surprised, because he on his own is spectacularly unimpressive – more of a wimp than a rising star. I wonder if Cutler has any hold over the youngster? Thanks, Maria. It always amazes me how much the computer boffins can trace back, and how quickly.'

'There were some early blocks in the trawl, but we overcame them, obviously, and Ginger says they suddenly seemed to disappear.'

'Interesting. I wonder why the firewalls, or whatever these guys do, were so quickly unblocked. I must ask Ginger.'

Edward looked at Michael and laughed.

'Michael, your computer knowledge is dangerous at the best of times, old boy; concentrate on what you are good at. I can always get you *iPad for Dummies* as an early Christmas present.'

'My friend, I could get you an early Christmas present too, and if Maria wasn't here, I would expand on that. There is nothing wrong with expanding my already vast array of skills into the world of cyber-spying and hacking.'

By now Edward was laughing out loud, and Maria had a smile on her face as well. Michael shrugged his shoulders, trying hard not to laugh as well, and pretended to be studying the report Maria had delivered.

'I will check with Ginger to see when he is available,' he said seriously. Maria, who knew how bad Michael's computer skills were, now started laughing as well. Just then, there was a sharp knock on the door and Colonel Torrens put his head around the door.

'Come on up to my office, you two, and let's see where we are at after your visit to Scotland Yard. Good to see you are not still angry about the police involvement.'

'On the contrary, sir,' Michael began, but the colonel had already left the doorway where he had been standing and was now walking towards the stairs up to his office. Michael and Edward quickly came around their desks and followed.

As they walked down the passage, Michael heard Maria saying, 'Michael Ashton: B.A., Masters and B.Sc. in Computer Science, now wouldn't that be something. The all-round master spy, more than just brawn, I like the sound of that for my man.'

She shut their office door and walked in the other direction down the passage before Michael could answer, but he liked what he had just heard and was determined to speak to Ginger about taking a crash course on computers and their mysteries.

Torrens frowned and appeared both annoyed and concerned when Michael related their meeting in detail to him. He shook his head once or twice, but waited until Michael had finished.

'The first thing we need to establish is why Superintendent Brownlee was not at the meeting. Bob Caldwell said he would be as he was the best suited to look further into the outline of what we gave him. Ginger can keep an eye on Cutler and the young fellow. What was his name? Ah yes, Hogan. Sounds like a lightweight – probably trying to prove himself to the older copper.'

Torrens lifted the grey encryption phone on his desk and dialled a number. A young, female police officer answered.

'Commissioners' Office, Constable Swan speaking. How may I help you?'

'Good afternoon, Constable Swan. This is Colonel Torrens. Is Sir Bob in and available?'

'Oh hello, sir, good to hear from you. I'm afraid the

commissioner is at 10 Downing Street with the prime minister. Can I help?'

'Could you ask Sir Bob to call me when he has a moment?'

'Of course, sir. I shall tell him you called the minute he returns, although that may not be until tomorrow morning, I'm afraid.'

Torrens thanked the constable and turned to Michael and Edward.

'Tomorrow morning, first thing hopefully, I shall find out what is going on and get straight back to you both. Let Ginger's boys do their stuff and we will meet again first thing in the morning.'

'Thank you, sir,' replied Edward, and he and Michael left the room.

23

Man Down

Michael and Edward decided to delay going back to Wimbledon Village and go instead for a couple of beers and a steak at Gaucho's Steakhouse off Regent Street. When they had finished, Edward persuaded Michael to stop off at Ronnie Scott's Jazz Club in Soho for a couple of hours of jazz. Edward had a friend whose daughter was singing there for the first time as a minor support act, and he persuaded Michael to tag along, not that he needed much persuasion.

Ronnie Scott's was just coming alive as the two men arrived at around 2200 hours. With its black façade, gold lettering and neon sax in the window, it looked every bit the jazz club. Inside, the brothel-red table lighting had been retained from the club's early days in the late 1950s. They chose to sit at a table up in the tiered rows above the main dining area where they could get a good view of the small stage. Edward ordered a bottle of Corolla Sicilian Red made from Nero d'Avola grapes, a little Sicilian gem and reasonably priced. They sat back and enjoyed a number of good artists and groups. Michael ordered some bread and olives and the room hummed with pleasant conversation. For the first time in days, Michael felt himself relaxing, although his mind never strayed far from the dark and sinister crime that was unfolding by the hour.

By 2.00 am, both men were feeling tired and mellow and decided to call it a night, so they moved out onto the Frith Street pavement. Further up the street, the sound of empty bottles and rubbish being put out echoed off the buildings, so tightly packed that they seemed to be crowding the narrow pavement. A lone, badly dressed man was slumped in a shop doorway.

'Looks like we are being chucked out with the rubbish, Michael,' said Edward.

Michael looked up to the night sky, but the street lamps and low, dark clouds blocked out the stars.

'Yes, good night, though. I needed that break. Why don't we wander down to Leicester Square? There are always cabs down there. We have probably missed the last night train, so we can cab it back to Wimbledon.'

'Good thinking, Batman. Good plan.'

They crossed over Old Compton Street and were just about to cross Romilly Street when they heard the sound of a car engine approaching at high speed. A dark C-class Mercedes sedan with blacked-out windows shot passed them, narrowly missing Edward who was slightly ahead of Michael. The brakes were applied heavily and the car skidded to a halt, about twenty feet in front of Edward, at an angle to the road as if intending to block the narrow lane. Michael's brain leapt into gear, as he immediately realised two things: the car had distinct, personalised registration plates, and the two men who were jumping out of its doors had on tracksuits and wore dark balaclavas over their heads.

Michael instinctively felt the immediate danger and

called out to Edward.

'Ed, watch out, fall back on me.'

Edward was a little slower to react. His mind had been in neutral, and he was enjoying the casual stroll and the early morning city sounds. He looked up and saw the two men bearing down on him at the same time as he heard Michael's warning. He turned and started to run back towards Michael who was now crouched down on the balls of his feet, arms outstretched towards the danger. But he was a second too slow: the larger of the two hooded men appeared to run into the back of Edward, and there was a dull thud, a sound like a fishmonger makes when throwing a large dead mackerel onto a wooden chopping board. Edward stumbled forward, his face contorted into a grimace, and he let out a cry of intense pain.

'Michael, the bastards have knifed me,' he called, as he fell to his knees on the pavement.

He stared at Michael in disbelief and rocked back on the cobbles, face up.

Michael leapt forward, directly into the path of the oncoming second man. He moved quickly, ramming his shoulder right into the man's body, then jinking a little to the left at the last minute. He took off in what in rugby terms would be called an illegal high tackle, his shoulder crushing the man's larynx, and his would-be assailant dropped like a stone. Michael landed in a crouch, and immediately spun around to see that his attacker was lying on the pavement, writhing in pain and struggling for air through his crushed windpipe. He was out of the fight. He turned to find Edward's attacker had pulled the blade from Edward's lower lumbar area and was now approaching Michael, arms forward and spread wide, a knife in his hand.

Michael recalled afterwards that the sound of the blade being removed was like the sound a plunger makes when the suction seal is broken – a deep sucking sound. Michael moved directly towards the man again, but then feigned a break to the right, before spinning onto his left foot and breaking wide, clear of the hand holding the knife. As he passed the man on the outside, he snapped out his right hand towards his opponent's knife hand. He felt the blade cut him across his hand, but gripped his opponent by the wrist, twisting it away from the direction in which the man was moving. He twisted hard, bending the man's wrist against its natural movement. Since Michael was six feet three inches, weighing nearly 200 pounds and moving away from the man at running speed, the wrist had no chance of staying in position. A second later, it had bent fully backwards and snapped, making a crack that echoed across the street. The man screamed, and the knife went sailing high into the dark night before clattering against the pavement on the opposite side of the street.

Michael noticed the back doors of the car open and two more hooded men get out. Hell, I can't run and leave Ed. The only thing I can do is to get next to him and do the best I can to protect and cover him. He glanced over to his friend's body and noticed a dark, almost black stream of blood running from beneath Ed and into the gutter. *He needs help fast*, Michael thought, as he crouched over Ed's body and faced the two oncoming men in a low crouch. To his surprise, they ran straight to their two downed comrades and began half-pulling, half-dragging them back towards their vehicle. The man with the crushed windpipe was in a bad way, struggling for air whilst his fellow assailant was calling out in pain about his shattered wrist. Michael watched the car pull away, noted the registration number and immediately turned to Edward. There was no way he could give chase on foot and he knew that, right at that moment, Edward needed his attention. He reached into his blazer pocket, noticing for the first time the pain from a deep cut on the back of his hand, just beyond the wrist joint. He pulled out his mobile phone, dialled 999 and called for an emergency ambulance. He then dialled the colonel's number and upon answering, Michael muttered one word: 'Reveille'.

He wrapped his handkerchief around his wrist to steady the bleeding and for a moment, London was silent except for Edward's shallow breathing. The City was sleeping around him. It was too early even for morning deliveries, most people firmly in their beds: some alone, some spooning their partners, all unaware of the drama that had unfolded below them.

Michael knelt on the pavement next to Edward, then gently lifted his head from the concrete and slid his blazer underneath.

'Stay with me, Ed. Don't close your eyes, mate.'

Edward stared back, trying hard to stay awake. He did not answer.

Short bursts from a high-pitched siren made Michael look up from his friend's face. Blue flashing lights reflected and bounced off shop windows and the damp street, signalling the arrival of the ambulance from Shaftesbury Avenue.

The ambulance pulled up right alongside the two men and out got two men wearing green overalls and yellow reflective overjackets. They both had a number of badges sewn onto their uniform chests, which identified them as a nurse and a paramedic. Michael could see the driver, who had remained in the ambulance.

The paramedic placed his hand gently on Michael's shoulder, 'Let's just move you to one side here,' he said. 'Let us get a look at your friend. What happened?'

'My friend was mugged and stabbed in the back,' Michael replied, standing up and moving to one side.

The paramedic looked up, and seeing the blood dripping through Michael's crude bandage, he said, 'We will need to have a look at that. Let's just get your friend stabilised and into the ambulance. What is his name?'

'Edward,' replied Michael.

'Edward, my name is Jim, and I am a paramedic. We are going to get you stabilised and on your way to Accident and Emergency. Can you hear me?'

Edward nodded slightly, although his eyes appeared dull and listless and he seemed to be falling asleep.

'Come on, Edward. Stay awake. We are just going to stabilise you.'

The other nurse was now kneeling alongside his colleague, and they both rolled Edward gently onto his side. The blood was flowing from a deep wound in his lower back. The paramedic leaned forward and gently cut away Edward's shirt. Michael noticed that both men were wearing latex gloves. Jim gently applied slight pressure to the wound; the blood flow had slowed so that the actions of the paramedic only caused fresh blood to seep out.

He looked up at Michael before speaking: 'We need to stabilise the patient and make sure he does not go into shock. We are also going to put him on an IV drip and cover him warmly. I am going to cover the wound with a temporary dressing to stem the blood flow and to protect the opening from infection.'

Jim was working all the time he was calmly speaking to Michael. The other nurse laid a stretcher alongside Edward, and when they had applied the dressing and covered him with a blanket made of a silk-like material that looked like it was designed for NASA, they lifted him gently onto the stretcher on his side, and in one steady and smooth movement, the stretcher snapped into an upright position on its wheels. They slid the stretcher into the back of the ambulance, and Jim called out to Michael, who was standing off to one side.

'Come on, sir, climb in and sit on the jump seat. Bert can have a look at that hand for you while we are travelling to the hospital. We are going to St. Thomas' Hospital at Waterloo, so it's only ten minutes away.'

Michael climbed into the ambulance, helped by Bert, using his good hand to pull himself up. Bert gently eased away the handkerchief.

'Nasty, but no tendons or veins were cut. A few stitches and some rest, maybe a little physio, and you should be fine,' said Bert.

'The mugger caught you as well,' said Jim, half-questioning.

'What? Oh yes. He slashed at me whilst he was getting away,' replied Michael.

'He wasn't successful by the look of things: your friend still has his wallet and watch.'

Before Michael could answer, Edward gave a low moan and Jim turned towards his patient, much to Michael's relief.

Michael sat back and rested his head on the ambulance bulkhead.

'What did the police say?' Jim was back!

'I haven't called them. I will as soon as we have Edward safe and tucked up in bed,' replied Michael.

'Should have called them immediately after calling us, young man. Our controller could have put your 999 call through.'

Jim gave Michael a curious look.

'I should have; you are right, of course – heat of the moment. I shall call them as soon as we have Edward settled.'

'Good man. Edward will be going straight into emergency theatre; we will have you stitched up in A & E and you can make the call then. They will send a police officer to take your statement.'

Michael nodded and stared out of the ambulance window in an attempt to cut off Jim's curiosity questions which were bordering on not believing Michael's story.

An hour after arriving at St Thomas' Hospital, Edward was in an intensive care unit, heavily sedated and resting in a semi-induced coma. The surgeon had explained to Michael that there did not appear to be any internal organ injuries, but the next 24 hours were critical.

Michael thanked him and made his way towards the front entrance of the hospital. As soon as he was outside in Westminster Bridge Road, he hailed a cab. There were a number of them heading towards Waterloo Station at this early hour.

'New Bond Street – the bottom end near Burlington Arcade, please,' Michael said as he climbed into the back of the black cab. 'Quick as you like, mate.'

'Righto guv'nor,' replied the cabbie.

Noticing the fresh bandage around Michael's wrist, he decided not to attempt conversation. The distinct clanking of the cab's diesel engine and its increased revving told Michael the cabbie was complying.

Michael knew his mobile call and one-word message would have spurred the entire team into action. The colonel, all active operatives not currently stood down, the backroom computer boys and the support staff would all be in situ and ready for whatever was required by the time Michael arrived at Excalibur.

He got out of the cab, paid the driver ten pounds without looking at the meter or waiting for change, and glanced up to the office above, where all the lights were on.

Michael struggled to get his Yale key into the dead-lock. Knowing that the fumbling would set off a silent alarm upstairs, he cursed, then using his left hand to steady his now painful right hand, managed to force the key in. As he gained access to the foyer, Tim Abrahams came bounding down the stairs and saw Michael half-stumble into the foyer.

'Are you okay, boss?' he asked, at once noticing the heavy bandage on Michael's wrist, and his drawn features and pale face.

'Good to see you, Tim. Yes, I'm fine, but the bastards caught Edward badly, knifed him in the back. He is in

St Thomas' in intensive care. I've just left there.'

'What happened? Were you guys ambushed?' asked Tim.

Michael held up his bandaged hand to silence Tim.

'Let's get upstairs to the colonel and I will tell you all what happened – saves repeating it again.'

Tim nodded and offered to help Michael, who again shook his head and started up the stairs. Tim followed closely behind, ready to support his boss if he stumbled.

Upstairs, all the lights were on, and as he reached the first floor, he noted with satisfaction that, although it had only been an hour and a half from his reveille call, everybody was there and on standby. He could hear soft voices, and the soft whirring of computers and TV screens; people were at their stations waiting for instructions.

The colonel, Maria and Sergeant McBride stood at the entrance to the boardroom. Maria, fully composed, looked concernedly across at Michael, and he smiled back. Beyond, he could see other members of his command.

'Let's go into the operations room, Michael,' called Colonel Torrens. 'We can call up whatever we need without having to relay things from the boardroom.'

Once they were inside in the operations room, Michael began recounting the full attack to his colleagues. He began with describing the dark Mercedes saloon, and told them its registration number.

'Ginger, get the registration up on your database and trace the registered owner,' the colonel instructed. 'If it's stolen, the police will find it quickly, I hope, and if not it's going to be locked up somewhere. The ownership will give us an idea of where to start looking.'

Michael described the four men and the clothes they were wearing as best he could, but they all had been wearing dark tracksuits and had balaclavas over their heads, which didn't help him. Something was nagging him about the second pair of assailants who got out of the car. *Was it something he had heard, something he had seen or recognised?* he asked himself. The harder he tried to concentrate, the less he could picture; his mind was drawing a blank.

'Okay, let's think about why this happened,' the colonel said.

'It's got to be linked to our investigation into the disappearance of the young girls,' Michael replied.

'Agreed. So we assume you and Edward were being followed tonight. Do you recall anybody who looked out of the ordinary at Ronnie Scott's?'

Michael shook his head. Everything had appeared normal; he did not remember being watched or followed in the club.

'So you were watched going in and picked up again coming out,' said the colonel.

'Agreed. There was a noise of rubbish bins being knocked over and we saw a homeless guy in a doorway.'

'Probably he was watching you and alerted the hit squad.'

'That was the only person I saw.'

'Send one of your boys back there and have him scout around. There is always a slight chance he might find something.'

'Will do, sir.'

Just then, Ginger looked up from his computer screen

and called out, 'We have an owner for that Mercedes registration, Colonel. It's our friends, Moonshoot Technical Defence Systems.'

'That's the link we need. They're the subsidiary of Rapier Systems that paid that Zimbabwean colonel,' said Colonel Torrens.

'Tekere,' replied Michael, reminding Torrens of the man's name.

'That's our man. Perhaps he was one of the two getting out of the car, Michael?'

'No, sir, it wasn't Tekere, I would have remembered him. It was something else about one of those two.'

'Okay, stay with the thought for now. Ginger, hook me up to the ops room of the Scotland Yard Serious Crime Squad and request they get them to link in Sir Bob Caldwell and Inspector Brownlee. Oh yes, and get those two clowns, Cutler and Hogan, who interviewed Michael and Edward, to be present as well. As soon as we have them all together, we can work out a plan of action. Maria, didn't you say that Lord Thackett has a townhouse here in London?'

'Yes, sir, he has a townhouse in Knightsbridge – sort of a mews house, actually. Very private: you cannot see into the courtyard.'

'Sergeant McBride, take Matt Birrell and get yourselves around there sharpish. Have a sniff around, see if you can find a garage and our missing Mercedes. Stay on comms with us here.'

'Aye, colonel, we're on our way,' replied McBride.

24

Teamwork

While the team was waiting for the Scotland Yard Serious Crime Squad to come online, they remained on post and at high alert. Coffee was organised and, as it was now around 0700 hours, some fresh pastries were brought in from a local deli. Maria called the hospital to get an update on Edward. She reported back that his condition had deteriorated a little, probably because of shock setting in and attempting to close down the body, the surgeon had said. They were considering putting Edward into an induced coma.

Michael sat quietly, trying to recall what his subconscious had picked up, his sixth sense. He drew a blank, but still his mind nagged him.

At 07.15, Ginger called out, 'We have visual with Scotland Yard Special Ops: Sir Bob Caldwell is there and ready to speak to you.'

The main screen lit up with a soft hum.

'Hello, Donald, early start. I am told one of your officers has been badly wounded. I am sorry about that,' said Caldwell, addressing Torrens by his Christian name.

'Yes, sir, it's bloody tough. Thank you for linking into the loop so quickly. We have a bad situation unfolding, but we are very sure we know who they are and what's going down.'

'Linked to our murder investigation, Donald?'

'Yes, we handed over a file of all our findings, dates, names, links and times and places to Detective Sergeant Cutler and his sidekick, Hogan. Have you been brought up to speed?'

'I am embarrassed to say this, but neither of them are at their desks, and there is no file we can find. So the short answer is no, I am no further into finding out more about the situation. Hogan called in this morning – or, to be precise, his wife did. She said he had a bad cough and was off to the doctor. Don't waste any time bringing me up to speed, we will back you from our end, Donald.'

'That's it,' Michael called out.

Both Torrens and Caldwell stopped speaking, and attention switched to Michael.

'That's it, sir. The second man who got out of the car, the slightly built one, he had a blue Mason's ring on his wedding finger; I recall it now. I will bet that the man under the balaclava was Hogan. If that is the case, then I would say the other man, the more thick-set of the two, was definitely Cutler.'

'Good God, man, are you saying there are police involved in this mess?' said Bob Caldwell.

'Yes, sir, that's what I am saying. The fact they are not there this morning only further confirms that they were involved. Why are both men absent from their posts this morning? Why was Superintendent Brownlee not part of the team that met Edward and I at Scotland Yard?'

'I had that looked into: it seems Brownlee was asked by Cutler to look into some intel on a major drugs bust we are bringing off in Manchester, something about needing senior eyes on it. Brownlee travelled up to Manchester, but it appeared there was no real need for senior involvement. Good team on the ground, well planned, and should end up an open-and-shut case. Brownlee found that odd, but put it down to Cutler being cautious,' replied Caldwell.

'It would appear now that he was taken out of the loop deliberately,' replied Michael.

Just then, the number two screen came to life, showing McBride and Birrell crouched behind a low white wall alongside a typical mews house garage.

'Bravo One, we are in position outside the building in question. I managed to get up close to the garage: it's a thick roll-back wooden design. If I slip a knife into the slats, I can see a dark Merc inside. Permission to enter and check closer.'

'Wait, One. Has anybody come in or out of the front door? I assume there is no exit other than into the mews?' asked Torrens.

'Affirmative on both counts: there is no back exit, and somebody in a dark suit carrying what appeared to be a doctor's bag did enter fifteen minutes ago, but has now left. Other than that, no movement.'

'Could be attending to the two men you were involved with earlier, Michael,' said Torrens.

'Or worse,' Michael said.

'McBride, hold your position; we are going to coordinate a number of operatives to visit various addresses simultaneously. We will need a little time to put it together,' said Torrens.

Sir Bob Caldwell cut in on the other screen.

'We will make available a small unit of armed

officers: highest clearance, and the best we have. I may not have seen all the evidence, Donald, but knowing you, you would not move unless you were absolutely sure. I have complete faith in you and your operatives. I will get the licence to arm and use weapons from the head of MI6 immediately. Even though we are internal now, it appears to be a several-continent operation; take it as read that you have clearance. We go back a long way. Operate as fully authorised to shoot to kill if necessary; your backs will be covered. Stay away from any public scrutiny.'

'Thank you, Sir Bob, we will also need some rapid deployment to the Kent coast. I'm running with that as the probable second location. Private estate on the clifftops, down an unmade road. I don't think we need to worry about Arran Castle, too close to home so to speak, family and all that,' said Torrens.

Right, I will put through a call to a police armed unit, which is off the radar and based at a barracks down there, next door to Dover Castle. We increased the number of armed officers after the illegal immigrant thing started kicking off in Calais. Officially off the radar, but attached to the Kent force. The public and tourists see the barracks and the men in unmarked combat kit and mistake them for soldiers based at the castle. Traffic will clear the route for you. All plain clothes and unmarked cars, but the ability to use sirens and blue lights when needed. We are now operating a couple of drones on that coast looking at human traffic, looking for suspicious movements. We can put one on standby for you, weather permitting.'

'Thank you, Sir Bob. That is about all we need for now,' replied Colonel Torrens.

The main screen went dead. Colonel Torrens stared at

the dark screen for a minute, gathering his thoughts, and then turned to the others in the room.

'Right, Maria, you and Robin Gibb sign out handguns from the basement armoury.' The office always kept a small supply of weaponry in a basement vault.

'Each of you collect a Range Rover and arrange to pick up the police armed response unit from the underground entrance area at Scotland Yard. No point in having too many vehicles near the mews house.

'Get Bravo One, McBride and Birrell to fall back on your position when you arrive and keep a watch on the place, but do not move until my order. Report anything suspicious; stay on the Bravo One call sign. My team, who will get down to Kent, will take Bravo Two. Ginger, you use Bravo Three.

'Ginger, hook my Range Rover into Sir Bob Caldwell and the Kent armed response team. See what you can do about coordinating the drone we have been allocated.'

Fifteen minutes later, two Range Rovers were speeding across Battersea Bridge into West London; from there, they continued down through Clapham and onto the A3 towards the M25, then headed eastbound towards Kent. Ahead and behind the Range Rovers, two unmarked BMW police traffic cars kept intersections clear and maintained a speed way above the normal limits. The cars alternated position, front to rear. Occasionally, they needed to use the blue flashing strobe lights, or a quick burst of the sirens, to alert road users to their presence. When they did, the other cars rapidly moved into the inside lane to allow them to pass. To the casual observer, this must have looked like some sort of protection unit escorting someone of importance, perhaps a royal.

Colonel Torrens had two young lads with him in his Range Rover. Michael had seen them around Excalibur, although they were not from his team. All operatives were trained to the same high standards and came from top army or navy units, so Michael had no doubt they would know what to do. In the front passenger seat of Michael's Range Rover sat a silent Tim Abrahams, his sniper rifle lying across the back seat. Michael's Glock pistol lay in the glove compartment, fully loaded and cocked and on safety.

They quickly reached the M25 orbital motorway, and the two unmarked police cars and two Range Rovers exited onto the eastbound carriageway. The traffic was already building; they were near the peak of the daily morning rush hour. One of the unmarked BMWs took up a position in the outside lane, going near 100 miles per hour, quick blue flashes from its lights getting surprised, half-attentive drivers to cut into the middle lane. The two Range Rovers followed in the same lane and the rear BMW prowled across all four lanes, pushing approaching traffic back and creating space.

These guys know what they are doing, thought Michael, as the Surrey countryside flew past his window. As the convoy approached the Clacket Lane motorway services, they flashed by a sign that said "Welcome to Kent". Within five minutes they were on the M26 and the traffic had thinned; the convoy had moved up to 110 miles per hour. Within minutes, they were on the M20 and coast-bound.

'Bravo One and Bravo Two, this is Sunray.' *That's the boss*, thought Tim.

'Listen up, Kent coast ETA in twenty minutes. There

is mist from the Channel over the cliffs, so although there is a drone airborne, call sign Sniffer One, it may not be any use to us. Our extra numbers are standing by at the top of the A2 roundabout leading down to the Dover docks. Bravo One, prepare to move from your current location onto your target in the next thirty minutes.'

'Bravo One, roger that.'

'Bravo Two, roger.'

The convoy slowed as the roundabout at the top of the road that led down to the docks came into view. The two BMWs crossed the roundabout and ran straight on down towards the docks. The two Range Rovers turned left onto the A258 towards Deal and a police armed response Transit van pulled out of a lay-by and fell in behind the Range Rovers. The air there seemed heavier and thicker than in London: swirling sea mist rushing across farmland from the direction of the cliffs and the English Channel. There was a damp chill in the early morning air. A new call sign came up on the radios, 'This is Blue Strike Three. We are on your tail and number six in bodies.'

'Police armed response,' said Tim quietly. Michael nodded, concentrating on the narrow A-road which the Range Rovers were now moving at speed along.

'Roger, this is Sunray, follow me, turning right shortly. Bravo One, stand by to move in; we have fifteen minutes to go.'

'Bravo One in position, ready to move.'

Colonel Torrens turned off the A-road onto a smaller road heading towards the cliffs. Michael could now see a village; it was in the distance, but it was fast approaching. A small church shot by, and then a country hotel appeared a little further on the opposite side of the road. At the next T-junction the vehicles turned into a village and slowed to the regulation speed limit; there was no need to risk a collision with a person or vehicle in the narrow village streets which wound towards the coast. As they drove through the small village, Michael caught sight of a small village shop and a couple of pubs. On his right, a large church rose from behind a flint stone wall, almost cathedral-like in appearance. *Seems out of keeping with the village, too big*, thought Michael – probably a lot of empty pews each Sunday. The spire vanished into the low mist, and the next thing that Michael caught sight of was a small hotel done out in New England style, with white clapboards and small curtained windows.

Suddenly, Colonel Torrens turned hard right down an unmade road, almost catching Michael unawares. He swung his Range Rover hard into the new road. The road itself was chalky and hard; there appeared to be flint stones buried in the white clay, making it a rough and bumpy ride. There were large potholes in the road, which was rapidly becoming a track. It was clear that no repair roadworks had been carried out recently. As they drove along the road, it narrowed to not much more than a path. They crossed a cattle grid, next to which there was a sign announcing that they were entering National Trust land. Thick bushy shrubs and wild trees hung over the path and Michael could see fallen trees on each side of the path. The swirling mist gave the place an eerie feeling.

'This track must be local traffic only,' said Tim, the last of the village houses now a mile further back down the track.

'Yes, wouldn't imagine many people live out here on

the clifftops,' replied Michael.

'No, perfect place to hide something, or somebody, you don't want to be seen. It reminds me of the time we hunted down that mafia boss in Namibia, same sort of out-of-the-way feel; different vegetation, but the same hide-and-seek principle.'

Michael, recalling the mission, half-smiled and nodded.

The colonel pulled into a clearing which looked like some sort of picnic area.

'Listen up, Bravo One, we are now ten minutes from our objective, so be ready to strike on my command. Bravo Two and Blue Strike Three on me. We will leave the vehicles here and move forward on foot. Follow me in single file until we are near the main gates. We will stop in the hedgerow near the gate and then decide how to approach the house.'

Overhead, they heard the faint sound of a light aircraft.

'Bravo Two and Blue Strike Three, that's our drone. It cannot see through the mist at this time, so we will have to rely on our own eyes. Bravo Three, confirm no visual?'

Ginger replied, 'Bravo Three, no visuals confirmed. There are intermittent breaks in the mist though, so Sniffer will stay on station.'

Michael, Tim and the armed response unit debussed from their vehicles and assembled in single file behind Colonel Torrens. Weapons were checked and safety catches applied.

'This is a favourite area for walkers, so we stay off the road and tracks. Let's go, chaps. Follow me in single file, six feet apart. Hand signals only from now on to keep noise levels down.'

The colonel disappeared into the thick undergrowth, followed by Michael and then the six armed response officers. Tim brought up the rear. The men moved down into a heavily wooded valley area. Michael could hear a woodpecker tapping loudly, and to his left, Michael noticed movement: a small herd of young cattle were moving quietly along the valley floor, grazing amongst the trees on the thick grass. The colonel followed the valley for ten minutes, before signalling to the group to spread out and into open file, standing in line abreast of each other and three feet apart. Then the colonel started to lead them up a steep embankment. Halfway up, he froze. He thrust his right hand into the air, signalling to the men to halt, then held it flat and pushed it downwards; instantly, all the men flattened themselves against the side of the slope. From further up the slope, voices could be heard. Two women out for an early morning walk with their dogs. One of the dogs started barking and headed down the slope towards the men.

'Coco, come back here,' called a female voice. 'Come back here, you naughty girl.'

The dog stopped 50 feet from the prone men, sniffed around in a circle, turned and headed back up the hill, towards the pathway along which the two women were walking.

One of the women, the one who had called the dog, said, 'There are so many young rabbits this time of year, and she chases them all. She is exhausted at the end of a walk – mind you, she sleeps all day afterwards.'

The other woman laughed as they passed by, within a few yards of where the heavily armed men were lying, prone against the slope.

The colonel waited for another full minute, before lifting his hand, signalling to the men to get onto their feet. After that, he continued his climb over the path the women were on and up through the bushes to the top of the hill. Off to his right, Michael saw a lighthouse beyond the tree line. The morning sea mist swirled up from the cliffs around the base of the lighthouse creating the effect that the top of the lighthouse was hidden.

The colonel turned off the top of the leas and headed west to avoid walking out onto the open grassland of the clifftop. They passed close to a couple of small cottages and into a farm field recently planted with wheat. Up ahead, behind a high brick wall, the start of Lord Thackett's estate appeared. The hedgerow that the colonel had referred to was just short of the unmade road leading to large, grey, wrought-iron gates. Off to the right, in a small copse set low in the muddy undergrowth, stood a World War II bunker, surrounded by concrete tank traps. The colonel signalled the team to move to the dark entrance of the bunker. He crouched down and removed a drawing of the estate boundaries and buildings from the pocket of his combat trousers. He signalled the men to gather around him, and they knelt down in a loose semi-circle, facing the colonel.

'Right, we are on the target.'

He spread the drawing on the dusty floor of the bunker. Piles of rubbish, and the smell of old urine and burnt wood, indicated that people had camped out here recently.

'This is a layout of the estate and its various buildings. You will see that there are four houses spread over twenty acres, as well as some sheds and barns. Here, here and here,' the colonel said, indicating the buildings by tapping on the drawings. 'The farm tractors and equipment are kept in these barns, close to the open fields. There is also an old oil-fired lighthouse in the grounds closer to the cliffs.'

The colonel's radio hissed to life in a soft squelch.

'Bravo Two, this is Bravo Three. The Sniffer has sent back some pictures taken through a break in the mist. There are a number of vehicles parked in the forecourt of the main house and one car at a small cottage near the cliff edge, about 200 yards from the lighthouse. There's some movement in an area of the barn alongside the first of the cultivated fields; looks like a couple of farm workers.'

'Roger that,' replied the colonel. He turned again to the men who were crouching in a semi-circle around him.

'Right, chaps. That confirms my thoughts on where to concentrate our efforts. The main house is only a few hundred feet from the far east wall. Beyond the house are formal gardens that run to a high brick wall with a large, heavy wooden gate, which leads onto National Trust land running along the clifftops. About 500 yards further down along the cliffs are the front of the two cottages we passed. The heavy undergrowth and wooded areas give way to open clifftop, grassland and a number of walkers' paths. To the left at this point is a small elevated copse further back into the forest area. Tim, get yourself over there, and pick a position where you can watch the clifftop and the open ground along the cliffs. You need to pick up anybody who manages to sneaks out of the back door and through the gardens onto the open ground.'

Tim nodded, then raised himself in one single movement and left the bunker silently.

'Michael, you and two of the officers take the front door head-on – no buggering about. Three of you chaps take yourselves over to the farm workers and make out you are on routine police business. Be wary in case any of the workers turn out to be armed bodyguards. Blue Strike Commander and I will cover the side of the house nearest the road. From there, there is nowhere to run except over the cliffs. Right, any questions?'

'Do we know the strength of the door, or anything about its locks?' asked Michael.

'No, Michael, but I want you to cover the open ground on the forecourt, using the cars as cover. Stay low until you are near to the door, then just knock on the front door. They don't appear to have guards or any sentries out, so with luck, somebody will answer the door.'

'Roger that. If we don't get a response within 30 seconds, we will blow away the lock and enter.'

'Any more questions?' asked the colonel, as once again the drone flew slowly overhead. Nobody spoke.

The colonel rose and folded the maps which he then returned to the pocket of his combat trousers.

'Check your personal area. Don't leave anything behind. Let's move out.'

At the entrance to the bunker, the colonel called softly into his radio.

'Bravo One, stand by. We are almost in position.'

'Roger that.'

25

Hit One

Maria, followed by Sean Ahearn in the second Range Rover, pulled up half a block away from the Knightsbridge address. The operation was now two hours old. Each Range Rover carried three heavily armed police officers. Maria had a Glock 17 pistol while the officers all had MPS semi-automatic carbines. Any qualms the officers may have had about being told they were being placed under her command disappeared as they watched her break down the Glock, reassemble it, insert a full magazine and cock the weapon with the safety catch still on, all in a matter of seconds. She knew exactly what she was doing. They all had flak jackets on. One of the officers in her Range Rover had a device used to break down doors resting between his knees. McBride and Birrell fell back from behind the small wall and joined them in Maria's Range Rover, which was parked half a block from the doorway. They, too, received pistols and flak jackets. Ahearn and the three police officers came forward, crouching behind the Range Rover door, which Maria opened in an attempt to hide the men and weapons. Maria's Range Rover was now both a little crowded and a little stuffy, so she lowered the blacked-out windows slightly. The air outside was crisp and cold.

'Now we wait until we get the go from the main group. They are in position in Kent. We have under ten minutes to go,' said Maria quietly. She handed McBride a stun grenade.

'When we get the go-ahead, lob the grenade through the letterbox, and you, constable, break the door down as quickly as you can. The rest of us will be out of the vehicle and with you in a matter of seconds. I will enter first followed by you, Birrell, then Ahearn, and then you, constable, Ahearn looked at the constable and nodded. Cover each other's backs and we will peel off from the front into each open doorway. Ahearn, you make your way to the basement with cover. Sergeant McBride, you clear the ground floor while Birrell and I will take upstairs. Make sure you are always covering each other. Clear each room and confirm verbally when you've done so. We don't think they are heavily armed, nor expecting us, but you never know. I don't want anybody shot in the back.'

McBride and the officer with the ramming device slipped out of the Range Rover, and crouching, crept forward quickly and quietly to the cover of the small wall. Midday was approaching, and there were a number of civilians in the streets, but fortunately there were none in the mews approach.

Maria's radio hissed into life: 'Bravo One, go, go,' the colonel called over Maria's radio.

Maria slipped the safety off her Glock and, followed closely by Birrell and the armed officers, she shouted out to McBride and the crouching constable.

'Go, go, get that door down.'

Almost simultaneously, there was an explosion and a

crashing sound as the stun grenade exploded inside the hallway. It had been thrown through the letterbox and the ramming device had been slammed into the door. The time for silence had passed. The door cracked and on the second blow, it burst open. Maria and Birrell, followed by the armed team, burst into the hallway of the mews house. Through the dust, Maria located the stairs, then ran up them. She could hear young girls screaming and crying out. As she reached the first floor, she indicated the right-hand door to Birrell, while slamming open the door in the opposite wall.

'Clear,' called out Birrell.

'Clear,' answered Maria.

They bounded up the stairs to the top floor of the mews house. Birrell tried the right-hand door; it was empty, and he called out clear. As he turned to leave, he noticed that there was a bed in the middle of the room. It appeared to be laid out in a similar fashion to a hospital operating theatre. White plastic sheets covered the bed, and on a chair in one corner, sheets that looked like they were made of silk were stacked along with pillows, and in another corner was a shiny metal bucket with a mop alongside it. Next to the bed, on a side locker, was a long thin knife and a brown bottle with no label, together with what appeared to be bandages.

In the seconds that it took for him to take in the unusual layout of the room he did not hear Maria call out from the room opposite.

'Are we clear?' he called out.

There was no reply. Birrell spun around, and holding his Glock with both hands, raised it in front of him, his forearms outstretched. He approached the open doorway slowly. He could see Maria's back just inside the door; she too appeared to have her weapon held in both hands at the level of the middle of her body. He could hear another person speaking in the room, but although he could ascertain it was a male, he could not see the person. His line of sight and fire was blocked by the doorjamb and by Maria's back.

Maria heard Birrell edging closer.

'Back up,' she called out.

Birrell stopped his advance, but kept his weapon in the firing position.

Maria spoke out calmly: 'Let her go, Tekere. Lower your weapon.'

After entering the room, Maria had come face to face with a scantily-clad Tekere and a young dark-skinned girl, barely into her teens. She was wearing nothing but white silk panties, which stood out against her dark skin. She was both shaking and crying softly at the same time. Tekere was holding her around the throat with his left forearm; in his left hand, he held a short-bladed knife. In his right hand he had a Russian Tokarev pistol, which was pointed at Maria's waist. He was nervous and sweating, and Maria noticed his fear at once. He shielded his face and body behind the girl by half-crouching.

'No, you lower your weapon, or I will kill this girl. You will give me safe passage from this house, or she dies.'

'Not going to happen, Tekere. Every floor of this house has armed officers. They will not let you pass; they are waiting for you and you will die before you get anywhere near the front door.'

'I will kill the girl. I have a knife, and I will shoot you as well if you do not guarantee my safety. Lower your weapon and kneel down on the floor, or I will shoot you first,' barked Tekere.

Maria started to slowly lower her weapon. Behind her, out of sight, Birrell crouched, waiting to spring into the doorway to open fire past her. *I hope she drops to the left*, he thought, as he readied himself. He still could not see Tekere or the young girl he was hiding behind.

Tekere pushed the girl slowly forward. His Tokarev shook slightly as he inched forward. Suddenly, the girl stumbled and slumped forward and downward. She appeared to have fainted from fear and lack of oxygen. Tekere pulled her upwards, but in doing so his left side of his forehead and the top of his skull were momentarily exposed. Maria snapped upright, lifting her Glock at lightning speed, and in a single smooth movement fired one round. The bullet missed the top of the young girl's head by less than a hair's breadth. It hit Tekere in his left frontal lobe and burst out sideways alongside his right ear, thundering into the wall to his right and behind him. He was dead before he hit the floor.

Birrell, on hearing the shot, had leapt forward into the doorway.

'Holy shit, ma'am. That was one hell of a shot,' he cried out.

'Thank you, Birrell, I didn't have much choice, he was going to kill me because he could not handle the situation and suddenly I had the shot.'

Underneath Maria's outward calm, she felt violently ill – not at having killed Tekere, but at the risk she had taken with the girl's life in taking the shot.

'What's happening? Are we good?' McBride called up the stairwell.

'Fine, everything is fine. All clear here,' Maria called back, as a heavily armed policeman hurried onto the third-floor landing.

'We have half a dozen young girls downstairs, ma'am. They had been locked in the basement. We have arrested a young male who was guarding the door. He was seated on a chair and could not get himself up and into a firing position. He has been disarmed and handcuffed. The rest of the house is secure. We have also found some body bags, or similar, but we won't touch them until we have forensics on site.'

'Thank you, constable,' replied Maria.

She turned and walked slowly across the room, then lowered her weapon and put her arms around the young girl, who was still sobbing with fear.

'It's over, child. Nobody is going to hurt you now.'

The girl shook her head, then buried her face in Maria's chest and continued to sob quietly.

'You are safe; we are here to save you from these evil people. What is your name?'

The girl spoke so quietly that Maria did not hear her reply first time, so she asked the girl again.

'My name is Happiness Muamba. My father is Chief Muamba,' she said.

Maria's heart nearly stopped as she heard the girl's name and recalled Michael's promise. Her thoughts turned to Michael and the assault on Thackett's farm on the cliffs. *For God's sake, Michael, keep yourself safe so that you're able to take this beautiful young girl home*, she thought.

Maria gently pushed Happiness away from her body and took her hand gently.

'Come, let's get you away from this place and back with your friends downstairs.'

The girl followed Maria down the stairs in a daze.

26

Hit Two

The colonel heard the affirmative from Maria and called softly on his radio: 'Bravo Two, this is Sunray. Bravo One is a go. Are you in position outside of the front door?'

'Bravo Two, roger that.'

'Bravo Two, go, go.'

Michael got up from his position behind the Bentley on the driveway, and using the large brass knocker, rapped loudly on the front door. Alongside him, the two police officers moved to the far side of the door away from Michael.

Michael listened intently for movement, and to his surprise, he heard feet shuffling towards the door. The door swung open and an elderly male in some sort of butler's outfit answered the door.

'Good day, may I help you?' the man enquired.

Michael pushed past the man, leaving one of the police officers to apprehend him. He signalled to the other officer to follow him, slightly behind and to Michael's right. Ahead, across the hallway, were closed double doors. On either side of the hallway, long sweeping staircases flowed up to the first floor, creating a galleried landing across the back of the hallway. Michael signalled to the officer to ready his weapon and pushed open the double doors to reveal a cavernous wood-panelled day room. There were several lounge suites laid out in sections and a huge open wood-burning fireplace. Soft background music was coming from somewhere in the room. There were heavy silk curtains hanging from the ceiling at the far end of the room, covering French doors which led to the gardens. The day room was empty.

Michael signalled to the officer to follow him, and they edged down a passageway towards the back of the house. A swing door led into an old and solid, thick-walled, spotlessly clean kitchen area. The kitchen itself was a tired off-white in colour, and there was a massive AGA cooker and a dolly maid wooden drying rack fixed to the ceiling with a series of up and down pulleys hanging from the racks. It was the kind of kitchen that fits well with a large country pile. There were two young girls sitting in dressing gowns at an old pine table, eating what appeared to be bowls of porridge. They looked up as Michael entered the kitchen. He held his index finger to his lips, signalling to the girls to remain silent. They stared at Michael, eyes wide open. One of the girls dropped her spoon on the table. From the far-off kitchen in the utility area a female voice was singing softly, and there was a clatter of plates. Michael walked slowly towards the young girls. He kept his finger to his lips, signalling the girls to stay quiet.

Suddenly, from around the corner to Michael's right, a young athletic-looking man appeared, carrying two glasses of milk.

'Here you are, you brats, the milk you have been bleating for.'

But before he could say any more, he saw Michael sideways-on. Michael was slightly in front of the man and was at a disadvantage for first visual contact.

As Michael turned to meet the new threat, he realised that the man had already drawn a pistol from behind his back. He probably kept one in his waistband, and so he was going to beat Michael to getting off a round by half a second.

Michael heard, rather than saw, a bullet hit his would-be attacker in his upper thigh, and simultaneously, he heard the explosive crack of a single round fired from a Heckler & Koch sub-machine gun set to single shot. There was a further sound as the round passed through the thigh. It hit the kitchen floor tiles, which disintegrated, and the round ricocheted off the floor and flew, emitting a high whine, into the ceiling towards the rear of the kitchen. The man crumpled into a heap on the floor, screaming his head off about how he had been hit.

Michael glanced over his right shoulder to see the armed response officer who had taken the shot, still standing in a firing position, covering the passage which the gunman had appeared from.

'Thanks, mate. He had me stone dead,' Michael said.

'No problem, sir,' answered the officer, eyes still fixed on the area of potential threat.

Then the silence was broken on all fronts. The girls started screaming; the cook from the utility area stopped singing and decided screaming was the best thing to do now; and Michael's radio came to life: 'Bravo Two, sitrep now. What's happening,' barked Colonel Torrens.

'We are clear – one bandit down, two girls located, but we are still looking for the main players. I think we should call back some of the officers sent to the sheds to assist in finding and apprehending them.

'Roger, they are on their way. They will arrive at your location in one minute. What area are you in?'

'We are at the back of the house in the kitchen area. We are moving to sweep the upstairs rooms. The officers can clean up here. There is a cook or somebody here – unarmed – as well as the two young girls.'

'Roger that.'

As soon as Michael had a visual on the two arriving armed response officers, he and his number two spun around and ran towards the staircase. There was no longer any need for stealth or caution: the little skirmish would have woken anybody within two miles!

As they reached the base of the stairs, young voices could be heard coming from somewhere upstairs, perhaps a bedroom; they were crying out and calling for help. Michael had one foot on the stairs and was being closely followed by two armed officers when he heard movement from behind a small doorway under the stairs that he had missed. He was convinced that the room had not been mentioned in the briefing. He hesitated only for a second, then signalled the two officers to proceed up the staircase and cover one another, before running across to the door and easing it slowly open, only too aware that he was now without a number two. Caution immediately became first priority. As the door opened, Michael's trained eyes immediately took in the contents of the room which was a snug-looking library: plush carpets, tartan-upholstered couches, leather chairs and mahogany walls, panelled with floor-to-ceiling book-cases. There was a wood fire burning in the hearth, and the room smelt of cigar smoke and good whisky.

Michael eased the door open a little further and his eye caught a movement at the far end of the library. Somebody had opened a French door and left the house into the rear formal gardens. A gentle breeze caused the lace curtains to rustle. Through the lace, Michael could just make out two men running across the garden towards the wall and the gate that led to the cliffs.

'Bravo One, I have two suspects in sight. They are heading through the formal gardens towards the back brick wall. I am in pursuit of them.'

'Bravo Two, roger that. We are coming around the roadside wall; we will approach from your left.'

'Roger that. Hang back, as I don't want you coming across my line of fire. I have them clearly in view; I suggest you stay against wall and proceed to the south corner, in case they break that way.'

'Roger.'

Michael bounded out of the French doors and leapt over a bed of dark red roses. A thought flitted through his mind as he passed: my mother would know what they were. He ran across an open section of lawn through an arbour area covered in wisteria. As he closed down the yards towards the two men who were now near the rear, high brick wall, Michael could see that the men were still dressed in what appeared to be smoking jackets or heavy gowns. As he raised his weapon, they flung open a heavy wooden door and disappeared from view. The door was slammed shut, and when Michael reached it seconds later, it appeared to be locked or obstructed from the outside.

Damn, I am losing time here, Michael thought, looking at the nearly two-metre high wall. To his left was a sort of brick buttress, built to stabilise the wall. He took several paces back, tucked his Glock into his waistband and ran up the buttress. Two paces from the top, he pushed upwards with his right leg, and leapt upwards and over the wall. He landed on his toes and rolled to his right in a parachute roll movement to break his fall.

'Bravo Two, clear of the wall. There is open ground ahead of me – some sort of grassed picnic area. Clear of civilians. The suspects are 100 metres clear, but moving slowly. They do not appear to be armed; I shall meet up with them in a minute.'

'Roger, we will come out of the front gate to meet you. The main house is secure – there are no further bandits and five girls have been recovered.'

'Roger,' replied Michael, short of breath as he was now running flat-out towards the two suspects.

As he covered the open ground he could see that the two men had run behind some thick scrub and bush away from the open ground and towards the cliff.

Michael's radio crackled and he heard Tim's distinctive voice say, 'I had visual: they have moved behind some low bushes and are still running away from the property. I should have full visual again in fifteen seconds, as the hedgerow runs out.'

'Roger, do not fire. I repeat, do not fire. I want these bastards to myself.'

'Roger that.'

Michael could see the two men were still running, but were slowing, constantly looking back towards him closing on them. The two men stopped suddenly and turned to face Michael. He could see them clearly now, and he stopped running as well, removed his Glock from his waistband and aimed directly at the two men. He approached with caution, never taking his eyes off the two men. They did not appear to be armed, and they were both in morning attire, the kind of clothing a country squire would put on after arising in the morning. *Toffs*, thought Michael: these have to be the main players.

As Michael approached to within 50 paces of them he recognised Lord Thackett. He was wearing a red velvet smoking jacket and was the more rotund of the two men. Next to him, in a full-length gentleman's dressing gown was the Shadow Chancellor Kenneth Smythe. Both men looked very out of place on the clifftop. Smythe looked somewhat alarmed, but Thackett's body language was both aggressive and arrogant.

Lord Thackett stepped forward towards Michael.

'Stand still. Keep your hands where I can see them,' barked Michael. He raised the Glock to firing position, held two-handed, level with the middle of the body and aimed at chest height towards the two men.

Thackett stopped moving immediately, but started to speak: 'What in heaven's name are you doing, you idiot? Do you know who I am, you whippersnapper? I am Lord Thackett, and this is Sir Kenneth Smythe, the Shadow Chancellor. You are trespassing on my land.'

'Let me correct you on two points, Thackett,' Michael said softly, fixing Lord Thackett with a cold, hard stare. 'You are on National Trust land which means this land belongs to the nation and not you, and secondly, I don't recall Smythe coming up in the honours list recently. He does not have a title.'

'Preposterous, you're arguing about semantics. You are in serious trouble, young man. I say again, I am Lord Thackett of Arran, and this is the Shadow Chancellor. You broke into my home like a common criminal, fired a weapon and acted like some sort of terrorist. Who the hell are you, and what do you want with us? I warn you: I have powerful connections at the highest levels in government, and my companies are of vital importance to Britain's national security.'

'Shut up, I will tell you what you really are. If you open your mouth again I will shoot you in the foot.'

Lord Thackett drew himself up to his full height and made to speak. Michael just shook his head and aimed slowly downwards, towards Thackett's feet.

'Bravo Two, I have the shot. Move to your right two feet; I can take them both out blindfolded.'

'Negative, hold your fire.'

Both men heard Michael's exchange over the radio with somebody out of sight. Smythe started to shake visibly.

Michael returned his attention to the two men.

'I'll tell you who and what you are, Thackett, and then I am going to kill you. You are a kidnapper, a trafficker of young girls from the DRC in Africa to the United Kingdom specifically for sex and exploitation. Even worse, there is no material or monetary gain: this is just pure sadism at its worst. You and your cronies, many of whom probably are, as you say, in high positions of power, use these girls for sex and then murder them. You are not only paedophiles; you are child murderers who must be stopped. Those in the wings must know that the punishment will fit the crime, and the price you and your friends will pay is the highest that man can mete out. You will forfeit your lives, I want you both to…'

Michael did not finish the sentence as Thackett cut in: 'You will not get away with this, you cannot shoot unarmed men, that's barbaric.'

'Don't talk to me about barbaric, you bastard. Enough talk – kneel down, both of you, facing the other way.'

Michael's radio crackled into life.

'Bravo One, move to your right, sir. You will not shoot these men; you are an officer and a gentleman. I know you will not fire. I have the shot and I am not an officer and certainly not a gentleman.'

Michael realised that Tim Abrahams was right: the most he could do was place them under open arrest and bring them to justice. He felt sick to his stomach at the thought of killing in cold blood, but he hated these two men with a passion. *You can do this*, he said to himself, trying to use his feelings of anger and hatred to make him carry out the execution. Why not move to the right? Tim is a trained sniper and has killed hundreds of men, none of whom had any idea that their lives were about to end when he shot them.

Smythe started to turn to kneel as Michael had instructed. As he did so, Michael noticed Smythe had pissed himself in fear; the urine was running down his legs. Michael steeled himself against feeling any sympathy. Suddenly, Smythe lost his footing and clutched at Thackett to steady himself. He did not, at first, comprehend that in turning to kneel, his foot had slipped over the cliff edge. His body now started to slip over the edge, almost in slow motion. At this point, the famous white cliffs are some 300 feet above the Channel below. Smythe screamed and grabbed Thackett's red smoking jacket with both hands. Thackett realised what was happening and tried to shake Smythe off to stop himself being pulled backwards, but he was too slow. Smythe's body was now a dead weight hanging in the air slightly above from the cliff face. He was not going to release his grip on the smoking jacket for a second: it was his only hope of staying alive.

Slowly, the two men slid over the edge. Smythe's grip released, and the two men started slowly spinning, each on his own axis, towards the rocks and sea below.

Michael ran forward and looked over the cliff edge. Below him, floating downwards through the air, the two bodies seemed to be performing a macabre cartwheeling dance. The bodies seemed to float for ever, although they were, in fact, travelling downwards at over 100 miles per hour. They both reached the jagged rocks at the same time. They bounced not once, but three times off the rocks before coming to rest at the base of the cliff in shallow, chalk-stained water. The way the bodies were lying, contorted and twisted, was confirmation that they were broken beyond repair.

Michael's radio came to life again: 'Result,' was all Tim said.

27

Homeward Bound

'Good evening, madam. Welcome to British Airways' Business Club Lounge' said the smartly dressed woman at the club lounge reception desk at Heathrow Terminal 5.

'May I please see your boarding passes?'

Maria handed over Happiness's boarding pass as well as her own to the receptionist. She gave both boarding passes a cursory glance, confirming their business class status, then handed them back to Maria.

'We hope you will enjoy your journey with us, Ms Mulvihill, and you too, young lady. Please do let us know if we can be of any further service during your journey.'

'Thank you very much, I'm sure we will be fine.'

Maria looked down at Happiness, and her face broke into a broad smile, her perfect white teeth shining. Maria smiled back, and as they entered the business lounge, she took Happiness by the hand. They passed by the display cabinets and area where food was laid out. Happiness saw the enticing displays of fruit and asked Maria whether she could have a lovely red apple from a fruit display. Maria assured her she could have whatever she wanted – except wine, of course. Happiness laughed and reached up to pick the apple from the display bowl.

The two moved over to the floor-to-ceiling windows. They looked out on the terminal stands, which were filled with aircraft. There were orange flashing lights on many of the vehicles buzzing around the waiting aircraft, all in varying states of readiness for their flights.

Happiness walked up to the glass and pressed her face against the pane, fascinated by the scene below.

She turned to Maria.

'Which is our plane, Maria?'

Maria looked at the boarding passes and then at the gate numbers above the telescopic boarding arms.

'There, Happiness: the one with 'A32' in yellow lights. Can you see it?'

Happiness ran her finger along the window pane silently mouthing the numbers.

'Yes, there it is. Oh, it is very big.'

'It's a jumbo jet, child, called that because it's big like an elephant.'

Maria found two full-length loungers. She lay back on one and tapped the other, indicating to Happiness that she should join her.

Maria looked at Happiness and wondered *will this beautiful and darling child ever get over the horror she and her friends have witnessed and been subjected to. Would taking her home to her family and the familiar ...*

A voice from behind them called out, 'Hi, how are my two favourite girls doing. Sorry I'm late; I popped in to see how Edward is getting on. He is up and about with the aid of a walking stick, but swears he will get rid of it as soon as he can. He is in good spirits. His field days are over, I'm afraid, but the colonel says he will be a very good mission controller and strengthen the back office. Heaven help me if I have to take instructions from him,' Michael laughed.

'Thank goodness he is recovering,' said Maria.

'Let me get my ladies a drink. Maria, I am guessing a large Sauvignon Blanc and you, little princess, a Coca-Cola. Have I got that right?'

Both girls nodded, and Michael moved away to the food and drink display area.

When he returned, he had their drinks on a small silver tray, together with a large glass of claret for himself. He sat down on a third lounger.

Maria was reading *The Times*, and she looked up and smiled at Michael's return.

Michael sat down on a chair next to Happiness. He handed her the Coca-Cola and leant forward and squeezed her arm lightly. *I cannot begin to comprehend what this child has been through*, he thought. He smiled at Happiness and started speaking.

'I am so looking forward to meeting your father, Chief Muamba, again, Happiness.'

Happiness smiled, but tears filled her eyes.

'I will miss my friends. They are gone forever because of those bad men,' she said.

'Those men are gone now, Happiness. I know it won't bring your friends back, but you must move forward. Are you looking forward to seeing all your family and your home?'

'Yes, very much. I wish we were there already.'

Michael lay back on his lounger and stared up at the early evening sky, towards London. He could see the approaching aircraft in the night sky, their landing and identification lights twinkling. *There must be fifteen aircraft in the landing leg alone*, he thought. He always wondered how many passengers were visiting the UK for the first time. He was shaken out of his thoughts by Maria calling softly to him. He looked across to her where she was sitting, with *The Times* in front of her.

'The paper is full of sad and depressing news,' she said, with a wry smile on her lips.

'Such as...?' asked Michael smiling back at Maria.

'There are a couple of articles. Firstly, it appears that the Shadow Chancellor, along with a close friend, Lord Thackett, fell to their deaths while on an early morning walk along the clifftops near Thackett's farm, Moonrise, in Kent. The police are saying it was an unfortunate accident, and they state they are not looking for anybody in connection with the incident as no foul play is suspected. Then there is an article about a Zimbabwean Army officer who worked as some sort of attaché to the embassy here. He was killed in a drugs bust-up between rival gangs, in Mayfair, of all places. The Zimbabwean Embassy has complained to the British Government about his murder while stating they have no knowledge of any of their staff or citizens in the UK involved in drugs or gang activity.'

'Probably right. They cannot know what all their embassy staff are up to,' replied Michael.

Then on page three there is an article which covers the apparent suicide of one of Britain's top MEPs, Simon Jones. He was the European Commissioner for Agriculture and Rural Development. He fell to his death from his third-floor apartment in Luxembourg; apparently neighbours heard him call out "no" just before he jumped.'

'Must have had a change of heart as he leapt,' said Michael.

'Then on page five, it reports that there has been a light aircraft crash near Luton Airport, reported to be on lease from a company called Executive Jet Solutions. A number of big industry leaders and a junior minister were on board. Engine fire, they say, no survivors.'

'What bad luck,' replied Michael, looking solemn.

Maria folded the paper and put it on the coffee table next to her lounger.

'Right, enough morbidity. Let's talk about this wonderful country of yours, Zimbabwe, and your spiritual home, Victoria Falls. I am really looking forward to seeing the place and going on safari with you.'

'You are going to love it, Maria. Zimbabwe is still God's country, the people are wonderful, and Kevin and Gail are going to love you. The only sad thing is our trip will be so short. The colonel has me earmarked for a new mission as soon as we get back here.'

Maria rose from her lounger, then stopped to give Happiness a small kiss on the top of her head.

'I'm off to find the ladies' cloakroom, Mr Michael Ashton. Oh yes, I meant to clear up one small but important point about this trip with you earlier. I trust you have booked separate rooms; can't have people thinking I am one of your casual affairs.'

Maria laughed softly as she moved away towards the cloakrooms, her silk flowing skirt swishing against her legs as she walked with the confidence of somebody who knows she has style and class. Looking back, she caught sight of Michael's distraught face. Her laughter could be heard across the entire lounge.

About the Author

Arthur Allison was born in Zimbabwe in 1948. As a young man, he spent a number of years in the Southern African bush as a soldier trained in terrorist warfare. In 1985, he moved to London to a career in finance that spanned thirty years. On his retirement, he returned to his first love, the African bush, setting up a successful safari planning business. This is his debut novel and the first in a sequence of novels featuring ex-Guards, Major Michael Ashton, and the team from Excalibur Security. He lives in The New Forest in Hampshire with his wife, Lynda.